The Last Tower

The Last Tower

ELIAS WITHEROW

THOUGHT CATALOG Books

BROOKLYN, NY

THOUGHT
CATALOG
Books

Designed by GloriAnne Rose Dairo and KJ Parish.

Published by Thought Catalog Books, a publishing house owned by The Thought & Expression Co., Williamsburg, Brooklyn.

First edition, 2018

ISBN: 978-1-949759-04-4

Printed and bound in the United States.

10 9 8 7 6 5 4 3 2 1

This is for John and June Tirone
You took my heart to the mountains
And it will stay there with you

CONTENTS

Chapter 1

Sam took a long pull from his cigarette and looked to the sky. Clouds wafted overhead like the smoke curling from his lips. Thunder rumbled in the distance as a storm stirred over the horizon. It would soon be upon them, the rains anxious to unleash across the dry wasteland. A fang of lightning caught the corner of Sam's eye and he turned toward it.

Tower 13 filled his vision, the massive black construct rising high in the far dusk. The bubble dome surrounding it shimmered, casting a distorted glimpse at what lie inside. He observed the familiar phenomenon but still felt unease ripple through him as he sucked on the last of his cig.

"You ready to go inside?"

Sam turned to his two companions, Alex and Luna. They met his gaze with weary eyes, every mile of the road written across their dirty faces. He could smell their fatigue. It was a familiar sensation, one he carried himself. Luna looked past Sam toward Tower 13. At the shimmering bubble that encased the objects of their fear.

"This is too close," she muttered, her voice raspy.

Alex hefted his backpack across his shoulders, "We'll be fine.

We've been closer. The Red Eyes won't bother us here. We're at least twenty miles from it, wouldn't you say Sam?"

Sam threw his cigarette down onto the hard packed dirt and stubbed it out with a dusty boot. He exhaled a bitter cloud from his nostrils and touched the pistol at his belt.

"We'll be ok. We'll sleep in shifts tonight, if the Lodge will have us."

Luna's eyes never left the Tower, "I hate looking at them."

Sam snorted, "Then don't."

"Tower 12 isn't far off either," Alex observed, retrieving a map from his pocket. He unfolded the worn parchment and stared intently at it. After a moment, he traced a finger down the center.

"Yeah, it's east of us, past the Lodge," he observed, "another thirty miles or so."

Sam stared down the road, "Yeah, I saw it earlier from one of the hilltops."

"So we're trapped on both sides," Luna muttered, "wonderful."

Sam shook his head, "We're not trapped. The Red Eyes won't leave their bubbles unless they absolutely need to."

"Or unless they send out a gathering party," Luna defended.

"Can we go inside?" Sam asked, irritated.

Without waiting for a response, he turned and faced the solitary building they had been headed for. It looked like it had been a hotel before The Impact. Considering how many times it had probably been looted, it looked to be in decent enough shape. A couple of the windows had been broken, the exterior was covered in dirt, but it still had a roof and that's all that mattered. Its four stories rose in sharp contrast to the barren wasteland it sprouted from, a single outpost standing watch along an empty road.

Sam coughed as the wind picked up, blowing dust down his throat.

Christ, he hated Texas.

"Let's head inside," Sam ordered, marching the final distance toward the painted glass doors of the Lodge. He heard Alex and Luna fall in at his back. He kept his hand on his pistol as they approached the building. Who knew what kind of crowd awaited inside. Three cars were parked out front, but they didn't look like they had been used recently. Gas was in shorter supply than cigarettes these days.

Gravel crunched underfoot as the three came to a halt in front of the double doors. Taking a deep breath, hoping for the best, Sam pulled them open and stepped inside.

The interior was dim and smelled like sweat, the high ceiling nothing more than a swath of shadow. Tables and chairs littered the lobby, forming a kind of common area for travelers. A dozen odd men and women filled the space, hard lines chiseled into their weathered faces. Grit, grime, and distrust filled the bags beneath their eyes. Food and drink sat forgotten before them. Battery powered lanterns lit the spacious room, casting darkness across darker gazes.

Sam gripped the butt of his pistol, his eyes meeting the cluster of travelers seated before him.

"We're just looking for a safe place to sleep tonight," Sam announced, his voice echoing.

Silence.

"You ever been inside any of the bubbles?" someone inquired after a moment.

"Never," Alex said at Sam's back. "Not once."

"You got guns," another stated, "you looking to sell?"

"Afraid not," Luna said, her voice carrying. "We just need a place to sleep away from the coming storm."

Sam looked to his left, at the reception desk, and spotted a bald man appraising them. Their eyes met.

"We're not going to cause any trouble," Sam said evenly.

The bald man stroked his bearded chin and then nodded, "Alright… come on over here. Let's get you sorted out."

That seemed enough to settle the room. Cautious eyes returned to their meals and bitter tongues dipped back into their drink. The loll of conversation rose once again.

Sam, Alex, and Luna approached the desk, thankful to be out of the spotlight.

The bald man nodded toward their guns, "You best keep those out of sight during your stay here. They make people nervous when the Red Eyes aren't around."

"We'll keep them in our room," Luna said, a hand absently touching the pistol at her hip.

"I'd appreciate it," the bald man stated, "hard enough keeping these folks at peace with them fuckin' Towers in plain sight."

"If I'm not mistaken, Tower 12 is east of here, yeah?" Alex inquired.

The bald man nodded, "Yup. You can see it if you go out back by the dumpsters. Two Towers within eyesight of one another. Ain't that just the shits? They're the only two that are like that."

Sam tapped his fingers down on the desk, "Yes, we know. Now, do you have a room for us? We're very tired and would like to get off our feet for a while."

The bald man nodded slowly, "I do, I do, but first I would like to know what brings you three to these parts."

"That's our own business," Sam said flatly.

The bald man sighed, "Well currently you're in *my* establishment which makes it *my* business."

Sam heard Luna sniff, but he ignored her.

"We're looking for someone."

The bald man cocked an eyebrow, "Oh? And who would that be?"

Sam lowered his voice, "We're looking for a man named Empire."

The bald man inhaled sharply.

"You've heard of him?" Alex asked quietly from Sam's shoulder.

The bald man nodded, his brow furrowed, "Course I have. Everyone has."

Sam leaned over the counter, keeping his voice low, "Have you seen him?"

The bald man bit his lip and suddenly looked nervous. He paused, as if chewing on the words he was about to speak.

"Out with it," Luna ordered.

Sam held up a hand, "Take it easy." Luna sniffed again.

The bald man wiped his hands down the front of his shirt and licked his lips, "Yeah...I've seen him. He came through here bout' a week past."

Sam felt something stir in his chest, like old fire. He clamped his teeth together, "He was *here*?"

The bald man nodded slowly, making sure no one was eavesdropping on the conversation, "Yeah. Took a pair of ladies up to one of the rooms. That's a service we offer here. At first,

I didn't know who he was. I had never seen him before, only heard the stories, like most."

"What did he do?" Luna snarled.

The bald man stared down at his hands, "You'd have to ask the two ladies who spent the night with him. But they haven't spoken since. They're sitting over there in the corner if you want to give it a go, but I wouldn't bother."

"How did you know it was him?" Sam asked fervently.

The bald man pressed his hands together, "Son...if you could have seen his eyes when he was done with them two...you wouldn't be asking me that question." He pointed to the old staircase leading upstairs, "He came swooping down there like all the night in the sky was on his shoulders."

"And you were here?" Alex asked, pressing a finger to the counter.

The bald man nodded, "I asked if he needed anything. And...and...." He bit his lip again.

"And what?" Sam pressed.

The bald man's eyes began to water, "And then he looked at me. I mean he looked right *fuckin'* at me. Like I was the only person left in the entire world."

"Did he say anything?" Luna asked.

The bald man swallowed, "Yeah. He told me he was sorry about the girls. And then he left."

"And you're sure it was Empire?" Sam inquired.

"It was him. I felt it shudder through me when he looked at me. Like he wanted me to know."

Sam balled his hands into fists, "And this was only about a week ago?"

The bald man nodded.

"We're gaining on him," Alex muttered.

"Should we keep going?" Luna asked.

Sam closed his eyes and took a long breath, "No. It won't do us any good to die from exhaustion on the road. We're not trailing him by much. We'll rest tonight and then we go hard tomorrow."

"I can live with that," Luna said.

"May we speak to the girls?" Sam asked the bald man.

"Like I said, you can try. They're over there, sitting at the table by the kitchen doors. Been like that since he left."

Sam nodded, "Ok, we'll square away the room in a second. I need to talk to them first."

"Suit yourself," the bald man shrugged, "I'll be here."

Alex and Luna followed Sam across the room, dragging eyes with them. The two women were young, not a day over twenty. Their faces appeared vacant and their skin was pale. Neither looked up as Sam slid into the chair across from them.

"I need to speak with you both," He said softly.

Neither even acknowledged his existence.

Sam placed both hands on the table, palms up, "I don't mean you harm. I don't want your services. I just need to ask you a couple questions about the man you saw a couple nights ago. The man named Empire."

There. Just a twitch at the corner of the mouth.

"It's very important," Sam insisted. "Please."

They turned to stone once more.

"This isn't going to work," Alex hissed at Sam's back.

Sam continued, "We've been tracking him across the country for a long time now. We've never been closer then we are right now. If you could just talk to us, I'd really, really appreciate it."

A tear suddenly trickled down one of the girl's cheek, a sad, lonely thing.

Sam rose from his chair and kneeled before the girl, "Sweetie, whatever that man did to you, I want to make it right."

"You can't," the other one whispered suddenly, "nothing will ever be right."

Luna was on her knees next to Sam, cradling the girl's hands in her own, "Listen hun, he's gone and we want to make sure he never comes back. If you could just talk to us, you can help make that happen."

The girl shook her head slowly, "It doesn't matter."

"What do you mean?" Luna asked quietly.

The girl closed her eyes, "You can't stop him. He knows things…"

"What things?" Sam asked, a little too sharply.

The first girl sniffled and wiped the tear from her face, "About what happens next."

Sam turned back to her, his eyes pleading, "Did he tell you something?"

"No…he showed us…"

"I need you to tell me," Sam begged, "it's very important."

The girls shuddered and in an instant, they were back to their familiar silence. They stared straight ahead like the world had vanished.

"Hey, girls," Sam called, looking up into their faces, "please, you have to help us."

Their lips remained sealed, white lines in snow white faces.

Sam looked up at Alex, "Get the phone."

Alex nodded and slid his backpack from his shoulders. He

unzipped it and retrieved a battered cellphone. Sam took it and held it up for the girls to see.

"Do you want to Listen?" He asked.

He saw their eyes light up, a longing across their frozen features.

"There's five voicemails on here," Sam said, "and I'll let you listen to one of them if you tell me what that man showed you."

The girls exchanged desperate looks, a need that was stronger than any drug.

"Do we have a deal?" Sam asked patiently. Slowly, hungrily, the girls nodded.

"How much battery is left in this one?" Sam asked as he powered up the cell.

"Twelve percent," Luna said. "Make it quick."

The cracked screen lit up and the girls audibly sighed, tears freely running down their faces now. Sam understood the feeling all too well.

Quickly, he loaded up the shortest voicemail on the phone. It was an eight-second message. A husband calling his wife to tell her he loved her and would see her soon. He put the phone on speaker and played the message back. They could all use it, not just the girls.

An unknown male voice chirped through the speaker: "Hi sweetie, just checking in. I'm almost to the restaurant. I'll get you something to drink. See you soon. I love you."

The message ended. Sam exhaled, feeling some of the tension leave his shoulders. The girls were smiling through misty eyes.

"Thank you," they said, almost in unison. Luna swallowed with some difficulty. Out of the three of them, it always hit her the hardest. The familiarity. The comfort. Life before The

Impact. Sam caught her eye and she looked away, almost ashamed.

"Turn it off," Alex said, his voice rough.

Sam powered down the phone and passed it back to Alex.

"You ok?"

Alex clenched his jaw and nodded, avoiding Sam's concerned look.

Leaving it be, Sam turned back to the girls, "Now…about that man."

One of the girls ran a hand across her nose, "Can I hear it again? Just one more time? Please?"

Sam shook his head firmly, "We can't waste the battery."

The other one sniffled, "Please…"

Luna patted her hands, "Maybe later, ok? Right now you need to tell us what happened. A deal's a deal."

The girls looked at one another and Sam felt some unknown conversation pass between them. A weight settled around the small group, an oppressive sensation that cloaked itself over each and every one of them.

The first girl looked at Sam, her lip quivering.

Her voice shook, "He's going to destroy the world. And all of us are going to play a part in it."

Sam blinked and he heard Alex shift uneasily.

"What do you mean?" Luna whispered, "What do you mean we're a part of it?"

"We can't stop it," the second girl interjected, "no one can."

"How do you know this?" Alex hissed.

The first girl looked up at him, her face painted with grief, "He showed us. We saw it happening…the bubbles…the Red Eyes…and…and something else…something awful…" she covered her face and began to cry.

"What else?" Alex pressed, "What else did you see?"

The girl didn't answer, unable to get past the tears now falling freely from her eyes.

Alex stepped forward, his voice hard, "Come on! What else did you see?"

"Hey, cut it out," Luna defended.

"Shut up," Alex snarled, suddenly angry, "we just wasted battery life on these two and for what?"

"Calm down," Sam instructed, standing, "we didn't waste anything. Just relax, ok?"

Without responding, Alex turned and sulked off toward one of the tables. Luna exchanged looks with Sam.

"What's his problem?"

Sam sighed, "You know how he gets after Listening."

Luna shook her head, "He worries me."

"He'll be fine. Just give him some space, let him work it out on his own."

Luna nodded, watching.

Sam turned back to the girls, his voice softening, "Thank you for speaking with me."

The first girl twisted her hands in her lap, "If…if you want some company tonight…"

Luna snorted and Sam looked at her.

"Do whatever you want," she said over her shoulder as she walked away to join Alex.

Sam closed his eyes and let his shoulders droop. He could feel a headache coming on. One to match the thunder outside.

"Sir?"

"I won't be needing your services tonight," Sam said, tired, his eyes still closed.

The girl looked at her feet, "I'm not expensive…maybe if you just let me Listen to another voicemail-"

Sam spun around, eyes burning, "I said NO!"

The girl whimpered and shrunk back into herself. Frustrated, feeling guilty, Sam strut away from them, back toward the reception desk. The bald man looked up as he approached.

"Seems you had some luck."

"I guess so," Sam said, dragging a hand over his face.

"You three want a room for the night?"

"If you can spare one."

"Sure can. Each room comes with water and a hot meal."

"That's generous of you."

"It's a dark world out there. No need to bring it in here as well."

Sam smiled wearily, "An optimist, even now, at the end of all things."

"That's a tad dramatic, isn't it?"

"I get that way when I'm tired," Sam breathed, his gaze drifting over to Luna.

The bald man cleared his throat, "Well, getting back to the business at hand, what do you have to trade for the room?"

"We got bullets and cigarettes."

The bald man groaned, "Please tell me you have something else."

Sam cocked an eyebrow, "You don't need ammo?"

"This is Texas. Bullets practically grow out of the ground."

"Ok, cigarettes then."

"I don't smoke."

Sam pinched the bridge of his nose and squeezed his eyes shut, "You don't smoke…"

"Come on, there's got to be something else," the bald man insisted.

Sam opened his eyes, "I have a cellphone."

The bald man lifted his eyebrows, "Oh?"

"It has five voicemails on it."

"Holy cow…how much battery?"

"Bout' twelve percent."

"Not ideal…"

"Oh yeah? When's the last time you Listened?"

The bald man paused and Sam saw need fill his eyes, "It's been quite a long time."

"Then keep it for yourself. Or sell it to someone else. I don't care. Regardless, that should be more than enough to cover our room for the night."

After a moment, the bald man nodded, "It's a deal."

"Thank you," Sam said, motioning for Alex to come over. Alex slumped up from the table, removing Luna's hand from his arm in the process.

"Let me have that cell," Sam said, "we're trading it for food and a room."

Without a word, Alex plopped the phone down into Sam's waiting hand. Then he returned to the table and sat in silence as Luna spoke quietly to him.

Sam handed the phone to the bald man, "Here you go. Enjoy. I envy you. Can't tell you how many times I've wanted to Listen."

The bald man smiled and made the cell disappear into his pockets, "Thank you, my friend. I will treasure every moment." He nodded toward Alex, "As for that one…I don't know your history, but maybe keep an eye on him. I've seen a lot of people come and go from this place. I've seen that look of his before, too."

"What's that supposed to mean?"

The bald man leaned forward and lowered his voice, "He has a rage in him. Just be careful."

"His wife and unborn child were taken away by the Red Eyes," Sam said darkly, "He's got a hell of a lot to be angry about."

"I was just saying…"

"Thanks for the room," Sam said, turning away and motioning for Alex and Luna.

Chapter 2

Sam sat with his back against the door. Night had fallen and he could hear Luna slumbering peacefully from one of the beds. His headache had come, just like the storm outside. Thunder rattled the walls and rain beat against the windows. Sam pressed his hands against his temples, shutting his eyes against the pain between them. His pistol lay between his feet.

In the darkness of the room, he saw shadows shift and float over to him.

"You should sleep, Alex," Sam muttered.

"Just making sure you're not," Alex said quietly, squatting down next to Sam.

"I'm fine for another hour or so."

"I can take over if you want," Alex offered.

Sam continued to massage his head, "Don't think I could if I wanted."

"Another headache?"

"They've been bad lately."

Silence drifted between them. Somewhere outside the door, someone walked down the hall to their room. Sam gripped his pistol until he heard a door close.

"Think they'll try to rob us?" Alex asked.

"I have no idea."

Alex grunted, "Let 'em try."

Sam cocked his head toward Luna, "She asleep?"

"Sounds like it."

Sam licked his lips, the food from earlier still staining them, "I'm surprised she's stuck with us for so long."

Alex said nothing.

Sam looked at him in the gloom, "Do you have something to do with that?"

Alex returned Sam's look, "I don't know. Do you?"

"What's that supposed to mean?"

"Doesn't mean anything, it was just a question."

"If you have something to say, then just say it."

Alex stared straight ahead, "You just going to pretend that night in Arizona didn't happen?"

"What are you talking about?"

Alex sighed, "I'm not an idiot, Sam. I heard you two. A couple times."

Sam felt his stomach sink, "You don't know what you're talking about."

Alex shrugged, "Ok, maybe I don't."

Sam scraped his teeth together, "Fuck."

Alex remained silent.

"I think she has eyes for you now," Sam finally confessed.

Alex took a moment before answering, "I think she's just lonely. Like all of us."

"Sure."

"Would it bother you?"

"Of course not, don't be ridiculous," Sam lied.

"We've just been friends for a long time, man. I wouldn't

want to do something that's going to piss you off. I've seen you pissed off. It's not pretty."

Sam looked down at the pistol in his hands, "Look, man, find your pleasures where you can. Before The Impact, I might have had a problem with it. But that was over ten years ago. Now? Do what you want. I don't care."

Alex just nodded and remained neutral.

"Look at us," Sam chuckled suddenly, "bartering Luna between us like she's a cellphone. Christ."

Alex cracked a smile, "Eighty-five percent of the world is destroyed in the most horrific event in history and guys are still assholes. Some things never change."

The smile fell from Sam's lips, "Yeah…"

Alex noticed the change in his friend, "Sorry…I know you hate talking about The Impact."

"It's been a decade since it happened and I still can't believe it," Sam said quietly. "Hard to believe North America is the only landmass that isn't ash." He sighed, "Why do you think that is?"

"Are we really talking about this again?"

"You got some place to be?"

"No, I just know it puts you in a rotten mood."

"I'm always in a rotten mood."

"Fair enough."

"I mean what *are* they?" Sam pressed as lightning flashed in the windows.

"The Towers? Shit if I know."

"And why twenty-six? Why not ten? Or three? It has to mean something."

"I'm sure it does. Maybe when we catch Empire we can ask him before we kill him."

Sam snorted, "There's a lot of things I want to ask him."

"We'll get our chance," Alex encouraged, "we're so close now."

The heavens bellowed and Luna stirred in her bed. Sam watched her roll over and couldn't help but feel something he wished wasn't there.

"What time is it?" He asked.

"Time for you to get some sleep, buddy."

Sam huffed a sigh, "Maybe you're right."

"Your headache gone?"

"Enough that I can ignore it," Sam winced, standing.

A loud crash erupted from downstairs, stealing his attention. Alex jumped to his feet and Luna sat up in bed, her eyes alert.

"What the hell was that?" She asked, sleep clawing at her voice. Shouting could be heard now along with another crash.

"Let's go find out," Sam said, hefting his pistol.

"Careful now," Alex cautioned. Luna sprung from her bed and retrieved her own pistol. She crept to the door, still in her clothes, and nodded to Sam. He opened the door a crack and listened. He could hear muffled yelling. Someone sounded angry. That meant trouble.

"Stay behind me," He whispered, inching the door open. Together, the three of them slunk out into the hallway toward the staircase. When they reached it, they peered down from the balcony, still wrapped in shadow. The glow of the electric lanterns painted the scene down below and after Sam recognized what was happening, he lowered his pistol.

"Is that a Red Eye?" Alex asked, leaning over the railing.

"Looks like it," Luna said.

The three of them descended the stairs, toward the tense situation unfolding loudly before them. Two men had a young boy thrown over a table on his back, a shotgun pressed to his face. The boy was crying, his red eyes leaving tracers in the air as he spun his head around in desperation.

The owner, the bald man, glanced at the newcomers as they reached the bottom of the stairs. The remaining occupants of the Lodge had formed a circle around the prisoner, glaring poison down at the scared kid.

"What's all this?" Sam asked as he approached the bald man.

"My men found him wandering around outside," he informed them, "they were coming back from Tower 12 and spotted him about a mile off, making his way toward the Lodge."

"What the hell were your men doing by Tower 12?" Luna asked sharply.

The bald man nodded at the two restraining the young boy, "I pay them to take measurements every couple weeks, see how far the bubble has expanded. I want to keep track of how long it'll be before this place is engulfed by it. I do the same with Tower 13. I don't want to wake up one day and find I'm a Red Eye, you know?"

"Stay still!" One of the men barked, a hand to the throat of the boy. The other dug his shotgun deeper into the kid's cheek. The child's eyes glowed a vibrant red, trails of color hovering like neon as he struggled.

"What are you going to do with him?" Sam asked, watching the small crowd as they sneered down at the hostage.

"What we do with all Red Eyes," the bald man sniffed.

The man with the shotgun chambered a round.

Alex stepped forward, "Don't waste your ammo." He leaned down and unstrapped the butcher's cleaver from his leg.

"What the hell was it doing outside its bubble?" Sam asked.

The bald man shrugged, "You got me there. Scouting? Boredom? Curiosity? Who knows why they are the way they are. They're mindless now, slaves to the creatures atop the Towers."

"I'm not mindless!" The child suddenly pleaded, "I just wanted to see what was out here, past the bubble!"

"Shut up!" One of the women surrounding the table yelled, "Don't you lie to us! You were hunting, weren't you? Looking for people you could drag back to your goddamn Tower!"

"No!" The kid cried, "I promise! Please, just let me go, I promise I won't tell the others you're here!"

Alex parted the crowd, cleaver in hand.

"You're an abomination," he growled, "and no one is listening to your bullshit."

"You don't have to be afraid of us!" The child begged, wept.

"Tell that to my family!" One of the men yelled, "You fucking freaks took them away from me, took them back to your Tower and turned them! They're gone! GONE!"

Alex pushed the man with the shotgun aside and stared down at the boy, "We aren't meant to share this world with you."

"Please!" The boy shrieked, fear igniting his blazing red eyes.

Alex raised the cleaver.

Suddenly, the boy's face changed and it became a snarl, his voice dropping to a whisper, "He knows what you're doing. He *sees* you."

Alex brought the blade down into the kid's throat. Blood exploded from the incision and splashed across the floor. Bone screeched as he jerked the cleaver back, pulling a splatter of red with it. Another thunderous hack and the child's head fell to the floor. The table filled with dripping gore.

"Fucker," Alex muttered, wiping the wide blade across the boy's carcass.

The crowd had gone silent, satisfied with the judgment Alex had executed. Sam watched as his friend strapped the cleaver back to his leg. Luna shifted at his side, her eyes trained on the headless body. Blood fountained to the floor. Someone picked up the head and went to the doors where it was discarded. The body went next.

"Now I gotta clean up this mess," The bald man complained, breaking the still silence.

"Sorry," Alex said, not really meaning it.

Luna touched Sam's arm, "What now?"

"We paid for the room," Sam said, watching as the crowd went back to their tables, "Might as well stay the rest of the night. We still have a couple good hours before sunrise and I'd like to make the most of them."

Leaving the visceral scene, the three retreated back to their room. Alex remained silent until he fell asleep, thirty minutes later.

In the morning, Sam gathered the water bottles he had left outside to catch the rain. He was pleased to find them overflowing. Water was becoming harder and harder to find the further they trekked across Texas. This would keep them going for at least a couple days.

"You get some sleep last night?" Luna asked as they stepped out into the growing day. The double doors swung shut as Alex joined them, looking bleary-eyed, but ready to get on with things.

Sam nodded, capping the last of the bottles, "Yeah, enough. Here, take these." He passed two water jugs to Luna who stuffed them into her backpack.

Alex stretched as the sun peaked curiously over the horizon. He sighed and looked at the three cars parked in front of the Lodge, "Sure wish we had some gas. I'm getting tired of hoofin' it. We must have walked a million miles at this point."

"Not quite," Sam muttered, digging in his pocket for a cigarette "But we should keep an eye out for more shoes. Mine are getting pretty bad."

Luna shouldered her pack, "You think we'll have time to scavenge today?"

Sam shrugged and lit his smoke, "Depends. I don't want to drag ass today though. We'll play it by ear. Maybe we'll come across a mall or something that hasn't been completely picked over. If we stop, I want to be quick. We seem to be gaining on Empire."

Alex stood shoulder to shoulder with Luna, "If nothing else, maybe we can find another cell phone. That was the last one we had."

Sam's eyes settled on the stretch of road before them, exhaling a stream of smoke from his nostrils, "Seems to be all people want to trade these days."

"Well," Luna groaned, "shall we be off?"

Alex pulled out the map and studied it intently, "If we stick to this road like we have been, we should reach Louisiana pretty soon."

"East we go," Sam sniffed.

"Hold up," Alex stopped, his brow furrowing, "Hold up, hold up. Sam, look at this." He turned the map and pointed to two circles drawn in marker. They intersected with one another, about twenty-five miles down the road.

"Shit," Sam hissed, "why are you just telling me about this now?"

Alex looked back at the map, "Sorry man, I was so focused on getting us to the Lodge that I wasn't really looking ahead."

"Care to fill me in?" Luna asked, irritated.

Alex tapped the map, "Towers 11 and 12. If what we've been told is true, then they overlap one another. About twenty-five miles down this road."

"Oh Christ," Luna muttered.

"Maybe the travelers we spoke to were wrong," Sam hoped, "I mean, that one guy seemed completely sun fried."

"Only one way to find out," Alex said, folding the map back up.

"What are we going to do if he's right?" Luna asked.

Sam shielded his eyes from the rising sun, "We'll deal with it." He tossed his cig to the ground, the ash smoldering.

Together, the three began to walk. The road unfurled before them like a long, dry tongue. Dust swirled in the morning cool, a luxury that wouldn't last past noon. After an hour, the flatlands began to ripple and the trail became more labored. Sweat stood out on Sam's face as the dull thud of his boots filled the bored silence. Luna walked beside him and Alex strutted a couple dozen feet ahead.

"Going to be a hot one," Luna observed quietly.

Sam wiped his brow, "That storm last night really pushed the heat on us, huh? We're going to have to be careful with the water."

Luna let her eyes travel down a side road, a longing revealing itself, "God I wish we could just hole up somewhere and let be what will be."

Sam glanced sideways at her, "That came out of nowhere."

Luna sloped a grin his way, "Don't pretend you haven't thought about it."

Sam nodded toward the side road, "What do you think is down there? A quiet little neighborhood untouched by all this? It's only a matter of time until all of this is gone. Squatting in a dark room and waiting for it to happen isn't going to do anyone any good."

The smile fell from Luna's lips like overripe fruit, "Jesus, lighten up, Sam. I was just saying."

Sam scraped his tongue over his teeth, "Is that really what you want, Luna? To hide away and just accept whatever happens next?"

"I don't know what I want," Luna said wearily.

"No shit," Sam muttered.

Luna shot him a look, "What's that supposed to mean?"

"Nothing. Forget about it."

"Are you pissed at me or something?"

"Of course not."

Luna stared straight ahead, "Is this about Arizona?"

Sam almost stopped dead in his tracks but managed to keep his composure, "Don't be ridiculous. We both knew what we were doing. We were lonely. Nothing more."

Luna gave him a look Sam refused to meet, "Ok, Sam. If you say so."

"I don't want to talk about this."

"Right. Let's just walk," Luna huffed, picking up speed, leaving him. He watched her fall in stride with Alex and her face lit up as they began to converse.

"Yeah, just leave," Sam breathed. He wiped more sweat from his face. It had to be almost ten now. Not that time meant anything anymore. There was day and there was night. That's all that really mattered.

He squinted in the sun and stared at Tower 12, still at least twenty miles away. The black abnormality rose hundreds of feet into the cloudless sky, a faceless wash of darkness against the dry blue. The twin spires at the peak sliced toward the sun. He couldn't see it from this distance, but Sam knew one of the Gargoyles was up there. There was one atop each of the twenty-six Towers across North America. They still puzzled him – the massive, isolated creatures. He had never seen one up close and wasn't even sure if they ever left the top of the Towers. They frightened him, though. He knew they played a crucial role in whatever purpose these mysterious Towers held. Perhaps they were responsible for the murky domes that descended from the summit of the ebony edifices. The Red Eyes territory. What the hell did they do in those bubbles? Was there purpose in any of this or was the apocalypse just as meaningless as life before The Impact?

Sam shook himself. He didn't want to think about that day, ten years ago. He had only been twenty at the time. Looking back, he hardly recognized his younger self.

Everything had been different before the Towers had come thundering from the sky.

Before most of the world had been lost.

Before The Impact.

"Sam!"

Sam snapped from his thoughts and directed his attention toward Alex and Luna who had come to a stop at the summit of a hill a couple dozen yards ahead. The wind whipped Luna's dark hair across her bright green eyes and Sam felt his stomach sink. God, she was pretty.

"Stop it," he muttered to himself, walking faster to catch his friends.

He reached the hilltop and followed Alex's finger down the

road. A gas station lay a half mile away. It looked mostly destroyed, stray garbage blowing across the vacant pumps. Past the station, down a winding road to the left, was a small cluster of houses surrounded by dying trees that stretched north over the horizon.

"What do you think?" Alex asked, his face flush.

Sam gnawed on his lip, "I don't know. We're making good time and haven't run into anyone. Those houses look a couple miles away. That's going to take some time on foot."

Alex nodded, "Yeah, but maybe there's a car down there. Sam, if the Towers overlap ahead, we're going to want some wheels."

Sam looked at the rising construct ahead of them. His stomach churned at the sight of it. Going around them would cost precious days. If they had to push through, they were going to want to do it as quickly as possible. The hills blocked their sightline to where he knew Tower 11 was. And the diameter of its dome.

Where more Red Eyes roamed.

"Sam?"

He sighed, "Shit...I don't know. I don't want to stop. Let's go to the gas station down there and see what we can find. We'll decide if we want to check out the houses afterwards."

"Sounds good," Luna said.

"I thought Tower 13," Alex started, pointing behind them, "and Tower 12 were the only ones within eyesight of one another."

"They are," Luna said patiently, "Apparently Tower 11's dome is massive. One of the biggest. If that's the case then it could very well overlap with 12's without being in eyesight of it."

"Why is it so much bigger than the rest?" Alex asked, confused.

"I don't know," Luna exhaled, "maybe there's more Red Eyes trapped inside."

"They're not trapped," Sam said, "They can leave if they want. They just don't very often."

"Thank you, Sam," Luna grated, "I forgot The Impact happened yesterday and I know nothing."

"Knock it off you two," Alex cut in, "We don't have time for this. If Sam wants to check out the gas station then that's what we're going to do. Now, unless you two wanna nip at each other a little more, I suggest we move on."

Without another word, the three began to descend the hill, following the barren road down toward the lonely gas station. The sun was in full blossom now, casting thick heat across the dry land. As they drew closer to the vacant building, Sam wished desperately for some shade.

"Easy now," Alex said, eyeing the blown-out glass panes lining the front of the station. "We don't know if anyone is inside."

Everyone drew their guns and Sam took the lead, inching his way toward the lonely doors. One of them was open, leaning back on its hinges. An empty chip bag blew across the tarmac, lost in the stale breeze.

Sam, pistol at the ready, stepped across the threshold, sweeping his eyes across the litter. The isles were in complete disarray. What little hadn't been looted was strew about without care. The coolers lining the walls were empty, the panel doors smashed or broken. Sam turned toward the counter, harboring hope for some cigarettes. Everything had been taken.

"We clear?" Luna asked at Sam's shoulder.

"I think s-" Sam started, but the words seized in his throat as something moved from the back of the store, behind one of the isles.

Alex stepped forward, his voice blasting through the station, "Hey! If someone's there, you better get out here right now! We all have guns and we *will* shoot you!"

A solitary second passed before a woman's voice began to whimper from the back, frail and scared, "Please don't kill me! I'm unarmed!"

"Come on out here!" Luna barked, sliding to the side to gain a better vantage point.

Trembling, a thin woman with ratty blond hair emerged from the isles. Her face was tear-streaked and dark blood stained her clothes.

"That's far enough," Alex ordered, keeping his pistol trained on her.

"Please," the woman begged, "I'm harmless. Just be on your way and leave me alone."

"Don't move," Luna ordered.

"What happened to you?" Sam demanded as Alex advanced and began to pat her down for weapons.

The woman shuddered beneath Alex's touch and when he was satisfied, she wrapped her arms around herself and stared at the floor. She seemed to be in shock.

"Who's blood is that?" Sam asked, a little more gently.

The woman just sniffled and continued to stare at the ground. Luna holstered her pistol and approached, her hands outstretched in a harmless gesture.

"She's terrified," Alex observed.

"We're not going to hurt you," Luna said quietly. "You don't need to be afraid." She placed her hand on the woman's shoulder, "What's your name?"

The woman hitched a sob, "Kristen."

"Ok, Kristen," Luna said softly, "can you tell us what happened? Where are you from? What are you doing here?"

The woman, Kristen, looked at Luna, her eyes threatening more tears, "We made a mistake. An awful, awful mistake."

"Explain," Alex said, earning a stern look from Luna.

"We just want to help," Sam soothed.

Kristen licked her chapped lips before continuing, "I-I lived in a community a couple miles from here. Maybe you saw it from the road."

"We did," Sam said.

Kristen ran a hand across her face, her voice thin, "Things were good there. Really good. We had food, water, guns, everything. We were safe." She shook her head, "And we got cocky."

"How so?" Alex pressed.

Kristen shook her head, "We thought we could destroy one of the Towers. We had so much firepower, so many willing bodies. Everyone was on board. We wanted to fight back. We had grown confident in our comfort. And so we formed a plan of attack. We had trucks, plastic explosives, rocket launchers, and a couple military men who trained us all how to shoot."

"How many of you were there?" Luna asked.

"About fifty went on the assault, myself included. We left behind about a hundred others. Children. Older folk. A couple men and women who couldn't fight."

"That's quite the community you had," Alex stated, "but there's also a lot of Red Eyes in the bubbles. Which Tower was your target?"

Kristen rubbed her arm, shaking her head, "Tower 12. We weren't worried about the Red Eyes. There were lots of them, but we had so many guns. Have you ever seen a Red Eye use a gun?"

"Can't say I have," Alex confessed.

Kristen closed her eyes, "None of it mattered though. We didn't even make it inside the dome."

"Why? What happened?" Sam asked.

Kristen's eyes rose to meet his, her voice a fearful hiss, "Because *he* got to us first."

"Empire," Sam whispered.

Kristen's face paled, "We saw him about three miles from the dome. We were all in trucks, armed to the teeth. He was alone, empty-handed, just strolling down the road toward us like he didn't have a care in the world."

"When did you know it was him?" Luna asked.

Kristen turned to her, "When he started to *massacre* us."

"Christ," Alex muttered.

Kristen continued, her voice pregnant with the horrific memory, "We didn't stand a chance. I managed to crawl underneath one of the trucks and play dead until it was over. I think I pissed myself. There was so much screaming. I can still hear it, ringing in my ears. It felt like hours, but everyone was dead in less than a minute."

"Fuck," Sam hissed.

Kristen looked at him, her eyes rimmed with red, "Yes. Fuck. But he didn't stop there. Oh no, he had to make an example of us. Don't fuck with the Towers."

"What did he do?" Luna asked cautiously.

Kristen closed her eyes, tears trailing through the dirt on her face, "He went to our community," She opened her eyes again, "and slaughtered *everyone*. I didn't know until I stumbled my way back there a few hours later. I was in a daze, shell-shocked

I guess. But when I got back to the community…I knew something was wrong before I even passed through the gate. It was so quiet. And when I made it inside…"

Luna swallowed hard and rubbed Kristen's shoulder.

Kristen drew the back of her hand across her eyes, "He didn't just kill them…he butchered them. Every last man, woman, and child. It didn't matter. They were all dead."

Alex exchanged looks with Sam.

"Do you know where he went?" Sam asked.

Kristen looked up at him, "Where he went? I don't know. And I don't want to know. This was days ago. I fled, fearing he would come back, like somehow he would know I had survived."

"And did he?"

"I don't think so. But there was one night, a couple back, when I thought he had. It was the first night I stayed here at the gas station. I was so tired and night had fallen hours before. I was sitting over by the counter there when I thought I heard…I thought I heard whistling on the wind."

"Whistling?"

Kristen nodded, "I know it sounds crazy, but when I heard it, I knew it was him. And I knew he was close. So I hid as best I could and covered my ears, like hearing it would somehow give away my position."

"But you never saw him?"

"No. The whistling stopped after a couple minutes and I didn't hear it again."

Luna traded eyes with Alex and Sam, "What do you want to do?"

Sam looked outside, "How long ago exactly did you hear the whistling?"

Kristen shuffled her feet, "I'm not a hundred percent, but I think about three days ago."

"Seems she bought us some time," Alex muttered.

Kristen glared at him, her voice suddenly venomous, "How can you say that?"

Alex turned away and began to rummage through the isles. Sam went to Kristen and stood before her, his voice solemn.

"I'm so sorry about your friends. What happened to them is awful. We've been on Empire's trail for a long time now, chasing him across the U.S. This is the closest we've ever been. Forgive my friend for his eagerness."

Kristen's eyes were wide, "Why are you chasing him? What are you planning on doing once you catch him?"

"We're going to *kill* him," Alex responded from the back of the store, "we're going to fucking kill him."

Chapter 3

Sam stood at the open doorway of the gas station, turning things over in his mind. Luna was comforting Kristen, calming her down. Alex was idly picking through the remains of the isles without luck.

Sam raised a hand against the looming sun. It was past noon now. He took a sip of water from his bottle and sighed. The news of Empire made his blood boil. So many dead. And for what? What did that accomplish?

Luna approached his side, her hand on his arm, "Hey. What are you thinking about?"

"Everything," Sam muttered, offering her the water bottle.

She took it and drizzled some into her mouth, "What are we going to do about her?"

Sam looked over his shoulder at Kristen, "What do you mean?"

"We can't just leave her here."

Sam raised an eyebrow, "We're not taking her with us. She's a mess. She'd slow us down and I'm not letting that happen, not when we're this close."

Luna's mouth compressed, "So we just leave her here to fend

for herself? Sam, she can barely keep it together. She won't last long."

"She's lasted this long," Sam said, turning back to the sun.

"How can you say that?" Luna whispered.

Sam felt irritation spike through him, "Did you ask Alex?"

"No."

Sam exhaled through his nostrils, "Of course you didn't. Because you want me to be the bad guy here, not him."

"What the hell are you talking about?"

Sam faced her, "She's not coming with us. There. Now you can hate me instead of Alex. Happy?"

"You need to stop with this," Luna said gravely, "right now."

"You already did."

Luna opened her mouth to respond, but the words died in her throat. A rumble filled the air. An engine. And it was drawing closer.

"Back inside," Sam hissed, pushing Luna away.

Alex poked his head out from between the isles, "Uh guys? Is there a car coming?"

"Yeah, and fast," Sam said, retreating back behind the counter, "everyone stay down. We don't know who they are. Hopefully, they'll pass."

"This is a gas station," Luna groaned, huddling in the corner with Kristen, "if they have a truck, they're going to check the pumps. That's what I would do."

"Shit," Sam hissed, ducking low and peering out at the road.

The vehicle came into sight, growling up a cloud of dust in its wake. It was an SUV, a grey one. Just as Luna predicted, it slowed as it approached the gas station. Sam tracked it, his heart racing. He pulled the pistol from his belt, his hands sweaty.

"Oh god," Alex said quietly as the SUV came to a stop. Sam saw it too. His pulse raced. His stomach rolled.

A pair of chains had been attached to the back of the vehicle. The ends had been fastened to two bodies, bound at the throat. The miles of burning road had shredded the flesh beyond recognition.

"Goddamn it," Sam muttered, appalled. It looked like a man and a woman. Maybe. It was hard to tell beneath all the gore and bone.

Three men loudly climbed from the SUV. One of them had a shotgun. The other two had machetes. They looked to be in their mid-forties and they were dressed in mismatching camo.

The man with the shotgun pointed at the front doors, "Hey! Anyone in there!? We need a fill-up!"

His two friends laughed.

Without warning, the man with the shotgun blasted a round into the isles. Sam heard Alex curse under his breath as shards fell around him. Sam met his eyes. Alex gave him a thumbs up. He was ok. Hidden, scared, but ok.

"Don't think anyone's home," the man with the shotgun announced. "Pity! We could use a couple more tag-alongs, don't you think fellas?"

One of the men gestured toward the dragged bodies, "Think them two are finally dead. Took long enough. Shit."

Sam gripped the pistol tighter in his hand. He looked at Alex and that was all it took. They were going to kill these monsters and take their ride.

No one misses monsters.

Sam slowly crouched and waited, a trickle of sweat running down the side of his face. From his position, he'd need to hop the counter if they entered through the doors. He didn't like that, but he was trapped where he was.

The man with the shotgun approached the storefront, "Check the pumps, guys. I'm going to see if there's any food inside."

Casually slinging the shotgun over his shoulder, the man entered through the doors. Sam braced himself. And then he heard Alex move.

In one swift motion, Sam watched as Alex stood, took aim, and blew the man's brains out the back of his skull. Without waiting for the body to fall, Sam hopped the counter and rolled across the open door, bringing his pistol up as he went.

The two remaining men were frozen, their mouths open in shock.

Sam shot one of them through the eye.

He trained his pistol to finish off the last, but Alex's booming voice stopped him.

"WAIT!"

Sam kept his pistol trained on the survivor. He saw him piss himself. Alex walked past Sam, out into the open air.

He unstrapped the cleaver from his leg.

"Alex, he's got a machete!" Luna screamed from somewhere inside the store.

It didn't matter. Alex was gone at that point. Sam could see his shoulders shaking, his fists trembling, the hell in his step. The remaining man took a desperate swing at him, but Alex sidestepped it and drove a fist through the man's teeth. He knocked most of them out. The machete fell and Alex kicked it away.

"You sick fucks," Sam heard Alex snarl, raising the cleaver.

Sam turned away and saw Luna and Kristen watching. Sam pointed to the back of the store.

"Get her away from here. She's not going to want to see this."

But they didn't move. The screaming had started.

The hacking.

The rage.

Reluctantly, Sam turned back to the grisly scene.

Alex was breathing heavily, his torso coated in red. His cleaver rose and fell, each blow shearing chunks off the still screaming man.

It seemed like an eternity before he died.

Gasping, chest heaving, Alex stepped away from the carnage. Blood dripped down his arms, across his face, from his hair. His eyes were wide, his teeth stained crimson.

He spit on the carcass, "Fucking cunt."

Sam carefully went to his friend, "Hey man…it's done. He's gone." Alex looked up at him, like he wasn't sure where he was.

"What? Oh…yeah…yeah I guess he is."

"Let's get you cleaned up a little, yeah?"

Alex swallowed, still catching his breath, "Sure Sam. Ok."

Luna was suddenly at Alex's side, her hand on his arm, her face riddled with concern, "Come on, I gotcha. Let's go inside and find something to get that blood off you."

Sam stepped back, going numb. He watched as Luna guided their friend back into the gas station, her hand never leaving him. Alex seemed to be completely out of it, his eyes vacant, his movement robotic.

Instead of allowing himself to feel anything, Sam went to the SUV and inspected it. The keys were still in the ignition. He checked the gauges and saw there was still a quarter tank of gas. That would help. He opened the passenger door and rummaged through the glove compartment for supplies. He was delighted to find a half-smoked pack of cigarettes. He stuffed them into his pocket.

In the back was a duffel bag full of canned food and a couple bottles of water.

At the bottom was a cellphone.

Heart racing, Sam turned it on. Twenty-six percent power. He went around to the other side of the SUV, so the others couldn't see him, and then checked for voicemails.

There was one.

Closing his eyes, he played it back and Listened.

"Hi Mark, the kids are at soccer practice right now and I'm stuck at work. Do you think you could pick them up? Shoot me a text and let me know. Love you."

Sam exhaled and powered down the phone. Memories of before floated back. Centered him. Cleared out some of the shit, the violence he had just conducted. He had needed that in the worst kind of way.

He pocketed the cellphone and decided not to tell the others about it. Not yet. As much as he hated to admit it, he was discovering how much he needed to Listen these days. As much as he wanted to fight it, he continuously felt the desire to remember.

"Everything ok?" Kristen asked, her voice startling Sam.

He turned, clearing his throat, "Oh. Yeah, just checking for supplies."

Kristen wrapped her arms around herself, "What the hell was with your friend just now? Is something wrong with him?"

Sam shook his head, "He just gets like that sometimes. He's fine."

"There was nothing fine about what I just saw."

Sam shrugged, "It's just how things are now."

"He doesn't seem stable."

Sam felt himself growing irritated all of the sudden, "Stability left us after The Impact. I know you've been safely tucked away in your community the past couple months, but this is the world now. Those men deserved what they got."

Kristen seemed uncomfortable, her voice thin, "Are you taking the car?"

Sam nodded and walked around to the back where the bodies were chained. Wordlessly, he began to remove them from the vehicle. Kristen followed him.

"Where are you going to go?"

"After Empire. Now that we have wheels, we'll roll the dice and race between the domes."

"You know the domes overlap right? There's no safe way between them. You should go around. There's going to be a lot of Red Eyes."

"Yeah, I know," Sam said without looking up, "But Empire is close and we can't waste time going around. We'll stick to this road and plow through. I can't imagine it'll be more than a couple miles under the domes before we're through."

Kristen stopped Sam from his work, a hand on his shoulder, "Don't throw your lives away. You can't kill him. Didn't you hear my story? He destroyed us in seconds. All of us. And we were heavily armed and knew how to fight. What makes you think you can fare any better?"

Sam looked up at her, his eyes hard, "He's just a man."

"You're wrong," Kristen whispered, "what aren't you telling me? What do you know?"

Sam finished unhooking the chains without answering.

Kristen shook her head, "Fine. Don't answer."

"I need to go check on my friends," Sam muttered, pushing his way past her. He walked around the SUV and went back inside. Alex was standing by the counter with Luna at his side. She was using a rag to mop off the blood from his arms. Her touch was tender and deliberate, her eyes concerned.

Sam approached them, "You ok?"

"He's fine," Luna said, dragging the rag across Alex's hand.

Sam looked at Alex, "You fine?"

Alex nodded, his color returning, "Yeah. Don't worry about me. How's the car? Can we use it?"

"It's got gas," Sam said nodding, "along with some food and water."

"So what's the move here?" Luna asked, finished up.

Sam crossed his arms, "We go through the domes. The overlap can't be more than a couple miles. We should be ok."

Alex nodded his thanks to Luna as she stepped back, "That sounds like a good plan. I say we go for it."

Sam looked at Luna, "You ok with this?"

Luna tossed the bloodied rag away, "You know how much I hate going near those damn Towers."

Sam sighed, "I know. But Empire can't be more than a day or two ahead of us. If we don't stick to the road, we're going to lose a lot of time."

Luna's shoulders slumped, "I'm aware of that, Sam. I just…" she looked at her feet.

"The Red Eyes," Alex finished.

Luna nodded, "I hate them. I hate them so goddamn much."

"We all do," Sam said, "and they've all taken something from us."

Luna's voice weakened, "They took away *everything*."

Alex touched her shoulder, "Sam and I care about you. You're not alone."

Luna's frown weakened, "I know that. We've just never been inside the bubbles before."

"You can do this," Alex continued, "remember when Sam and I found you in Arizona? Hell, we thought you were dead. You were surrounded by about a dozen bloody Red Eyes, all blown to bits. And there you were, sitting against the wall with that shotgun in your hands. Do you remember what you said when we approached you?"

Luna smirked, "I told you that just because I was out of ammo didn't mean I couldn't kill you."

"You sure did," Alex smirked. "Put some of that ice back in your veins."

Luna's mouth coiled and then she exhaled, "Alright. Fine. Let's get this over with."

Alex looked at Sam, "Our ride ready to go?"

"Sure is."

"Hold on," Luna said, "what about Kristen?"

Kristen was standing off to the side, watching the conversation. When she was mentioned, she took a step back, raising her hands, "What about me?"

"You're all alone," Luna said.

Kristen took another step back, "So?"

"You should come with us," Luna continued.

Sam was about to object, but before he could, Kristen spoke, "No thanks. I think I'm better off on my own. I don't want to get anywhere near those Towers. And no offense, but your friend seems a little…unstable."

Alex cast his eyes aside.

"Are you sure?" Luna pressed.

Kristen nodded.

"Then let's move," Sam said, pushing past everyone. "We're wasting time."

Alex followed in stride. Luna went to Kristen and placed a hand on her shoulder, "I can tell you won't change your mind so just…just take care of yourself, ok?"

"You too."

Sam had climbed into the driver's seat and had started the engine by the time Luna joined them. She took the backseat and crossed her arms. Alex glanced at her from the passenger's seat.

"You ok?"

"I just feel weird leaving her like this."

"She knows what she wants," Sam said, shifting into drive, "you can't change that."

"We could have tried."

Sam let the statement die as he pulled out onto the road. Alex stared out the window as the SUV picked up speed. An unspoken weight settled around the car. Tower 12 soared in the distance like a black knife slicing the sky in two. The dome shimmered around it, a transparent bowl that engulfed the surrounding land.

As they drew closer, Sam spotted the overlap of the domes, a pair of low arches, like a cartoon heart cut across the middle. He drove toward it, his knuckles tightening on the wheel. Alex sensed his tension and began cleaning his cleaver. His eyes were empty, but the creases along his mouth gave him away.

When they were about a mile away, the landscape a flat brown carpet littered with abandoned buildings, Sam heard Luna speak from the backseat.

"Sam. Red Eyes."

"I see them," he answered. They were milling about the edges of the domes, watching the car approach. A few of them wandered past the divide, their heads cocked curiously to one side.

"They're on the road," Alex muttered.

"I know," Sam hissed. A cluster of six were standing shoulder to shoulder, blocking the way. Did they seriously think he would slow down?

"Hold on," he growled, gunning the SUV right for the middle man. Their eyes flared dangerously, red light wafting from their sockets like neon smoke.

"Oh hell. Guys look!" Luna yelled from the back, her face pressed to the window, her eyes trained up.

Sam leaned forward and looked to where Luna was pointing, to the top of the Tower. His heart skipped a beat and dread filled him like poisonous water.

From the top of the Tower, the Gargoyle moved. It's long dark limbs extended and it pointed a gnarled finger directly at them. Its eyes were open and writhing on the long stalks that hosted them. Its wide, massive head twisted on its long, boneless neck and it reminded Sam of a worm in agony. As the SUV raced closer, he saw the Gargoyle step to the edge of the Tower summit, its two long legs making short work of the distance.

It continued to point at them.

"It's taken control of them!" Luna shrieked as the Red Eyes began to form up on the road. They were seconds from hitting them, the engine roaring.

"SHIT!" Sam screamed, jerking the wheel to the side, the pack now seven deep. The car bounced violently and Alex leaned away as his door brushed past them, knocking a few of the Red Eyes back a couple steps.

"Go, go, go!" Luna cried as Sam adjusted the wheel and steered them back onto the road, past the cluster.

And for the first time in ten years, since the Towers fell from the heavens, they entered the bubble.

Something shuddered through them as they passed the barrier, a quick shiver that reached for every nerve in their bodies. It passed in an instant and they were back on track. The base of Tower 12 dominated the view outside Alex's window, a thick, dark column surrounded by milling Red Eyes.

"I've never seen a Gargoyle move before, ever," Alex said, his face pale. "Jesus Sam, look at all these Red Eyes. They're coming right for us."

And they were. As soon as the SUV passed through the dome, the swarms began to sprint toward the fast-moving vehicle. Sam felt his forehead break out in a cold sweat, his eyes trained on the road. Just a couple miles and they'd be through. Just a couple miles.

"I can't see the Gargoyle anymore!" Luna yelled from the back, her face twisted against the window, "the Tower is too high! Go faster, Sam, PLEASE!"

Gritting his teeth, Sam floored it.

"Where the fuck is the other side?" Alex called, squinting into the distance.

"Sam, the Red Eyes are filling the road again!" Luna cried from the back, clutching his seat.

"Goddamn it!" Sam yelled, jerking the wheel again, taking them off the pavement. The SUV sloped to one side and shuddered across a steep ditch, drawing an angry growl from the shocks. Up on the road, the Red Eyes blurred past.

More were coming from the left, about a half mile ahead.

Dozens of them, streaming from the remains of a busted

auto garage. They were yelling and pointing at the car, completely lost beneath the Gargoyle's control. Sam aimed back for the road, and as he did so, his heart stopped.

From one of the garage bays, a semi-truck roared into their path.

"Oh FUCK!" Sam screamed.

"Watch it!" Alex yelled, pointing ahead.

The wheels tumbled back onto the road and Sam directed his eyes back to the semi. It spit gravel from its massive wheels and spun out onto the road, headed directly for them. Sam could see a Red Eye at the wheel, a woman, her face empty of emotion.

"She's going to hit us!" Luna screamed, bracing herself as the truck roared for them.

At the last second, Sam jerked the SUV to the right, into an approaching cluster of Red Eyes. The semi clipped the back wheel and they went spinning into the swarm. Blood sprayed the windows and bone crunched loudly from outside as they made contact. Sam heard the back wheel blow out and the crunch of metal as the bumper was ripped away.

Fighting the wheel, Sam wrestled to keep them from flipping over as flesh thundered against the windows. Blood splashed wetly across the windshield and from the backseat, he heard Luna grunt painfully. He didn't have time to check if she was ok as he stomped on the gas and righted the SUV. It shuddered painfully and limped along, the back wheel thumping loudly.

"Get us back on the fucking road!" Alex screamed through gritted teeth.

"SHUT UP!" Sam roared, the SUV finding pavement once more. Behind them, the snarl of the semi revved up as it turned around for another pass.

Sam made the rubber sing as the wet tires skidded across the tarmac, toward the other side of the domes. More Red Eyes raced for the road, clogging their passage. Sam chanced a glance back and saw Luna rolling down the window. A Red Eye was clutched the side, smashing its head against the glass in a crazed attempt to get in. Luna raised her pistol and stuffed it down the man's mouth. One shot later and the SUV was free of the clinger.

Eyes back on the road, Sam's heart raced as he tried to put distance between them and the approaching semi. The smashed back wheel was like a weight, dragging them down, and the massive truck roared on approach.

"It's going to hit us again!" Luna cried.

"Well then hold the fuck on!" Sam screamed, bracing himself.

With diesel roaring in his ears, Sam felt his spine whiplash as the semi made contact. His teeth clicked together and his forehead battered off the wheel. Stars momentarily consumed his world before he shook his vision clear. He tore through a pair of Red Eyes who had made it onto the road, their bodies crunching against the grill.

"There's the other side!" Alex called. Blood ran from the side of his face, but he didn't seem to notice.

Sam made the engine wail as he accelerated, the semi-hot on their trail. He leaned forward, counting off seconds before another impact. Sweat stung his eyes and his heart raced frantically. The other side of the dome was right in front of them. They could make it.

And then they were through.

Another shiver ran through them as they passed the barrier. The Red Eyes following them continued to sprint past the transparent wall, but as soon as they did, they slowed and began to look around, like they had no idea where they were. As their eyes fell on the SUV, their brows furrowed with hatred, but they did not pursue further. The Gargoyle had lost control of their bloodlust, their consciousness returned to the individuals, along with their will to live.

The semi rolled through the dome as well, but as the driver passed the divide, she sat up straight and slammed on the brakes. Sam watched this through the rearview mirror, his breath returning to him in a relieved wave. They hated this side of humanity, but they didn't want to throw their lives away. Not unless the Gargoyles made them.

"Don't slow down," Luna urged.

"That's the last thing I want to do," Sam said, still tense. His eyes continued to flicker across the mirrors, making sure they actually were leaving their pursuit behind.

Ten minutes later, he finally allowed himself to relax a little, his shoulders melting from stone. The back wheel thumped loudly, but Sam didn't stop.

An hour later they passed a filthy sign and Alex chuckled.

"Welcome to Louisiana, everyone."

Chapter 4

Sam leaned against the SUV, smoking a cigarette. Alex and Luna were huddled around a campfire they had made, the light pushing back the deep shadows of night. They had stopped when darkness had fallen, the headlights smashed to pieces in the crossing. Sam didn't feel comfortable driving without them so they had decided to stop until sunrise. They had entered a patch of woodlands and had found a clearing to pull off onto. After their ordeal earlier, everyone needed a breather.

Alex scooped beans out of a can and offered the rest to Luna. She took them and held them up for Sam.

"You eating tonight?"

"Already am," Sam said, flicking his cig.

Luna shrugged and dug in. Alex opened a water bottle, one of the ones from the SUV and took a long pull from it. The flames from the fire danced across his face and his eyes looked distant, troubled.

"That was some wild shit today," Luna said around a mouthful of beans.

"Yeah, but we made it," Sam said, exhaled smoke.

"Was worried there for a second," Luna muttered, casting the empty can aside. She folded her arms and scooted across the ground closer to Alex.

"You alright, man?" Sam asked, finishing his cig.

Alex looked up, distracted, "Huh? Oh…yeah. I'm fine."

"What are you thinking about?" Luna asked quietly.

Alex rolled his head back, "Everything. The Towers, the domes, those goddamn Gargoyles…the Red Eyes."

"You saw how it took control of them, right?" Luna asked.

Alex nodded, "Yeah. We heard they could do that – Sam and I back in Nevada. We ran into some woman who studied the Towers. She was fascinated with them. That's how we learned so much about how all that works. If the Red Eyes are under the domes, the Gargoyles can control them."

"But why? Why do they usually stick to the domes then?"

Alex shrugged, "I don't know. You'd have to ask a Red Eye. We know they hunt the rest of us, though. We know they can change us."

"What do you think they want?" Luna asked softly.

"No idea. But we know once they take us into the Towers, we don't come out ourselves. They do something to us inside. They change us. They make us one of them."

Luna huddled into herself, "It's so awful. I can't imagine being one of them. Even if I'm not a mindless drone…hell, you've interacted with them. You see what they're like. They're completely brainwashed by whatever their endgame is. Whatever their purpose is. Whatever the hell those damn Towers are here for."

Sam heaved himself away from the SUV, "We should get some sleep."

Alex nodded, absently.

Luna wrapped her arms around herself tighter and scooted even closer to Alex, "I don't know if I can sleep tonight."

Sam felt something twist in his gut as Luna laid her head against Alex's shoulder. She closed her eyes and breathed softly, visibly trying to shake the memory of the day away. Sam pulled another cig from his pack.

"I'm going to walk a little. Make sure we're alone."

Alex just stared into the fire and Luna nodded, her eyes still closed, her cheek pressed against Alex. Sam couldn't look at it any longer and strode off into the woods. He lit his cigarette as he went, forcing himself to calm. It was the end of the world, there wasn't time for that kind of thing. At least, that's what he tried to tell himself.

The woodland grew around him as he pushed into it. Dry twigs and leaves crunched underfoot, but the ground was soggy from the recent storm. It was also quiet, the absence of animal nightlife glaringly apparent. It was something growing more and more common these days. It wasn't just humans who hated the Towers.

He let his mind wander, thinking back on the day he set out with Alex. He loved Alex, had grown up on the same street as him. They were like brothers. When the Towers came, he was one of the first people he had sought out. He had been with his wife, barely two weeks married, just back from their honeymoon. Whether her pregnancy was a catalyst for their marriage or not, it made no difference to Alex. He had always planned on marrying her. The discovery that she was with child only sped up the inevitable.

Those were the good days.

Before Alex learned to hate the Red Eyes.

Before they dragged his wife and unborn child off to the Towers.

Sam crunched through the underbrush, milking the last of his smoke. Christ, that had been a bad day. Alex had lost his mind.

They had run to the store to grab some food and supplies. No one knew what was happening, everything was in chaos. At that point, it seemed like a safe idea, though. The Red Eyes were a new threat, one that was unknown. And Alex wasn't going to let his new wife go hungry while the world tore itself apart. He was going to take care of her, no matter what. That was something he had drilled into Sam's head as they had run to the store to stock up. They had formulated a plan. They were going to stick together. They were going to make it through this, whatever it was.

They couldn't have been gone more than fifteen minutes. When they got back to Alex's house, it was overrun with Red Eyes. The whole street was. And they had taken his wife, along with everyone else who couldn't fight or hide.

"God, we tried," Sam muttered, the memory lingering.

But she was gone. And it was either stay and be taken or run. They had run.

Alex had never been the same after that day. Neither of them had been.

Sam stopped suddenly, his ears perking up. He looked around, slightly lost. He hadn't been paying attention where he was going and moody forest pressed close. Did he hear something moving out there?

He slid behind a tree, hand going to his pistol. It had been stupid to smoke. The smell was like a signal flare to anyone around. Sam paused and listened again. Was someone walking through the woods? A breeze stirred the treetops and blew across his face.

His heart froze.

Faintly, he heard whistling on the wind, a gentle, soft melody that ignited every alarm in his mind. It rose with the air and swirled through the darkness without a care in the world. The hair stood up on the back of Sam's neck and his eyes darted between the trees. The whistling died and was replaced by the rustle of leaves overhead.

Heart in his throat, he slowly drew his gun.

Someone was watching him. He could feel their eyes on him, consuming him. But no matter where he looked, he couldn't see.

"Where are you, you son of a bitch?" Sam whispered, clutching the tree he was behind with his free hand. He needed to alert Alex and Luna. He needed to get back to the SUV. But where the hell was it? Where was he?

His skin crawled as the whistling came again, dancing across the currents of night. It fluttered around him and twisted with the wind, echoing into the black. Sam licked his lips, his mouth suddenly dry. He could feel his pulse thundering in his ears as he scanned the forest, desperate to spot the source.

Suddenly, on the wind, a voice whispered to him, a soft calling.

"*Sam Sam Sam Sam Sam Sam Sam Sam….*" and then it died, lost beneath the breeze.

Slowly, Sam backed up. He kept his eyes glued to where he thought the voice had come from, but it was impossible to be sure. He had to get back to camp. Now.

And then, without warning, coming from all directions.

"*I see you…*"

Sam broke into a run, back the way he had come, praying it was the right direction. If he got caught out here alone, he was dead. He needed Alex.

Underbrush crowded his path, snagging and slowing him. Invisible branches reached for his clothes and face, angry claws that swiped at him as he passed. He raised his hands to his face to protect himself as he thundered away from the voice, terror rippling through him in full bloom now.

The wind began to laugh, a rising cackle that chilled Sam to the bone.

Half falling, he stumbled out of the woods and into the clearing. The fire was low and offered nothing but muted shadow. Alex and Luna were nowhere to be seen.

'Oh no," Sam hissed, fear sour across his tongue. He spun around, staring fiercely at the treeline, convinced the horrors he dreaded would come roaring from the darkness. When it didn't, he raced to the SUV and tore the door open.

Alex and Luna were inside, half-naked and on top of one another. Their heads whipped up and Luna let out a startled yelp. Alex met Sam's eyes and something unspoken passed between them.

"Get out here," Sam snarled, turning away.

Alex scrambled for his shirt, "Look man-"

"He's here," Sam growled, pushing away everything else.

"Shit," Luna hissed, pulling her clothes back on. Sam stepped away from the SUV, pistol at his side. His eyes returned to the woods. His heart hammered in his chest and the breeze chuckled innocently through the clearing.

After a moment, Alex and Luna tumbled out of the car, guns at the ready. Luna trained her shotgun in the direction Sam was staring, her eyes wide, her face flush.

"Where?" Alex asked darkly, armed with his pistol and cleaver.

Sam didn't look at him, "I don't know, but I heard him. In the woods."

"What do you mean you heard him?" Luna whispered.

Sam shot her a venomous look, "I mean I heard the fucker calling my name."

Alex grit his teeth and walked to the fire. He stood over it, the light revealing the darkness beneath his eyes. He swung his head to either side, waiting, anxious, his cleaver bouncing slightly in his grip.

"Get out here," he whispered, his voice grating.

Luna went around the SUV and propped the shotgun up on the hood, one eye shut as she stared down the barrel. Sam went to Alex's side, the hairs on his forearms rising.

"You sure you heard him?" Alex asked out of the side of his mouth.

"I'm sure."

"Did he follow you?"

"I don't know."

"What do you want to do, here?"

"I don't fucking know, Alex," Sam snapped, "it's not like he's standing right in front of us."

Luna called to them from behind, "You see anything?"

"No."

The seconds ticked by, a brutal run of the clock. With each passing moment, Sam felt the tension in his shoulders lessen. He wasn't going to show himself. Not yet. Not now. He had just been toying with him.

And that enraged Sam.

"Get more wood on that fire," he finally said. "This isn't happening tonight."

Alex didn't move, "Sam, if he's here…"

Sam shot him a glare, "He's gone."

Finally, Alex moved. Luna came around to their side.

"What are you doing? Shouldn't we go?"

Sam shook his head, "If he wanted to confront us or kill us he would have already. Let's just keep the fire going and stay alert. We'll sleep in shifts tonight, just in case, but I think we'll be fine until morning."

Luna lowered her shotgun and placed it on the hood of the SUV. She went to Alex and helped him gather more firewood. Sam reached into his pocket and fumbled for his pack of cigarettes. His fingers brushed against the cellphone he had found earlier. He felt a sudden overwhelming urge to Listen, but he pulled his smokes out instead.

No harm in it now.

By the time he finished smoking, Alex and Luna had brought the fire back to life. They stood huddled around it looking unsure and anxious. They made a point not to meet Sam's eyes.

Finally, Alex nudged Luna, "Why don't you get some sleep. I'll take the first shift with Sam."

Luna looked up at him and then at the ground. Alex nudged her again and she walked slowly to the SUV. She pulled the door open and looked back at them and then at the woods. She looked like she was about to say something, but instead, she climbed inside and shut the door behind her.

Sam pulled out another cigarette and Alex stared at him from across the flame. His face was riddled with caution and smoke blew through the clearing like a catalyst.

"Look, man," Alex started.

Sam faced the forest, exhaling smoke from his nostrils, "Don't."

Alex sighed and rubbed his arm, "We have to talk about this."

"Why?"

"Because it bothers you and I hate that."

"It doesn't bother me, Alex."

Alex shrugged, "You don't have to lie to me. I'm your best friend."

Sam turned, "Yeah. You are."

Alex deflated and sat down, crossing his hands over his drawn up knees, "Jesus man, I didn't plan for this to happen."

"But it did. It's fine."

"Don't do that."

"Do what?"

"Don't dismiss me like I'm some asshole."

Sam clenched his fists, his cigarette clamped between his teeth, "I don't want to talk about this."

"I'm not going to make excuses," Alex pressed on, "and I'm not going to bullshit you. I like Luna. This isn't going to go away."

Sam hissed smoke.

"I know you and her had a thing there in the beginning."

"It wasn't a 'thing'. It was one night. We fucked. That's it."

Alex nodded, "Right, right. I just don't want you to be pissed at me. Or whatever it is you're feeling. I need this. I need her. There's so many things that are wrong right now…I just need something to be right. And what we have – it's right. It might be skin deep, but it's enough. It helps me…keep things under control. For the most part. I mean Christ, Sam, you know how I feel about what we're doing and why we're doing it."

Sam's voice was low, "Are we talking about Empire now?"

Alex looked at his hands, his eyes dark.

"Look at me, Alex."

Alex raised his head.

"I don't give a shit about you and Luna. Seriously. We're cool."

Alex snorted and then nodded, "Thanks, man. Means a lot."

Sam stepped toward the fire, his voice low, "Just promise me one thing."

"What's that?"

"That we'll catch Empire and figure out what the fuck is going on."

Alex's face hardened, "Of course."

Sam grit his teeth, "And then we kill him."

Alex balled his hands into fists, "Sam. He's dead. Count on it."

They stared at one another a second longer and then Sam nodded. He relaxed some and slumped, sitting opposite Alex. The flame shuddered and popped between them, the night silent and empty.

"I can't believe he was so close," Alex muttered.

"We'll get him," Sam whispered.

"What's the plan for tomorrow?"

"Keep driving. Keep searching. He's out there. We just have to find him."

"You think the busted wheel will hold out?"

"It will until it won't. Nothing we can do about it."

Alex sighed heavily.

"What is it?"

Alex ran his hands over his face, "I'm just…tired."

"Yeah. Me too. We've been through a lot."

"Why don't you get some sleep? I'll keep my eye on things," Alex offered.

Sam wanted to protest but found he didn't have the energy. He nodded and rolled over on his side. The heat from the fire was warm against his face and he closed his eyes against it. He listened to the wood crackle and it was the last thing he heard before sleep took him.

He dreamed of the Towers, rising up into a blood red sky. The alien beings, the Gargoyles, were standing, watching him as he walked between the foreboding structures. The massive giants were all pointing at him, their dark fingers tracing his path across the ruined land. Past the sky, past the color, something moved. Something shifted.

Something…approached.

"Sam."

He stirred, the dream slipping.

"*Sam.*"

He opened his eyes. Immediately, he knew something was wrong. Alex was crouched down next to him, one hand shaking him awake. Sam blinked himself from sleep and sat up, fear rising from the urgency in Alex's voice.

"What is it?" He whispered, going on full alert.

Barely audible, Alex pointed to the woods, "Look."

They were surrounded by Red Eyes. They lined the forest front, unmoving, crimson smoke wafting from their icy glares. They didn't speak, they didn't flinch. They only watched, as silent as the night around them.

"What is this?" Sam whispered, heart hammering.

Alex leaned into his ear, "They appeared out of nowhere. They haven't moved."

Sam reached down and retrieved his pistol, "Where's Luna?"

"She's still asleep in the SUV."

Sam's grip tightened around his gun, "There's too many to fight."

Alex ground his teeth together, "We could take them."

Sam grabbed his friend's arm, "Don't be ridiculous. It's five to one."

The Red Eyes continued to watch, their faces carved from raw hatred.

"This is his doing," Alex growled, "He's trying to scare us."

"It's working," Sam whispered back.

Suddenly, Alex stood, his voice booming across the clearing, "What do you WANT!?"

If the Red Eyes heard him, they showed no sign.

Alex took a step forward, "If we're going to do this then let's DO IT!"

Sam scrambled to his feet, his voice an urgent hiss, "Alex!"

"Come on then!" Alex yelled, unstrapping his cleaver, "Let's get it over with!"

"Stop it!" Sam cried, grasping for his friend's arm, "What are you doing!?"

Alex, unmoved, met the Red Eye's burning stares, "I know you can see me," he called, his voice a snarl, "so why don't you come out here yourself."

Slowly, one by one, the Red Eyes began to back up into the night.

"I'm not afraid of you!" Alex roared, "I know who you ARE!"

"Shut the hell up," Sam pleaded, "do you want to die?"

But the Red Eyes showed no signs of aggression. They continued to fade back into the forest like they had never been there at all. Soon, all they could see was a wall of night, as quiet as if nothing had ever happened.

After a few moments, Alex shivered and looked at his feet, "Christ…"

Sam shook his head, "What the hell was that all about…?"

"He wants us to stop."

Sam clenched his teeth and the wind whistled all around them.

"We should leave," Alex said, finally.

"I agree."

The two of them walked to the SUV, feeling uneasy. Luna was awake and half crawling out of the vehicle, her eyes wide and confused.

"What the hell is going on? I heard shouting."

"Red Eyes," Alex muttered.

"Here?" Luna sputtered, "Did they attack you?"

"No," Sam responded, casting a glance over his shoulder, "they were just watching us."

Luna looked at them both and her eyes settled over Alex, "We're leaving right? Yes? Good. I'll drive. You've been up all night and it'll be dawn soon. You need to sleep."

"I'll be fine," Alex said, brushing it away.

"I'm not asking," Luna said, going to him and placing a hand on his arm.

Alex looked like he was about to protest, but after seeing Luna's face, he sighed and nodded without arguing. Luna sniffed and pulled open the driver's door.

"I can go for a while," she said. Sam silently went around and took the passenger's seat. He heard Alex lie down in the back as Luna brought the engine to life.

"How much gas do we have?" Sam asked.

Luna checked the gauge, "Not much. Probably an hour or two at best. If that back wheel holds out."

"Let's go," Sam said.

It wasn't long before they heard Alex snoring softly from the back. Sam was relieved. His friend needed the rest and who knew what the day would bring.

"Can you see ok?" He asked, shooting Luna a look across the cab. The sky was tinted with the slightest hints of dawn, pushing away the darkness by a fraction.

Luna was squinting over the wheel, concentrating, "It'd help if we had headlights. You want to just stick to this road?"

Sam nodded, "Yeah. Hopefully, we won't run into any trouble. There are no Towers in Louisiana. We won't hit one until Mississippi."

"That brings little comfort considering we were just ambushed by Red Eyes," Luna muttered.

"No shit," Sam said, pulling his cigarettes from his pocket.

Luna nodded toward them, "Give me one of those, will you?"

Sam lit the one between his lips and passed it across the seats, "Didn't know you smoked."

"It's been a while," she said, taking the cigarette and inhaling deeply.

Sam's hand fell against his leg. The cellphone in his pocket bulged beneath his fingers. He retrieved it and powered it on. Luna exhaled smoke, cocking an eyebrow.

"How long have you been hiding that?"

"Not long."

"Were you going to share?"

"Probably," Sam said, watching as the screen came to life.

"You're not very good at that, are you?"

"Huh?"

"Sharing?"

Sam looked over at her, his eyes dark, "The fuck does that mean?"

Luna sighed, "It was a joke."

"Hilarious."

Luna transferred the cigarette to her opposite hand, "Do we have to talk about this? I know you and Alex already did – bartering for me like I'm not even allowed a say in the matter."

"That's not what happened."

"Sure, Sam."

Sam closed his eyes, "Look…just…"

"Just what?" Luna snapped suddenly.

"Just be good to him. He's lost a lot."

Luna stared out the windshield, "So have I. There are things I want too you know."

"Clearly."

"Christ, Sam, be an adult. It was one night."

Sam examined the phone, growing numb, "I'm well aware. Don't hold it against me, please. It wasn't just about the sex…"

"Uh…what's that mean?"

Sam squeezed his eyes closed, "It was my first time."

Luna coughed smoke, "What?!"

"Oh, piss off."

Luna cleared her throat, "That night…with me…that was the first time you've ever slept with a woman?"

"Yeah. Get over it. It's not like there's been a ton of women around. The world is ending, in case you didn't notice."

Luna flicked her cigarette out the window, "Wait, hold on.

I thought you were married? You know…before shit hit the fan?"

Sam shook his head, "No. Just Alex."

Luna looked across at him and he saw her soften slightly, "Jesus, Sam. I'm sorry."

Sam grit his teeth, "Don't do that."

"Do what?"

"Don't feel sorry for me."

"I don't! It's just…"

"Can we drop this? Please?" Sam growled, staring out the window.

Luna attempted to collect herself, but her face gave her away, "Alright. I just…yeah, alright."

"Thank you."

Silence grew between them. It wrapped itself around the interior of the SUV and clouded Sam's head. Feeling unbearably uncomfortable, he brought up a voicemail and put it on speaker. The message played and they Listened. When it was over, he heard Luna sigh.

"God, I miss those days."

"So do I," Sam said quietly, shutting the phone down. He shoved it back into his pocket and returned his eyes to the window. The sky was starting to exhume color, a precursor to a hot, clear day.

"You know," he started, "you've been with us a couple months now and I've never asked you about when we found you."

Luna shrugged, "What about it?"

"Before you joined us on this mad hunt…what were you doing?"

"I don't know. Trying to survive. Trying to understand what

the hell was happening to the world. I mean it's been years and we're no closer to understanding what exactly the Towers are. Or the Gargoyles."

"Did you have a family?" Sam asked, a little too casually.

Luna's knuckles turned white against the wheel, "Why do you ask?"

Sam ran a hand over his face, "It's just you've been with us for a while and I don't know much about you."

"Why the sudden interest?"

Sam exhaled, "Just making conversation."

Luna took a moment to gather herself, "Did I have a family…yeah, I did. I had twins. Boys. They were two when everything changed. Before the Impact."

Sam quieted, "Shit."

"The father was never part of the picture. He left soon after I became pregnant. He blamed me and was furious I wanted to keep the babies. He left soon after."

"So you raised them yourself?"

"My sister helped," Luna confessed, softly, "they were with her when the Red Eyes came."

"They took them?"

Luna nodded, "I was driving back from my house. I just went to get some things. Things for my babies. When I got back, everyone was gone and the house was torn apart. I knew what had happened."

"Sounds familiar," Sam said gently.

Luna looked across at him, "You mean what happened to Alex? Yeah."

"What did you do?"

"I looked for them. What else would I do?"

"I don't know."

Luna sighed heavily, "But it didn't matter. They were gone. The Red Eyes had them and they weren't coming back."

"Christ, Luna…" Sam muttered.

"But I still hold out hope," Luna said, "I know it's stupid. I know I'll never find them. But I can't stop looking. I can't let them go."

"So when we found you in Arizona…"

Luna nodded, "When you found me I was headed East, just like you and Alex. I had spent the last ten years tearing apart the West Coast in hopes someone had seen my kids. Of course, no one had. The ones that talked to me seemed doubtful and looked at me kind of like how you're looking at me now."

"Sorry…"

"It's ok. I get it. A crazed mother hunting for her long-lost sons. How else are people supposed to react? I mean hell, it's been ten years. I don't even know if I'd recognize them."

Sam checked to make sure Alex was still sleeping before continuing, "So you decided to team up with us, despite the suicide mission, in hopes we'd run across your children?"

Luna snorted, "Why not? Figured I had a better chance of survival."

"Makes sense."

Chapter 5

Not long after, the SUV began to sputter as it choked on the last remains of the fuel. Content to let it die, Luna waited until they had come to a complete stop before releasing a foreboding sigh.

"I guess that's that," she muttered, leaning back in her seat.

The sun was up now, spreading a buffet of color across a colorless landscape. In the distance, they could see a town, a lonely vertical cluster that sprang from the dry earth. The road gutted it right down the middle and Sam knew they would have to go through it now on foot.

From the backseat, Alex growled to life. He sat up, rubbing his eyes, which hosted heavy bags beneath them.

"What's up?"

"We've stopped," Luna stated.

"Was it the wheel or the tank?"

"Out of gas," Sam said, opening his door.

Alex ran a hand over his face, "Awesome. Surprised the wheel held out for as long as it did, though. Any chance of finding some more gas?"

Sam climbed out onto the road, "Looks like there's a town

up a couple miles down the road. We can check there, but I wouldn't hold your breath."

"Where are we?" Alex groaned as he followed Sam and Luna out onto the road, abandoning the SUV.

"Still in Louisiana," Luna muttered, "you weren't out that long."

"God, I hate the South," Alex grumbled as the morning light swathed his face with heat.

Sam pulled on his backpack and surveyed their surroundings. Rolling hills composed of dead grass stretched all the way to the distant town. A smattering of crooked, rotting trees littered the landscape like broken bones jutting from the earth's crust. Past the town rose a wall of mountains, a brown, imposing line that ran north to south. Sam prayed they'd find another vehicle before having to traverse them.

"Back to walking," Alex muttered, coming to Sam's side, "can't say I missed it."

"Just keep your eyes open," Sam instructed, "we're wideout in the open right now and completely exposed."

"Yes, chief," Alex groaned, "now can we please get to that town and out of the sun? It's going to be hot as hell in a couple hours and I'd rather not get a sunburn to go with my sleep deprivation."

Together, the three began the familiar trek. Sam had gotten used to it during their travels. The constant dull ache, the dangerous boredom, the heat. It didn't make any of it more enjoyable, but it was a familiar sensation that he shouldered like an old injury. As they walked, he kept his eyes moving, scanning, searching for anything that might be moving. It was a small comfort, not having a Tower in sight.

He took the lead, his boots eating up the miles. Luna hung

back with Alex and he could hear them rationing out conversation as the hours dragged by. He left them alone, content to save his breath for the next step. His shirt was soaked through by the time the sun reached its midpoint in the sky. The town ahead had grown close and he began to make out details as they approached the first cluster of looted stores and shops.

"Guns out," Sam said, slowing so Luna and Alex could catch up. As one, they drew their weapons and began to creep into the belly of the ruins. Everything was in disarray and destroyed, the years of wear and pillaging apparent on every sign and building. The road led them past empty windows, smashed doors, and total abandonment. Garbage bled out onto the street like the last remains of an opened vein. Rusted out cars pocked the road and everything was eerily silent. At the end of the street was a church, its steeple a monument to a time when people believed in something that hadn't saved them.

Before they reached it, Sam held up a hand, "Hold on. We should take a second and check a couple of these places, see if they have anything we can use."

Luna cocked an eyebrow, "I think this place has been pretty much picked clean, Sam. You really want to?"

Sam exhaled and wiped sweat from his brow, taking in the state of chaos the street was in.

"I'm all for taking a break," Alex said, his face red from the heat, "but I think she's right. I don't think we're going to find anything of use here."

Sam nodded slowly, "Maybe you're right. Shit. You think any of these cars still have gas in them?"

Alex snorted, "I think ten years hasn't changed much in this shithole town. I wouldn't count on scavenging anything from here. Any gas that might have been here has probably been claimed, probably a long damn time ago. It's getting harder and harder to find anything we can use. And it's only going to get worse. I hate to say it, but we could be walking for a long damn time."

Luna clutched her pistol, "What I wouldn't do to run across a community with a working generator."

"We came across one in Nevada," Alex said, "they let us charge the phones we had. Nice bunch of people. We gave them one as thanks. They hadn't Listened in years. You should have seen their faces when they did. You would think The Impact never happened."

"That's the appeal," Sam said, distracted. He itched to find gas or a working vehicle. Something to get them to the next Tower ahead of Empire. If that was where he was headed. He looked past the steeple toward the far terrain. The mountains waited patiently and Sam felt his heart sink. It would take them entirely too long to get over those if they couldn't find transport.

As he struggled to decide what to do next, Luna's voice cut through his thoughts like a knife, "Oh no…"

Sam whipped his head over and saw her face go white. Alex immediately went on full alert and seconds later, it became clear what had alarmed Luna.

"Shit…" Alex hissed, his voice dropping.

Sam turned and looked up the street. His ribs clamped over his heart.

Dozens of Red Eyes were emerging from the church ahead. They walked calmly and with purpose, down the road toward them. There was no urgency, no bloodlust, just icy hatred as they approached.

"What is this?" Alex growled, taking a step back.

"A gathering party?" Luna offered, her voice shaking.

Sam swallowed hard, "Why would they be so far away from the Towers? There's no one here to take!"

"Except us," Luna whispered, back peddling.

Sam raised his pistol and retreated with his friends, sweat stinging his eyes. This wasn't right. None of this was right. They shouldn't be this far out.

The Red Eyes continued forward, their eyes blazing with barely controlled rage.

"He's trying to scare us again," Alex snarled suddenly.

Sam squeezed the grip of his pistol, "Which means we're doing something right."

"We need to leave," Luna said, "right now. We aren't getting past them."

Alex suddenly stopped, planting his feet in the road, "Hold on."

"What are you doing?!" Luna breathed, gripping his arm, "Are you insane? There's too many of them! This isn't something we can fight, we need to LEAVE."

"Alex, she's right, let's go," Sam muttered.

But Alex didn't move and Sam saw something enter his eyes that he was all too familiar with.

Rage.

"He doesn't scare me, Sam," Alex snarled, "and neither do they."

The Red Eyes were a dozen yards away now, a wall of shimmering red faces illuminated by the burning yellow sun.

"Alex!" Luna cried, trying to pull him back.

The Red Eyes stopped. They formed a line across the street, ten deep. Each one looked ready to rip the three apart at a moments notice. They stood, unmoving, with clenched fists, their teeth revealed behind bloodless snarls.

Alex took a defiant step toward the crowd, his voice echoing across the sun-bleached sky, "What do you want!?"

Silence greeted him.

Alex raised his pistol toward them, "What the FUCK IS GOING ON!? WHERE IS HE?!"

A Red Eye stepped forward, a mountain of man with a full beard and overalls. His voice returned back to them as a thunderous command, "You need to leave. You need to stop this."

Alex shook his pistol at that man, "Why!? Why is he trying to scare us away? What is it he's so afraid of!?"

The burly man's face contorted beneath an onslaught of furious creases, "Afraid? He's not afraid of anything. There's nothing you can do to stop what is coming."

Alex ground his teeth together, "And what, exactly, is coming?"

The Red Eye's face melted beneath a sinister smile, "Join us and find out."

Sam had a death grip on Alex's arm, "Stop talking to them, we need to get out of here right fucking now."

But Alex wasn't finished. Sweat dripped from the tip of his nose as his voice dipped into a quivering challenge, "If you don't tell me where he is, I'm going to shoot you right in your ugly fucking snout."

The Red Eye continued to smile, spreading his arms to the crowd around him, "He is here. Right now. With all of us."

"I'm warning you!" Alex roared, cocking the hammer back.

"Alex!" Luna pleaded.

The Red Eye took an aggressive step forward, "He sees you, Alex."

Alex's breath fled his lungs as he was named, a horrible draining that exhumed all defiance in his stance.

"Jesus Christ," he whispered, lowering his gun with a shaking hand.

Sam, along with Luna's help finally pulled him back, "This confrontation is over, don't listen to them."

Alex let himself be pulled along, but his eyes never left the wall of Red Eyes. As the three retreated back out of town, Sam couldn't help but feel like they had escaped certain death. Or capture. When they reached the outskirts, he chanced a look over his shoulder and saw the Red Eyes still watching them. They hadn't moved, but all of them were smiling now, a horrible, sickening display that inspired both confusion and terrible fear.

"What the fuck is going on?" Sam whispered to no one.

The sun was fleeing daylight by the time they made it back to the SUV. During their return, no one voiced why they were going back to it. Their plan had been cut off and it left them all shaken and unsure on how to proceed. This new development with the Red Eyes was new and it seriously hampered Sam's plan to stick to the road right on through the state. If they were going to have to get creative, then things were going to take way longer than he wanted. And each second they weren't moving forward, Empire was going the opposite direction.

Panting, they reached the SUV. The evening sun cracked the humid air with splinters of color that extended out like rainbow fingers. It was an observation that inexplicably depressed Sam a great deal.

Luna pulled open the back door and collapsed inside. Alex followed, throwing his backpack to the floor.

"I can't believe we're back here," he muttered, leaning back and closing his eyes.

"Neither can I," Sam muttered, looking down the road where they had come from.

Luna rested her head against Alex's shoulder, "We need to figure this out. The Red Eyes today…that's not a problem that's going to go away."

"I know," Sam said, frustrated. "I'll think of something."

Alex opened one eye, "We could just go around the town. Sneak past under the cover of night."

Luna groaned, "Not tonight. I can't walk another step. Between the heat and the road, I'm done for today."

Sam ran a hand over his face, his frustration growing, "Ok, ok. Let's sleep on it. We'll figure it out in the morning. Regardless, we're moving forward. Right?"

"Sure thing," Alex assured, closing his eyes again.

Restless and exhausted, Sam had no choice but to climb into the SUV as well. He took the passenger seat up front and placed his pack next to him. He needed sleep. His body felt drained, beaten, and dehydrated. His feet ached and his face itched with sunburn. He closed his eyes and pushed his irritation away as best he could. For now, he needed to rest. Everything else would be waiting for him when he woke up. That was something he could always count on.

"Sam?"

Luna's voice forced his eyes open.

"Yes?"

"We'll get through this. I promise."

A ghost of a smile lit his lips, "I know, Luna. Get some sleep."

Ten minutes later, the car filled with gentle snoring.

A dream slowly approached Sam's weary mind. It crept up

on him like a predator, circling its prey. It was a dream he had seen before.

He was standing beneath the Towers under a blood red sky. He was on the edge of a cliff and he could see all twenty-six of them, expanding across the United States. The domes were huge, engulfing the land and swallowing it up. The Gargoyles were all watching him, their eyes swaying on their long, thick stalks. There was no wind. There was no sound. There was nothing, like he was standing in a vacuum. The only thing he heard was his own heartbeat drumming in his ears.

In the dream, the Gargoyles slowly raised their arms as one and pointed directly at him. As they did so, he felt himself go weak. His legs turned to liquid and he felt a dread so real that it drove him to his knees, gasping for air.

A voice cut through the perfect stillness, a gentle whisper that hissed from the crimson heavens.

"*I…see…you…*"

He tried to scream, but couldn't seem to release it from his throat. A shiver ran through him, snuffing the energy from his body.

Something moved…above him…

Sam ripped his eyes up past the Towers, past the Gargoyles…past the eeric sky…

…and something *shifted* beyond the vermillion canvas of space.

Gasping, Sam sat up in his seat. Sweat coated his face and his chest heaved as he sucked in oxygen. He blinked and then squeezed his eyes shut, rubbing them furiously, extinguishing the afterburn images of the nightmare.

"What the hell…?" he panted, forcing himself to calm. He checked the back seat and saw Alex and Luna still asleep.

Shaking himself, needing air, he climbed out of the SUV. The night was mercifully cool and a slow breeze dried the sweat on his brow. Trembling, clawing the cobwebs of the dream away, he walked away from the car, smacking a cigarette from his pack. He sat down on the edge of the road, facing the barren wilderness, and lit his smoke.

"Christ," he breathed, smoke snaking between his lips. His heart was finally slowing and reality began to cement around him.

"This shit is starting to get to you," he said to no one. He took another drag from his cigarette and turned his eyes to the dark earth sprawling out before him. Nothing moved beneath the moonless sky, nothing breathed, nothing lived.

Sam squinted and leaned forward. His eyes slowly adjusted to the night. Was there actually something out there? Scattered across the earth, only a couple dozen yards away, were mounds of darkness, inky black lumps that littered the land.

Rocks. They were rocks.

Sam ran his hands over his face, "Pull yourself together, man."

The wind died. Everything grew impossibly still.

"Tough night?"

The sudden voice turned Sam to stone. His eyes went wide as he swiveled to see a man casually sitting right next to him on the side of the road.

Empire grinned, "Easy there, man. Easy."

Every alarm and trigger exploded through Sam's body, screaming, howling to rise and call for his friends. But no matter how hard he fought to move, to call out, he simply could not.

Empire brushed a strand of black hair from his youthful

face, his dark eyes meeting Sam's, "Relax. Hey. I mean it. Relax. Can you do that for me?"

Heart roaring in his ears, Sam slowly nodded, his eyes bulging. Why couldn't he scream? Why couldn't he move? He fought against the horrible sensation, but it felt like he had been encased in ice.

Empire motioned to the dying cigarette clutched between Sam's fingers, "Got another one of those?"

Painfully, Sam nodded, his mouth as dry as the earth beneath him.

"If I let you go, are you going to try and shoot me?"

Sam shook his head and heard his bones creak.

Empire smiled, "Good. That wouldn't be wise. I don't want to be vulgar, but if you try anything, if you try to alert your friends, then I'm going to take that woman in there and rip her apart right in front of you. And Sam? There wouldn't be a thing you could do to stop it." Empire clapped his hands together, "So. Bum me one of those smokes and be smart. Deal? Cool? Can you handle that, man?"

Sam nodded once again, chest heaving. All at once, he felt the pressure surrounding him vanish like smoke. He gasped and then shivered, wrapping his arms around himself. Fear surged through him like a disease, consuming his mind and flesh beneath its vicious teeth.

Empire snapped his fingers, "Cigarette?"

Hands shaking, Sam pulled out his pack and handed one to Empire.

Empire clamped it between his teeth and cocked an eyebrow, "I'm assuming you got a light?"

Swallowing hard, Sam pulled his lighter out. Empire took it

and lit his smoke. He inhaled deeply, but after a moment, he hacked violently and held the cigarette out for Sam.

"Nope, still hate them," Empire coughed, "here, take it. You look like you need it more than me right now."

Is this really happening? Sam thought, almost blind with dream-like horror. He took the cigarette back and sucked desperately on it.

Empire sighed at the night sky, "Nice, isn't it? I love the night. This southern heat really sucks the piss right out of you, huh?"

Scrambling for words, Sam opened his mouth, his voice a trembling mess, "What do you want?"

Empire cocked his head to the side, "Want? I want a lot of things. You're going to have to be more specific."

"What are you *doing* here?" Sam heaved, his breath like burning steam.

Empire rolled his neck, groaning, "Oh…that." He sighed heavily, "Come on, Sam. You know what I'm doing here."

"We're going to stop you, one way or another," Sam said weakly, not sure what else to do.

Empire snorted, "Huh…maybe. Maybe not. I'm not invincible you know, despite the rumors. People are scared shitless of me, aren't they? Crazy right? Who would have thought…"

The initial shock was beginning to wear thin. Sam felt his hands ball into fists, crushing his cigarette, "Why are you here?" His fear was slowly giving way to a deep, throbbing anger that pushed through to the surface.

Empire's face turned serious and he met Sam's gaze with a sureness that would have stilled the sunrise, "I'm putting an end to this little hunt of yours."

Sam's body rose and fell with each labored breath, "We're not going to stop. None of us. Not me, not Luna, and certainly not Alex. You'd have to kill us, but we both know that's not going to happen."

Empire shrugged, "Maybe. It's true – I don't want to kill you."

Sam grit his teeth, fighting the urge to draw the pistol strapped to his thigh, "Then I'll ask again…what the hell do you want?"

Empire's eyes hardened, "I want you to join me. To join us. Something is coming, Sam, and there's nothing you can do to stop it. No one can."

"You want to turn us into Red Eyes?" Sam snarled, "Is that what this is about? You want to brainwash us and force us to join your fucking army of psychos?"

Empire suddenly barked a laugh, "MY army? Oh, brother, I wish. Sam, I may be able to seize control of the Red Eyes, but they're not MY army."

Sam felt confusion explode over him like a depth charge, "W-what are you talking about?"

Empire pointed to the night sky, "They are for the Gargoyles. When the time comes, they will be used as needed. To fulfill their purpose here on Earth."

"I don't understand," Sam sputtered, feeling lost, confused, and horribly exposed.

Empire's voice grew low, "Something approaches, Sam. And we are close. We are very, very close. The Red Eyes, you, me, we're all just a part of it. When the time comes, the Red Eyes will be the ones to change…everything." Empire leaned forward, "And Sam…I want you to be a part of it. I want Alex to be a part of it."

Sam shook his head, his eyes dark, "It's not going to happen so you might as well kill us and get it over with."

"I told you, I don't want to kill you."

Sam felt an ember in his chest, "Quit fucking around. It's not that you don't want to…it's that you can't."

Empire gave Sam a look that bled fire, "What makes you so sure?"

Sam pointed to the SUV, "Because of that man in there."

The air heated between them, a dangerous, violent omen.

Sam leaned toward Empire, his voice hot and venomous, "Because Alex is your fucking *brother.*"

Empire's eyes suddenly exploded with red light, hot color that smoked from his sockets, "Careful Sam," he hissed.

But Sam pressed on, "If you killed me, then you know deep down that Alex would never forgive you. He would never join your cause. Because that's what you want more than anything isn't it? When everything goes to shit, you're afraid you'll be left alone without your big brother at your side. Because that's the way it's always been, hasn't it, Will?"

"Don't you fucking call me that," Empire snarled, his eyes blazing.

Sam shook his head, "I don't know know why you're pretending to be someone you're not. I don't know why you've taken on this new persona. I don't know why you're helping destroy the world and everyone in it. I mean Jesus, I grew up right down the street from you. I teased the hell out of you when we were little. You remember? When you, me, and Alex would hang out?"

Empire turned his glowing eyes to the night, "That's not who I am anymore. I've been chosen to lead this world into something greater."

"You got lucky," Sam growled, "you were in the right place at the right time. The Gargoyles needed someone on the ground to keep an eye on the Towers. You just happened to be the one they picked. You're not special." Sam leaned toward Empire, "You're a goddamn tragedy."

Empire bared his teeth, "Don't act like you're somehow better than me. You have no idea what I've been through. What Alex and I went through all those years ago. What our parents were like."

"Alex told me."

Empire whipped his head around, "No Sam, he only told you *some*. He didn't tell you everything. The hell we went through…it really showed me something."

"And what would that be?"

Empire's voice crawled to a rumble, "That people are evil."

Sam shook his head, "Oh yeah? And what about me? Am I evil?"

"Fuck you, Sam. You didn't help us. No one did. I have scars on my body that would give you nightmares."

"So that's what this is about? You had bad parents and so you're going to destroy the rest of us?"

"You couldn't possibly understand. And I'm not going to ask you to. Don't insult me by trying. Things have been set in motion that can't be undone. I'm going to see this thing through to the end."

Sam sighed heavily, "Christ, Will. Don't you hear what you're saying? Think of all the people you've changed. All the people you've killed. That you've taken and turned into Red Eyes. What the hell did they ever do to you?"

Empire stood, a tower in the darkness, "What did they do? They remained silent when I needed them most."

"You can still stop this."

Empire looked down at Sam, "No, I can't. The Towers are almost ready. We have the numbers. Soon, now. You'll see."

Sam climbed to his feet, "I hope you know me well enough to know I will never stand behind you. And neither will Alex. There is nothing you can do to convince him otherwise. Not after what you did to his wife and child."

Empire met Sam's stare, "I was stripping away his distractions. It's always been the two of us against the world. Nothing can change that. No man, woman, wife, or child. I needed to remind him of that."

Sam cast his eyes to the ground, "You ruined him, Will."

"Stop *fucking* calling me that."

Wearily, Sam exhaled, "So…what now? You know you'll never be able to talk Alex into this insanity."

A smile crept around the corners of Empire's lips, "I know that. But *you* can."

Sam felt something sink into his gut, "What are you talking about?"

Empire raised his hands to the dark landscape. His eyes flared red and his voice gurgled from his chest, "Take him."

Sam suddenly felt himself encased in an unseen coffin, his body compressed with icy claws. His mouth was sealed shut and he was powerless to just stand and watch as something moved out in the quiet black.

The rocks. The rocks were rising.

But they weren't rocks. They were Red Eyes. They had been lying in wait, flat on their stomachs, listening for their master's command. As one, they rose, pinpricks of crimson dotting the night.

They approached, smiling, hungry.

Empire looked at Sam almost apologetically, "I'm sorry. This is the only way. Don't worry, you'll see your friends again. But first…first you need to be baptized."

Sam struggled to scream as the Red Eyes swarmed him, rough hands grasping at his arms, legs, and throat. They lifted him off the ground, hoisting him up like a sack of dead meat.

Empire walked to his side and stared down into Sam's terrified face, "I'm going to take care of you. And soon…soon you'll understand exactly what is going to happen."

He turned and faced the sky, "You'll know what is coming."

Chapter 6

Alex woke up soaked in his own sweat. He looked down and saw Luna nestled against him in the backseat. He gently pushed her off him and scrubbed his damp face. The sun was coming up. Had he really slept through the night?

He looked around, feeling stuffy and claustrophobic. It was sweltering inside the SUV. After a second, he realized that Sam wasn't in the front seat anymore. Groaning, he opened the door and climbed out onto the road. He heard Luna stir behind him.

Taking a moment to gather himself, he looked along the length of the road. Warm sunlight swathed the land in soft yellow. Shadows extended to their peaks and a thick breeze whistled across his flush face.

Where the hell was Sam?

He walked around the car, eyes roaming the horizons. When he didn't see his friend, he felt the first pings of worry enter his bloodstream.

"Luna!" He called. When she didn't respond, he repeated the call.

Finally, she crawled out of the SUV. Her eyes were puffy with sleep and her bangs stuck to her forehead in sticky clumps.

"What is it? What's wrong?"

Alex felt panic beginning to rise, "Sam. Where the hell is Sam? Have you seen him? Did he get up in the middle of the night and go somewhere?"

"I don't think so," Luna said groggily, "Why, where is he?"

"That's what I'm asking!" Alex cried, spinning around, praying he'd spot his friend. "He's not here! What happened!? Where is he!?"

Luna was suddenly very awake, "I don't know, Alex. I slept through the night and didn't hear anything. Is he gone?"

Alex spread his arms, frustration lacing every syllable, "Clearly!"

Luna bit her lip.

"Do you think he went back into town?"

Luna shook her head, "Not without telling us. That's not like him."

Alex paced the road, head on a swivel, "What the fuck...what the FUCK..."

"Do you think he got up and the Red Eyes took him?"

Alex stopped, "Don't say that."

"Well, SOMETHING happened! He wouldn't just leave without telling us!"

Alex ran a frantic hand through his hair, "Shit...aw shit..."

Luna went to him, "Hey, calm down. We don't know anything yet."

Alex jerked away, eyes wild, "We know that he was here and now he isn't! What the hell are we supposed to think?"

Luna stepped away, her voice neutral, "I don't know. But let's not panic, it'll only make things worse. Maybe he did go back to town. Maybe he'll be back in a little bit."

Alex began to pace again, his fingers twitching at his side,

"This is bad...this is really bad...did you see anything last night before we fell asleep? Anything at all?"

"Like what?"

Alex stopped again, shaking his head, "I...I don't know. Fuck Sam, where the hell did you go?"

Faintly, he began to hear something coming down the road. He spun, eyes attuning to the source of the sound. He squinted in the morning light and then took a step back, gripping Luna's arm.

"We got company."

Luna looked down the long carpet of pavement, back the way they had come, and her eyes widened. Two pick-up trucks were hauling ass in their direction.

"You think it's Sam?" Luna asked, reaching for the shotgun in the backseat.

"I have no idea," Alex growled, "but we're not going to stand out here in the open just waiting for them. Get in the car and keep your head down."

"Alex, they're going to stop."

"I know, but I'd rather not give them an easy target if they're assholes."

Together, they piled into the back seat and shut the door. Alex felt his heart hammering against his ribs and sweat coated the back of his neck. He propped his pistol against the headrest, taking aim out the back windshield as the trucks roared closer. Luna took position next to him and chambered a round into the shotgun.

"Don't shoot unless they do," Alex said quietly, feeling his ears throb beneath his pulse.

"Thanks, Alex," Luna responded sarcastically.

The trucks slowed on approach, spitting gravel against the

SUV. The cabs were filled with people, as were the truck beds. Alex counted fifteen. If they were hostile, he knew he had just seen his last sunrise.

The trucks idled a dozen feet back from the SUV. Men and women climbed out, guns raised, looking pissed. Shotguns, assault rifles, pistols – it was clear to Alex that if a firefight ensued, they'd be dead in seconds. The mob looked weathered and sweaty, the men sporting wild beards and hard lines around their eyes – the women just as rugged.

"Please don't be assholes," Luna whispered as the mob circled the SUV.

One of the men raised his voice, a raspy, dry call, "Hey! We can see you in there! Come on out! Don't be stupid, we got you outnumbered!"

Alex didn't move, tracking one of the crowd with his gun.

"What's the play here, Alex?" Luna hissed.

The man who spoke called again, "Cut the hogshit! Come on out and we won't harm ya!"

Alex wiped sweat from his face, "Hell of a time to start trusting people."

"We don't really have a choice," Luna responded, lowering her shotgun.

Alex squeezed his eyes shut, "It was nice knowing you."

He kicked the door open and raised his hands in a sign of surrender. Immediately, the mob jumped back, yelling to drop his gun. He complied and heard Luna sliding out next to him. Her shotgun clattered to the pavement. She kicked it away and sighed, giving in to whatever happened next.

The mob closed in on them, weapons trained on the defenseless two. The man who had spoken earlier stepped forward, his overalls stained with months of grime, his beard a wild nest growing from his face.

"Who in the hell are you two?" He asked aggressively.

"We're just passing through," Luna said loudly, "We seem to have lost our friend and are looking for him."

The man cocked an eyebrow at the rest of his companions, "That true? You're not working with the Red Eyes are you?"

Alex let his shoulders droop, "What kind of stupid question is that? No, of course, we're not working with the Red Eyes!"

The big man shot him a hard look, "That so? What happened to your friend then? You turn him over to the Red Eyes or something?"

Alex slammed his teeth together and was about to respond, but Luna gracefully swooped in, "We don't know what happened to him. We all fell asleep last night, right here, and when we woke up he was gone. I know it sounds ridiculous, but that's the truth. We just woke up a couple minutes ago and were looking for him when you pulled up. We didn't know what kind of people you were so we took precautions. We're not bad people, we're just looking for our friend."

The man licked his chapped lips, "What kind of people are ya then, huh?"

Alex put a hand over his chest, "We're hunters. We're hunting someone."

"Who might that be?"

Alex's eyes brimmed with hatred, "We're looking for Empire."

The big man blinked like he couldn't believe what he was hearing. One of the others in the mob, a gruff looking woman, spoke up.

"The hell you doing that fer?"

Alex turned to her, "We're going to kill him."

A murmur ran through the group and then the big man slowly lowered his weapon, his voice reproachful, "You wouldn't be lying to me now, would you boy?"

"Wouldn't fuckin' dream of it."

The man scratched his beard and met the eyes of his companions, "What do ya'll say? Think they're cool?"

A handful of them shrugged in response, but most nodded. Alex felt the boulder on his back fall away.

The big man cracked a grin then and stuck his hand out, "Name's Percy. I'm kinda in charge of this whole operation."

Alex shook the man's hand, "Alex. Thanks for not killing us."

"I'm Luna," Luna said, shaking Percy's hand next, "and if you don't mind me asking…what exactly is your operation? We haven't seen many groups since…well, shit, since entering Texas, really."

Percy nodded, "Yes ma'am, not a whole lot of us left. Most are either dead or have been taken to the Towers and turned into Red Eyes. But there are indeed a couple of us left, yes ma'am there certainly are. We got a whole network spread out through multiple states."

Alex raised his eyebrows, "No shit?"

Percy shrugged, "No shit, man. We've worked hard to get some kind of system running. Passing information, keeping tabs on the Red Eyes, that kinda thing. It hasn't been easy, but it's something. We got six Lodges now, safe havens for travelers such as yourselves."

"I think we might have stayed in one of those just across the Texas border," Luna said.

Percy turned to her, "Probably one of ours. Was the owner a bald fella? About my age?"

"Yeah, that'd be him," Luna said.

"Look," Alex butt in, "I'd love to stay here and chat all day, but we really need to find our friend."

"You sure they didn't just leave ya?" A scrawny man asked from the crowd.

"He wouldn't do that," Luna said firmly, "There's just no way."

"Then the Red Eyes probably got him," another offered, a woman holding a revolver.

Percy nodded, "Hate to say it, but she's probably right. Don't know if you've seen it, but there's a town down this road that's infested with em. We were just headed that way to clear em out."

Alex snorted, "Why? Why bother?"

Percy planted his feet, "Why? Because we're not going to let them push us around anymore. That town is where a lot of these folks grew up. They want it back. And if —when—we get it back, then it'll extend our network that much further."

"Just how many of you are there?" Luna asked.

Percy grinned, "A lot."

Alex waved a hand dismissively, "Do what you want, but we got our own shit to figure out."

Percy sucked on his teeth, "Yeah...finding your friend, you mentioned that. And hunting Empire." He lowered his voice, "If you don't mind my asking...the hell are you doing going after that nut?"

"We're going to kill him," Alex repeated.

Percy didn't seem convinced, "Sure, but how? No one's been able to touch him since he showed up all those years ago. That psycho is a friggin' terror."

Alex shook his head, his mouth a sour twist, "No, he's not."

Percy took a moment and then simply shrugged once more, "Hell, I've never been the type to tell folks what to do. If that's what you want then God go with you." He jerked his chin to the SUV, "this thing work?"

"Out of gas," Luna said, "and the back tire is kind of fucked, but it works well enough."

Percy pursed his lips together like he was thinking.

"What, you want it or something?" Alex finally asked.

"I think I do," Percy said slowly, "we got people who can fix it and it seems to be in pretty good condition, considering." He suddenly raised his voice, "I'll tell you what! How bout we trade? You take one of these pickups and we take the SUV. I'll even throw in half a tank of gas."

Luna's eyebrows climbed her forehead, "Are you serious?"

Percy barked a laugh and turned to his companions, "Listen to her! She just can't believe it!" He laughed again and then addressed Luna, "Yes ma'am, I'm very serious. You can stop looking so shocked. I'm a fair man."

"Why wouldn't you just take it?" Alex asked, "I mean, Christ, there's not a thing we could do to stop you if you tried."

Percy's face slumped, like he was hurt, "Breaks my heart to hear people talk like that. Just cause the world's gone to piss and beans doesn't mean we gotta stop being decent to each other now does it? You have a need – finding your friend – and we could use a better vehicle. Everyone wins. What do you say?"

"You got yourself a deal," Luna grinned, offering Percy her hand. Percy's face split into a wide smile and he shook her hand vigorously.

"Well all right then!" He beamed. He turned to the others in his group, "Ya'll hear that?! We're taking the SUV. Grab one of them gas cans and give this baby some juice!" He pointed to one of the pick-ups, "Make sure that one is at half tank and pile out. We're making a trade here!"

Alex couldn't believe what he was seeing. The people followed his orders without question and soon one of the men was handing him the keys.

Percy placed a hand on Alex's shoulder, his eyes twinkling, "Don't have a stroke, son. There's still some good people in this world. Don't forget that."

Alex, wordlessly, met his stare.

Percy squeezed Alex's shoulder, "Promise me."

Alex slowly nodded, "Yeah, sure. Ok."

"Good boy!" Percy cried, slapping him on the back, "Now if everything is up to par, we got some Red Eyes to clear out!"

Dumbfounded, Alex watched as the group gassed up the SUV, checked the wheel, and then piled in. Luna was quick to grab their packs from the back, handing them to Alex who took them and turned to Percy.

"Thank you."

Percy brushed him off, "Don't sweat it, son. Best of luck to you. Hope you find your friend." He leaned in close, lowering his voice, "And between you, me, and God? I hope you find that bastard Empire and find a way to put a bullet between his eyes."

Alex took Percy's hand, "Maybe we'll see you around."

"Stranger things have happened!" Percy laughed over his shoulder as he went to the SUV and climbed in. The engine was brought to life and he threw his hand out the window, waving goodbye.

Alex and Luna stood shoulder to shoulder and watched as the group left, hauling ass down the road toward the abandoned town. Soon, they were surrounded by silence.

"That couldn't have gone better," Luna eventually said, breaking the trance, "I mean holy hell, can you believe them?"

Alex shook his head, "No, I can't. But I'm not complaining."

Luna took the keys from his hand, "So. What's the play here?"

Alex turned around in the road, looking east to west, "I don't know. You think they were right? You think Red Eyes took Sam?"

Luna rolled her shoulders, "It's the only explanation I can think of. It's not a pretty one, but it's the only one that makes sense. Maybe he got up to take a leak or something and got snatched. I really don't know, Alex."

Alex exhaled slowly, "Jesus, what a mess…"

"Which way are we going?" Luna asked.

Alex ran a hand along the back of his neck, "If Red Eyes really did take him then they're going back to one of their Towers. The closest one is Tower 12…the one we passed through."

Luna winced, "You're probably right. Shit. I mean, SHIT."

Alex faced her and gently gripped her shoulders, his voice softening, "We gotta try. I'm not going to abandon him."

"I know you're not," Luna said, "and neither am I. If you think that's where he might be, then that's where we'll go." She took his arm, "I'm with you, Alex."

Alex allowed himself the slightest of smiles, "Thanks. You wanna drive?"

Luna bounced the keys in her hand, "Hell yeah I do."

"Then let's go find Sam."

Chapter 7

Sam felt the full force of the sun upon his face as he marched. It was past midday and they had left the road hours ago. He knew where they were going now and it terrified him. Empire walked slightly ahead of the group, his stride confident and quick. The Red Eyes around Sam were clustered tight, keeping a watchful eye on their prize. His weapon had been taken away, but he had been allowed to keep his cigarettes. He smoked one now, trying to calm his nerves.

The dry earth crunched beneath his boots and sweat rolled past his lips. Smoke unfurled from between his teeth and his heart raced. Where were Alex and Luna right now? What were they doing? Were they looking for him? Could they even help him? His eyes found Empire again and his stomach sank. No. There would be no rescue for him. But he was not giving up. He would not let this happen.

He needed to do something before they reached Tower 12.

Up ahead, Empire stopped. The Red Eyes did as well. Sam looked around, wondering what was happening, a trickle of perspiration stinging his left eye. He wiped it away, flicking ash from his cigarette.

Empire turned, muttering to himself, "Something's happening..."

A Red Eye stepped forward, a woman, "What is it?"

Empire held up a hand to them, "I need to see."

He dropped his hand to his side and his body went completely still. An instant later, his eyes exploded in a flurry of red. Crimson tendrils rose from his sockets in great wafts of swirling smoke. A crackling sound emanated around him, like dry leaves being burned. A couple tense seconds passed before Empire's eyes returned to normal.

"Idiots," he growled, shaking his head.

"What is it?" The woman asked.

Empire looked up at her, clearly irritated, "That resistance group is trying to retake the town back there. We're going to lose some people, but we'll win. Still...they should have already returned to their Tower though...idiots."

He looked directly at Sam, "It's not all easy, is it?"

Sam tossed his cigarette to the ground and didn't answer. He felt sick. Resistance? Who? Was he talking about Alex and Luna? No...that didn't make any sense. It had to be someone else. Some other group?

"I've instructed them on how to handle the situation. There's nothing more we can do right now," Empire continued. "I'll check in later. Let's continue. Our ride should be here soon."

Sam opened his mouth, "Ride?"

Empire snorted, "Did you really think we were going to walk all the way?"

Sam cleared his throat, "What's happening back at the town?"

Empire mopped sweat from his face, "Fools acting like fools. There's an organized group that's been giving us some trouble lately. Seems like they're at it again. Nothing to be done about it now. If we lose some people, so be it. We already have the numbers for what we need to do."

"Why don't the Gargoyles do something?" Sam asked.

Empire cocked an eyebrow at him, "Why are you so concerned?"

"You know why."

Empire turned away, "Alex and the woman aren't with them. Don't worry. I didn't see them."

Sam decided to press his luck, "So you're just abandoning your people?"

Empire spun, "As much as I appreciate your sudden worry for the Red Eyes, I'm going to have to ask you not to talk about things you don't understand." He stepped toward Sam, "And the Gargoyles aren't doing anything because those Red Eyes aren't inside the bubbles. They are on the *outside*. And when they are on the *outside*, they fall under my control. And Sam? They're fine. A few dead doesn't mean anything. They'll take care of the attackers and march right back to their Tower."

"Who is this group that's been on your ass?" Sam continued, thinking in some vain way that he was buying time for himself.

Empire took another step toward Sam, his voice a grating slur, "What do you care? Your time on that side is drawing to a rapid close."

"So then tell me. What's the harm? We have to wait for our ride anyway, right?"

Empire snorted, "They're a network of people who, against all odds, have established some semblance of organization. They have towns, outposts, Lodges, and guns. Their reach extends across the southern states. We've had a few run-ins with them, but nothing we couldn't handle. None of them have harmed the Towers."

"Do these people have a name? Something they call themselves?" Sam asked.

"No, they don't have a *name*. This isn't some hopeful resistance group who leaves their calling card around towns they've liberated. These are desperate souls who don't know they're dead yet. They are people just barely scraping by, fooling themselves into thinking they can make a difference."

"Isn't that what we all are?" Sam asked quietly.

Empire jabbed a finger at Sam, "No. We're not. Now smoke your cigarettes and keep your mouth shut. You're exhausting."

A Red Eye motioned ahead, a finger pointed to the hazy horizon, "Sir, look. Someone's coming."

Empire turned and followed the man's finger. The air vibrated as a trio of vehicles grew out of the background, engines howling as they sped toward the group.

"Is that ours?" One of the Red Eyes asked.

Empire stiffened, tension turning his body to stone, "No."

Sam felt the first pings of actual hope ignite his mind, giving him a surge of adrenaline. The cars were approaching fast, only a mile or two away. He could see they were packed with people.

"What is *with* today?" Empire growled. He turned to face the Red Eyes. "Stay back. I'll take care of this."

Sam's heart leaped into his throat, "Wait! Don't hurt them! Maybe they're just passing through!"

Empire looked at Sam over his shoulder, "No, they're not just passing through. They want to hurt me. They want to hurt us," he turned back to the cars, "and I'm done being hurt."

Unable to do anything but watch, Sam bit his lip as Empire

marched toward the cluster of vehicles. After a couple dozen steps, he stopped and planted his feet.

And the air...shifted.

Empire didn't move. He didn't flinch. He simply watched and waited, each second bringing the trio of vehicles closer. Sam could hear their engines, their determination, their need to extinguish the Red Eyes.

Fifty yards from Empire, the three cars suddenly slammed into something, like they had hit an invisible wall. Metal screamed and crunched in on itself. Glass exploded from the windows, bodies flew out of the ruined windshields, and one of the vehicles upended, flipping over itself and landing with a crash, obliterating the riders in a bloody eruption.

Empire stood motionless before them, his hands at his sides. Smoke wafted from the wreckage as he watched the survivors begin to crawl out of the broken mess. Cries of pain filled the air and the dirt turned to mud beneath countless lacerations.

A man bleeding profusely from the head managed to find his pistol. From his belly, he let out a defiant roar and took aim at Empire.

A second before he pulled the trigger, his arm dislodged itself from his body. Screaming, the man rolled across the ground, fountaining blood as his severed limb was cast aside.

Empire towered over the carnage, a statue of rage and power.

Slowly, he raised his hands to the scattering of survivors. Sam watched in absolute horror as something extended and grew out of his fingers, two trails of squirming red that flickered like elongated tongues. As the twin channels of light grew, they began to splinter off into a hundred different rays, pencil thin and sparking with heat.

Empire strode toward the gasping people, hands at his sides, the whip-like strands spooling out behind him like scarlet claws.

"Stop this," Sam whispered, his voice shaking, "someone please stop this." One of the Red Eyes next to him grinned and licked her lips.

Empire stopped amid the bodies and surveyed them, his gaze scornful and brimming with hatred.

"Is this what you wanted!?" He roared suddenly.

The survivors inched themselves toward the nearest weapon, agony and terror written plainly across their faces. Empire spun around, watching them, shaking his head.

"No one can save you," He snarled, his voice echoing across the sky, "no one is coming to help you." His voice dropped, but Sam heard his next words clear as day.

"You're all *alone*."

Something cracked through the air and the red whips around Empire's fingers came to life. They sprang toward the survivors as if they had minds of their own.

What followed next was something Sam would never be able to forget.

Empire began to flay his victims alive, his glowing creations rising up like cobras and falling upon the bleeding bodies. He tore their flesh from their bones, one chunk at a time, each lash from his burning whips bringing screams that chilled the afternoon heat.

Blood fell like rain, gore showered the earth, and through it all Empire remained silent. The Red Eyes around Sam watched the display of violence with hard stares, each one drinking in the horrific scene.

"My god…" Sam whispered as Empire snuffed out the last ruins of life before him.

The world stilled.

What lay scattered across the ground would never be described as human. Ribbons of stripped skin littered the dirt. Pools of red spread like fire on gasoline. Shards of bone and hair lay in chaos. Smoke curled from the wrecked cars, bits and pieces of metal interwoven with the gore.

The light extending from Empire vanished in a flash. And in its absence came a great shuddering breath. His shoulders shook and he stumbled forward, catching himself. The Red Eyes took a step back, pulling Sam in their wake.

He was about to ask what was happening when Empire sank to his knees.

And then he began to cry.

His body trembled beneath the onslaught, a merciless wave of grief that exploded from his lips in a howl. He slumped over, balling his hands into fists, a hoarse sob rattling the air.

"What…what is he doing…?" Sam whispered.

A hand fell across his shoulder, hot breath on the back of his neck, "Leave him be."

Empire covered his face in his hands, tears pouring between his fingers. His teeth chattered violently as he choked on his own rising shrieks.

After considerable effort, he began to calm. His breath steadied and he visibly fought to regain control. His chest hitched once, twice, and then he wiped his eyes and crawled to his feet. He craned his face to the sun and inhaled deeply.

When he turned back to Sam and the Red Eyes, it was as if it never happened. He walked to them, a smile teasing the corners of his mouth.

"Well, that's that I guess," he said cheerily. "Shall we be on our way?"

Sam didn't move, his heart, racing, "What is wrong with you?"

The smile sputtered across Empire's face, "Maybe it's best you didn't talk for a while."

But Sam wouldn't let it go, his mind spinning, "You...you don't have to be like this. I can help you. Alex can help you if you just ask. I know he will. We don't have to keep going."

Empire's eyes began to tint with crimson, "Sam...I'm not going to warn you again."

Sam reached out and touched Empire's arm, his voice low, "Will, you don't have to be alone anymore."

Empire ignited and Sam didn't have time to react as a fist plowed into his face, blasting him into a void of total darkness.

He was back in the dream. The crimson sky soared overhead, a vast canvas that stretched beyond the limits of his vision. He was standing on a cliff and the Towers rose before him.

But something was different.

The Gargoyles were gone. The domes were gone. The world was deathly silent and Sam felt like he would be consumed with an unbearable wave of sudden loneliness. He spun, searching for someone, anyone, to take the sensation away. His breath came in short gasps and he reached for his throat, begging for oxygen.

Sam Sam Sam Sam Sam Sam...

He twisted toward the voice, toward the Towers. His eyes grew wide and his body went cold.

Empire stood on the summit of every one, his eyes blazing. A violent smiled ripped up his face and Sam knew he was about to die.

But then he realized something that filled him with rippling terror.

It wasn't Empire.

It was Alex.

Gasping, Sam woke up. A scream soared along his vocal cords and his eyes bulged, momentarily paralyzed. He jerked his head around, frantic to get his bearings, to escape the claws of the nightmare.

Rough hands battered his body and constricted his movement. He tried to sit up but realized he couldn't. He blinked and discovered he was being carried.

Four Red Eyes had him over their shoulders, tightrope binding his legs together. He twisted his head, the night sky above filled with twinkling stars. A warm breeze wafted across his face and he coughed, dust filling his mouth.

"Where are we?" He rasped.

Empire answered from up ahead, "Your last stop."

Before Sam could respond, his eyes settled on their destination.

Tower 12 cut into the night sky, a massive obstruction directly ahead of them. They were inside the dome. Oh, Christ, they were already inside the dome!

Help me, Sam thought frantically, *oh god someone please help me!*

Thousands of Red Eyes stood by the wayside, watching as Empire led the procession toward the base of the construct. Squirming, Sam looked up along the seamless black walls. A Gargoyle stood at the summit, its eyes peering down from the ends of its stalks. It long dark arms hung motionless at its side. It was watching him. Watching Empire.

"Please don't do this," Sam begged, trying to free his body

from the ropes. The Red Eyes carrying him tightened their hold.

"Don't be afraid," Empire responded without turning. They had almost reached the base of the Tower. Each step forward felt like a nail in his coffin.

"I don't want this," Sam cried, "Please don't do this to me!" Empire didn't respond. They had reached the titanic edifice. The Red Eyes halted behind him, adjusting Sam across their shoulders. The air filled with a buzz of excitement and Sam's stomach plummeted. This wasn't happening. This couldn't happen. Someone would stop this. Someone would save him.

Empire extended his hand and brushed it against the exterior of the Tower. An instant later, a doorway slid open, exhaling a wash of cool air.

"Put him down," Empire commanded.

Gently, Sam was lowered. His eyes bore into his captors, a desperate, weak plea.

"Cut his ropes. We go in alone."

The order was followed. As his bindings fell away, Sam was overwhelmed with the urge to run. Instead, he looked at Empire and awaited whatever came next.

Empire smiled and cocked his head, "Go on. I'll be right behind you."

"Will…." Sam fumbled one last time. "I'm begging you…"

"Get inside, Sam."

Trembling, he obeyed, unable to do anything else. He slowly stepped toward the open door, took a deep breath, and entered the mouth of Tower 12.

His boots echoed beneath a hard floor, his senses overwhelmed by a rush of altered atmosphere. His breath billowed out before him, the cold increasing with every step. His eyes fought to adjust to the darkness, helped by a rising red hue that emanated from a central pillar that rose the height of the Tower.

The circular walls of the interior were lined with massive sockets, like empty coffins. Hundreds of thousands of them spiraled up and up and out of sight. The red light from the center pillar illuminated these strange, barren cavities, and Sam's imagination didn't have to work hard to understand their purpose.

"The Red Eyes…" he whispered, his voice echoing up above him.

Empire walked to his side, the door closing at his back, sealing them both in silence.

Sam turned in place, taking in the empty slots in the walls, "Don't tell me…"

"Soon this Tower will be filled," Empire said quietly. "Soon they will be called to take their place here."

Sam's heart raced, "But why? What is all this?"

"Come with me," Empire instructed, taking Sam gently by the arm, "and I'll show you."

He led them closer toward the pillar in the center, its red glow painting their faces a soft crimson. As Sam was brought deeper inside, he saw that a staircase wrapped along the length of the center column. He followed it up and out of sight, the endless stairs disappearing as they reached for the summit.

Empire guided them beneath the stairs to another hidden door which he activated with ease. As it slid open, he stepped back.

"You need to do this alone," he said softly.

Sam turned, fear rising, "What's in there?"

Empire smiled, all traces of malice gone, "Everything."

Cautious, feeling sick, Sam turned and faced the open door. Blue light trickled from the blank space and it was all he could see.

"Go on," Empire cooed.

Closing his eyes, Sam took a deep breath, stepped toward the door, and knew he would never be the same.

As soon as he crossed the threshold, the door closed at his back. The noise startled him and he clutched a hand to his chest, begging his heart to slow. Spinning, he scanned the interior. It was cylindrical and encased with a thick fog, lit only by unseen blue light. For a second, he feared it was poison, but found himself breathing without trouble.

As far as he could tell, the room was completely empty.

But then…slowly…everything began to change.

The fog swirled lazily around him and the blue light began to fade. The room seemed to expand, the walls falling away as darkness pressed in. Faintly, from the black, something stirred and was brought to life. The cold slithered from Sam's skin like it had never been there at all. From beneath his feet, something blinked and soared up toward him. The world shifted and everything vanished before this new vision, a glimpse down into something completely alien.

Tower 12 was gone.

Everything he ever knew…was gone.

He was standing on a cliff, the sky a cloud filled blanket of deep red. Below him were millions of Gargoyles, each one upside down with their heads buried beneath ashen earth. Their bodies extended from the soil as if frozen in place. Their arms were locked to their sides, their elongated feet paralyzed in the air.

The world was a gray haze of smoldering ruin. Smoke rose

around the upside down Gargoyles, a burned, charred landscape that stretched past the horizon. Rising from the scorched vista…were structures.

Towers.

But they were different, each one burning with a brilliant red energy. The power surged from the soil and traveled up to the summits, pulsing with blinding light.

As Sam observed this terrifying sight, a thought plunged into his mind without warning.

This is how things are meant to be.

The Gargoyles remained as they were, buried up to their shoulders in ash. The Towers glowed. Silence overtook the world.

This is how things are meant to be.

Despite the change in temperature, Sam shivered.

Let them feed.

And that's when Sam realized that the Gargoyles *were* moving. It wasn't easy to spot from his vantage point, but he saw that the upside-down bodies were breathing. They were alive. And they were eating.

They were eating the ash.

The world shifted.

The ash was gone. The Towers were colorless. The Gargoyles were standing upright, staring at nothing, their eyes unmoving atop their stalks. It was like the entire planet was stuck in time, a picture of a world gone numb.

Shift.

Millions of Gargoyles standing around a colossal pit. They encircled the enormous hole, pressed close to the edge, staring down into the empty black. Shoulder to shoulder, they began to emit sound, casting their eerie voices down into the mouth of the world. It held no melody, no cadence, no joy. It was a desperate howl that echoed across the blood-red sky and plummeted down, down, down into the darkness.

Shift.

Sam could now see the entirety of the planet, a black smudge across the star-choked cosmos. A red tinge wrapped itself around the world, a tease of bloody atmosphere.

A deep rumble filled Sam's head, a bellowing moan that was almost unbearable. It reached into his skull and hammered at the bone, a droning growl that consumed his senses.

And then the planet began to crack apart.

It started from the center, a splinter of ebony that raced across the solid mass of land. It webbed out as the groaning continued, a spider web across the world. Pieces of the planet began to break apart, continent-sized chunks that were lazily pushed out into space.

From the wreckage, something reached out.

It was a hand, a tremendous, god-sized spectacle. It was grey and attached to an arm that extended from the destruction. It was triple jointed, bending once, twice, three times, reaching out toward the galaxies.

Sam's eyes went wide as he saw the arm was connected to a titanic shoulder that edged its way through the planet's surface, breaking pieces of the world apart as it went. It was like watching an egg hatch, a slow, pained birth that revealed hidden horrors that chilled him to the bone.

Next came the face, a moon-sized terror that squeezed through shattered earth and followed its shoulder out into the universe.

It was a hairless thing, a snouted, humanoid looking monstrosity. It was grey, its jaw protruding from its face like a disjointed growth. At the end of the snout was a colossal twist of flesh, a tube or some kind of hose that twisted around its face and back into the core of the planet. Its eyes grew similar contortions, the flesh extending from the sockets, twin tubes of grey matter that trailed around the sides of its mountainous head and back into the world from which it had been released.

The creature groaned, a sky-splitting earthquake of noise that rippled to the ends of space and time. As it did so, it reached out with its free hand, its joints twisting, and began to pull the planet forward. Its cluster of gnarled fingers seemed to grasp and grip the emptiness of the galaxy, dragging the shell of its planet forward. The organic tubes jutting from its face quivered, as if it was gasping, bubbles of unseen substance pulsing through the hideous flesh, causing it to bulge, like a snake swallowing its prey.

Shift.

Sam was back on the planet's surface. The Gargoyles surrounded the Towers. They were climbing them. One for each of the twenty-six. When they reached the summits, they walked to the center and knelt. The two spires on either side sparked with color, just a flash of red as if struck by lightning.

The Gargoyles below stepped back.

The earth shuddered and the Towers began to tear themselves from the barren world below. They jolted and jerked, swaying left to right before finally freeing themselves from the planet in a great explosion of rock.

The Gargoyles on the surface bowed their heads and remained silent as the Towers began to ascend, crawling up the ladder of the sky.

They were leaving.

Shift.

Twenty-six comets soaring through space leaving long bloody tongues in their wake.

Shift.

The birthed titan pulling the consumed planet across the universe, its one arm and repulsive head extending from the hatched world. The tubes wriggled out from its abhorrent skull, pulsing as something passed through them and back into the planet.

Shift.

The Gargoyles sitting aimlessly across the empty surface, a barren, smeared ruin of rocky wasteland. Amid the millions, Sam saw one of them convulse, buckle, and then fall onto its back. None of the others moved. After a moment, another did the same.

They were dying.

Shift.

The Towers, rocketing through space. Rocketing towards a planet that looked all too familiar. Earth.

Shift.

New York City. Houston. Phoenix. City after city rose like film, flickering and rushing past. Life. Humans. People going about their days. Working. Walking. Talking. Laughing. Yelling. Fucking.

Shift.

Sam was standing in the middle of one such city, staring up at the sky. He looked to his left and saw the Space Needle. Seattle. He was in Seattle. He turned back to the heavens in time to see a streak of crimson explode through the blue sky and roar towards the world below.

Shift.

He was in another city. He looked up. Another Tower

loomed above, plowing through the clouds towards the surface.

Shift.

He was standing in a field, surrounded by motionless cows. He cast his eyes upward and saw another Tower, a long finger of red trailing in its wake.

He was floating above the world, above North America. Twenty-six tails roared toward the earth below him. Twenty-six Towers exploded into the world, a massive, deafening collision that rattled the teeth in his head.

The Impact.

As the outer Towers slammed into the coasts, Sam watched as something rippled out from them. It was a massive wave of power, a fiery wall of immense destruction that shot out from both coasts, east and west. They screamed across the oceans and met in the middle, obliterating everything in their path in a matter of seconds.

Sam felt his mouth go dry.

The world had ended without warning, without any chance of survival. In a moment, the evolution of mankind had been erased as if it had been nothing at all. Cities were consumed, towns were erased, families were snuffed out, and the world burned beneath it all, leaving nothing but mountains of ash in its wake.

Sam looked back down to North America, the one landmass that had been spared. Twenty-six beacons of glowing light dotted the land, protected from total annihilation.

Shift.

Government officials scrambling in DC. Armies and air forces were assembled. Order was desperately gathered from the chaos – broadcasts assuring the confused, terrified citizens that everything was under control.

Shift.

Colorado. The Rocky Mountains. Denver. Tower 22 rising above it all, a monument to something completely alien, a symbol that all was not right in the world. The Gargoyle atop its summit was climbing down. The bubble dome expanded outward as it did, the first birth of a new mystery.

Everyone was evacuating, fleeing, getting as far away from Tower 22 as they possibly could. Highways were clogged, streets were filled, screams filled the air, and disorder triumphed over reason.

Shift.

A lone man walking toward Tower 22, the Rocky Mountains at his back. Sam knew the man.

Empire.

Will.

Shift.

The Gargoyle stood at the edge of the bubble, its Tower looming over its shoulder. Empire stood on the outside of the strange, transparent dome, his eyes wide. He was speaking to the Gargoyle. Sam couldn't hear what he was saying. The Gargoyle nodded. Empire stepped into the bubble and immediately collapsed to his knees as the Gargoyle touched him.

Shift.

Empire on top of Tower 22, screaming as the Gargoyle channeled something into him, a red worm of light that vomited from the creature's open mouth. Every vein and tendon stood out on Empire's body as he howled, seconds from breaking beneath the flow of power pouring into him.

Shift.

A wall of infantry, tanks, the skies screaming as aircraft whistled overhead. They rumbled toward Tower 7 just outside of Washington DC. As they approached the dome, they began to open fire, an explosion of might that rocked the earth.

Nothing hit the Tower. Not a single shell, bomb, or bullet. They all whistled off course, around the dome like something had swatted them aside.

Sam's vision tightened and drew close to the top of Tower 7.

Empire stood at the summit, radiating with crimson energy. A Gargoyle stood at his back, its giant hands on his shoulders. Empires slowly raised his own hands to the army of opposition below him.

His fingers curled into fists and the dirt beneath the troops exploded as massive, writhing tentacles of red light erupted from the earth. They thrashed about, thick, pulsing coils hundreds of feet wide. They twisted into the air and then thundered down across the terrified military, pulverizing their forces in seconds.

Shift.

Another Tower. Another mass of military opposition. Another slaughter. Another step toward complete ruin, another blow dealt to the dwindling remains of organized government. Another glimpse of Empire, sparking with power.

Shift.

A missile flying overhead headed right for an unspecified Tower. It was alone, somewhere across the Midwest. The missile soared closer, a nuclear warhead. Empire was visible, hands at his sides, watching as complete destruction roared ever nearer.

The missile suddenly shot upwards and curved back the way it had come.

Shift.

Washington DC vaporizing.

Shift.

Thousands dead across a silent, ruined city.

Shift.

People, gathering before the Towers. They were terrified, submissive, looking for answers. They stared up at the Gargoyles, tears running down their faces, pleas on their lips.

Shift.

Hundreds entering the domes. Then thousands.

Shift.

Changing…they were changing.

Shift.

An army of Red Eyes, grinning, emerging from the structures.

Shift.

The barren planet filled with Gargoyles. More were dead, at least half.

Shift.

The titan crawling across the expanse of space, its one arm pulling the planet behind it.

Shift.

Darkness.

Shift.

Red.

Shift.

Nothing.

Shift.

Nothing…

Sam gasped and clutched his eyes, falling to his knees. The void consumed him, a cold fog that cloaked his skin. His head howled, his skull burned and he felt like he would lose himself to madness.

Worthless...

Sam grit his teeth, begging the pain to stop.

Worthless...

He fought against the voice cracking through his mind like thunder.

You are worthless.

Sam nodded, tears budding in his eyes.

Feed them.

He choked back a cry, his world on fire.

Worthless. Feed them.

"Yes," Sam whispered, spittle leaking from his lips.

You are nothing. Feed them.

"Of course...yes..."

You are fodder. You are nothing. Give them what they need.

Tears rolled down Sam's face, "Yes, yes I know...I will..."

Worthless...worthless...worthless...

Sam opened his bloodshot eyes, his mind reeling, "I am worthless. I am nothing."

And to his amazement, he believed it. He was nothing. An indescribable, insignificant speck, a stain of waste and ruin. How could he not have seen it before?

Toxic...you are toxic.

Sam nodded, "I know...I'm sorry. I'll make it right."

Then show them the way.

Sam arched his back, disgust and self-loathing rocketing through him. He opened his mouth and let out a cry, a shrieking, repulsed howl. It tore at this throat like a revelation. The human race was a conglomeration of waste. A plague. A disease to the universe. Why should they be allowed to continue?

Why did they deserve to exist? What did they *contribute*? What did they fucking *do*? War, cruelty, unrest, political squabbles, deceit, hatred, murder, death...these were the things that defined them. These were the staples, the traits, the fucking DNA of mankind.

Sam screamed again, his eyes bulging, images racing through his head. He saw the entirety of existence, the timeline of the world. He saw every merciless, horrible act ever committed. He saw endless suffering, selfishness, and countless encounters of unrelenting sadism. He saw how truly evil humanity was. He saw every act ever committed behind closed doors. Every secret hidden from sight. He saw domestic abuse, cheating, child abuse, neglect, pornography, drunks, drug addicts, thieves, liars, and the sloth of the uncaring.

Howling, Sam fell forward and vomited, his body buckling. And as he spewed forth the bile, the bile in his mind continued to churn. His eyes watered, bulged, and he was consumed in the deepest repulsion he had ever experienced.

Humanity...was worthless.

Feed them.

Sam wiped his mouth, coughing. Yes. Yes of course. He could still save himself. He could still mean something. He could still redeem his toxic existence. He could die and turn to ash. He could feed the Gargoyles. He could still be of use.

Dazed, consumed, Sam crawled to his feet. Through his nightmare haze, he realized he was back in the Tower, back in the room with the blue light and fog. It swirled and danced around him, the soft glow coming from all directions.

Die. I need to die, Sam thought desperately.

He stumbled to the wall and braced his hands against it. He

cocked his head back and slammed his face into the hard surface. The contact brought stars and his teeth rattled in his head.

Die. Die quickly. Feed them. DO SOMETHING.

Sam brought his head back for another blow but felt himself suddenly restrained as powerful arms wrapped around his body, stopping him.

"It's ok, Sam. Take it easy, buddy."

Sam struggled against the grip holding him back, "No! Let me go! I have to die! I have to do something! Please!"

Empire leaned into Sam's ear, his arms like a vice, "I need you, Sam. You can't die, yet."

Sam choked back a frustrated cry, "But I'm nothing! I don't deserve to fucking exist! PLEASE!"

Empire slowly pulled Sam further from the wall, his chest pressed tight against Sam's back, "I know. I know, Sam. None of us do. But the Gargoyles need us. We have to light their way. Don't you understand?"

Blinking back tears, Sam looked at Empire, "The Towers...we have to fill the Towers. We have to power the beacons."

Empire smiled gently, "That's right. But not you. I need you for something else."

Sam finally stopped struggling, "Anything. I'll do anything. Just please...give me a purpose. I can't bear the weight any more...I feel..." his chest hitched, "I feel so fucking empty. That I've always been empty like I'm nothing."

Empire released Sam and turned him so they stood face to face. His voice was calm, "I need you to get Alex."

Sam nodded slowly, "He deserves to die for the trouble he's caused."

"No!" Empire said sharply, "No, Sam, don't kill him. I want him to join me. I want him to *choose* to join me. I know I can't do that myself. He's too angry with me. His family…he'll never forgive me for that. For the Red Eyes taking them away." Empire touched Sam's cheek, "But you…you're his best friend. You've been with him through it all. Show him the way. Show him how you feel. Convince him to come back to me. I want him. I need him there by my side when the world ends. Can you do that for me? Can you convince him?"

Sam ground his teeth together, "Count on it. I'll get it done."

Empire smiled, almost lovingly, "Thank you, Sam."

Sam smiled back, his eyes pulsing the deepest red.

Chapter 8

Alex slid the truck between the trees and shut the engine off. Night had fallen hours ago. The darkness, along with the towering cluster of foliage, cloaked the vehicle. Tower 12 rose before him, its dome a reflection of shimmering power beneath the starlight.

"Do you really think he's in there?" Luna asked quietly from the passenger's seat.

"I don't know," Alex said, his eyes never leaving the massive construct.

Luna sighed, an exhausted exhale, "Even if he is, how the hell are we going to get him out?"

Alex leaned back in his seat, "I don't know, Luna. But I'm not going to just abandon him."

"That's not what I said," Luna said, "I want to find him too. But we've been driving all day and we haven't seen anyone. No people, no Red Eyes, nothing."

Alex closed his eyes, his temper rising, a result of his own fatigue, "So? What are you trying to say?"

Luna placed a hand on his arm, "I'm not saying anything. I just want to know what you're thinking."

Alex pulled a hand over his face, "I just want him back."

Luna squeezed his arm, "Alex?"

Alex kept his eyes closed, his voice growing soft, "I'm so fucking tired of this shit…"

Luna leaned into him, her cheek resting on his shoulder, "I know. So am I. We'll get him back, one way or another. We just need to figure out how."

"What if they changed him? What if he's not even in there? What if we've driven all this way and he's somewhere else?"

"Then we'll go somewhere else and find him," Luna assured.

Alex laid his head back against the seat, "Yeah…yeah we will. I'm not ending this without him."

Luna went quiet for a moment. Her hand remained on Alex's arm. Red Eyes wandered in the distance beneath the dome.

"Alex?"

"Hmm?"

"Can I tell you something?"

"Sure."

Luna sat up, choosing her words carefully, "I want you to know that…that…" she trailed off, searching.

"What is it?" Alex prodded.

Luna wrung her hands together, "Sam told me about Empire."

Alex bristled, "What do you mean?"

Luna looked into his face, her eyes soft, "Back in Arizona…Sam told me who he was."

Alex held her eyes, saying nothing, his face an unreadable mask.

"It's ok," Luna continued, "I understand. What he did to your family…I don't know if I could ever forgive someone who took them away like that."

Alex turned to stare out the window, refusing to speak. His

heart thundered in his chest and his pulse raced.

"His name is Will, right?" Luna pressed gently, "Your brother?"

Alex nodded, gazing out into the night.

Luna looked down at her hands, "I know the Red Eyes took your wife and unborn child away from you. I know why you're so angry at Empire. At your brother. I know you want to kill him for what he did. When my kids…" the words died on her lips.

"It's more than just that," Alex said, breaking the growing silence.

Luna looked at him, her face a mask of sadness.

Alex let his forehead fall against the window, his eyes staring aimlessly, "I was always there for him growing up. Every time he needed me, I was there. Our parents…they were fucking monsters. The things they did to us…I can't think about those days anymore. I blocked them off, tried to erase them."

Luna's hand found Alex's arm again, but he brushed it off, his voice growing thick.

"I worked my whole life to forget my childhood. And when I met my wife, when I met Maddison…" Alex closed his eyes, "When I met her everything evaporated. She took all that darkness away. She was the only person I had ever met who could do that," Alex's voice grew quiet, "and I loved her to pieces for that."

"Hey…" Luna whispered, her hand returning to Alex's arm. He let her.

Alex grit his teeth, "And then she was taken away, months before giving birth to my child. My son. It was a boy. I couldn't believe it. For the first time in my life…I felt hope. Like I had a chance of living a normal life. But then The Impact…and then the Red Eyes…" Alex's voice turned to a snarl, "And then my own fucking brother took it all away from me. And for what? Why would he do something like that?"

He turned his bloodshot eyes to meet Luna's, "Because he needed me again."

"Why did he do it?" Luna asked after a second. "Why did he offer himself up to them? Why protect the Towers?"

Alex closed his eyes again, "Because I abandoned him."

"What do you mean?" Luna asked, her voice cautious and caring.

Alex heaved a labored breath, "Once we escaped our parents, I left. I ran away to California. I couldn't be around him. I didn't want to. It was selfish and I knew it, but I didn't care. I couldn't stand him. I couldn't stand what he reminded me of. Of all the bad shit we went through. I had to escape. I had to start a life for myself."

"You did what you had to," Luna affirmed.

Alex shook his head, "No. I did what I *wanted* to. I left him. And in his place, I took my best friend with me."

"Sam…"

Alex nodded, "He came to California with me. We found a place, found jobs, and he helped me build a life for myself. He helped me realize I could do this. That I could exist without all the fear. He even introduced me to Maddison. I owe him my life. I owe him everything."

"Where was Empire during all this?"

"His name is Will," Alex said, "No one called him Empire until he started killing everyone. Until he built a new persona for himself. A new life. Just like I did. Don't you get it? It's my fucking fault he's turned into the monster that he's become. It's because I fucking left him. My own brother…"

Luna reached up and placed her hand beneath Alex's chin.

She leaned forward and kissed him on the lips, allowing the sensation to last. When she pulled away, a stillness emanated between them.

"I'm glad I met you," she said quietly, breaking the trance.

Alex let out a slow breath, "Yeah…"

"Can I ask what happened to your parents?"

Alex turned away, his voice low, "No idea. I hope they died miserably."

Luna nodded, "What happened between you and Will, the reason you left…everything that happened before…I'm sorry. You don't deserve it. Any of it."

Alex nodded numbly, "I guess. It doesn't matter though. None of it does. That life, that world, it's gone. What's left, what's left of us…it's all we got. There's no point thinking about things before The Impact."

Luna kept her hand on his arm, the two of them staring out the windshield, through the trees at Tower 12. Red Eyes stood in clusters around the perimeter, talking to one another. Alex watched them, wondering what they could possibly be discussing. They were too far away to see if any of them were Sam. The thought made his stomach clench. What the hell had happened last night?

"Where are you…?" Alex muttered.

Luna glanced at him and then twisted in her seat to look out the back. Her grip on Alex's arm tightened.

"Alex. More Red Eyes."

Alex turned and let his eyes roam the darkness until he spotted a small group making their way down the road toward the Tower. They staggered slightly and looked terrible, their stance limp and weak. It looked like they had just been through hell.

"They're going back to the Tower," Luna observed.

"How many do you count? Six?"

"Yeah, six."

Alex grated his teeth together, feeling his blood pressure rising. Just the sight of them, their glowing eyes, their subservient behavior, everything they stood for – it made him furious. It enraged him. He felt it fill his head.

Luna leaned forward, "Hold on. Look. There's someone with them. One of us."

"Where?"

"In the middle of the pack. His eyes aren't glowing. Don't you see him? The one with the beard?"

Alex's eyes narrowed, "What do you think they're doing with him?"

"No clue. Changing him? Seems odd they'd take only one. What do you want to do?"

"Get out of the car," he growled.

Luna cocked an eyebrow, "What?"

"I have an idea."

"Care to fill me in?" Luna asked, one hand on the door handle.

"I'm going to flash the lights. Just enough to get their curiosity up. Draw them over here. When they come, we're going to ambush them."

"Why the hell would we risk something like that?" Luna asked, perplexed.

"Because I bet you anything one of them knows where Empire is. And maybe, if we're real damn lucky, where Sam is."

"That's quite a stretch," Luna said, "we don't even know if Sam was taken."

Alex unstrapped his cleaver, "Well, we can always ask."

Luna held his eyes a moment longer and then slid out of the

car like a shadow passing through the night. He heard her walk around to the back of the truck and stop. When she did so, Alex took another look at the shuffling Red Eyes on the road. They were almost parallel to the truck, off to his left, about twenty yards away.

He leaned down across the seats and then flicked the headlights once. Immediately, he crawled across to Luna's side and out into the night. He got to his feet and saw Luna retreating into the trees, her eyes trained on the road.

Alex did the same, allowing some distance between them. As he did so, he directed his attention to the Red Eyes. From behind a tree, he saw they had stopped and were staring down at the truck.

"Come on," Alex whispered, "come have a look, you bastards..."

They were talking to one another, their voices muted by the distance. Then, finally, they began to walk toward the truck, keeping their prisoner between them. They were cautious, as if unsure what they had really seen. They spread out and approached the cluster of trees. Alex looked to his left and saw Luna a couple feet away. She was pressed against the trunk of a large oak, knife in hand.

"I'm going to circle around behind them," Alex called. Luna simply nodded. Using the trees, Alex began to flank the approaching group. His heart roared in his ears and as he got closer, he felt something fill his mind, consume it like a disease. It pulsed through him with every beat of his heart, an angry, hungry urge that threatened to overtake his senses. He tightened his hold on the cleaver, his teeth bared. The Red Eyes were close now. They had seen the truck and now appraised it with trepidation.

Alex slunk closer, fighting against the rising tide. It burned through him like wildfire. The Red Eyes. The Impact. Will.

Maddison...

So much had happened, his life an unrelenting continuum of misery and violence. It swelled up in his chest, exploded through his senses and overtook him without warning. Every memory, every terrible day, every heartbreak and injustice. As he watched the Red Eyes, the horrors seemed to sharpen in his mind and take on new life. It was like he was staring at a reminder of how horrible everything had been for him, his entire, lonely life. He grit his teeth, seething.

As the first of the Red Eyes reached the truck, something overcame Alex and his vision went white.

He felt himself push through the trees, but it was as if someone else were controlling his body – like he was floating above the conflict.

A flash of blinding white coursed through his head. He was running. Running toward the Red Eyes. They hadn't seen him yet.

Fire. Fury. Christ, it was so fierce he thought he would scream.

White.

Red. He was bringing his cleaver down, a silent assassin upon the unsuspecting group. Distantly, he heard bone crunch and felt the splash of blood against his face. Something was snarling. It sounded like an animal.

White.

He was slamming someone against the truck. He heard a skull crack hard against the window. His cleaver streaked before him and severed a jawbone. More blood. Wet, slick blood. It was everywhere.

White.

Something was clawing at his back, driving a battering ram into his ribs. He gasped and spun. The cleaver bit deep and flesh parted, split, and then fell away.

White.

His head pounded, his muscles cramped, his eyes streaked and tried to focus. He was choking someone. His fingers dug deep into soft skin and he heard gurgling beneath him. His mouth filled with a coppery liquid and he realized he was biting his victim's face. He tore it off and spit out the chunks.

White.

He was holding someone up by their hair, dangling their body in front of him like a puppet. He raised his blade once more, but a voice hissed in his ear, begging him to stop.

"Alex no! We need him! Stop!"

Hands on his arm, then on his cleaver, lowering it. He blinked and saw a bloody, dazed face hanging in the air before him. Teeth were missing, the lips were swollen and the eyes glowed a dim red. The sight of it brought the volcano back and he raised the cleaver once more.

"Alex! NO!"

He felt himself jerked back and he dropped the beaten Red Eye to the ground. Someone was at his side, shaking him, the voice urgent.

"Hey! Alex, snap out of it! Stop it, they're all finished!"

The world bled color and everything seemed to sharpen. He blinked and sensation filled his body like warm water. Something was dripping down his face. His arm ached. He couldn't seem to catch his breath.

Luna reached up and cupped his face, her bloody knife glinting in the starlight, "You here?" she asked carefully.

Alex nodded slowly, lowering his cleaver. He looked around and saw the ground littered with dead Red Eyes, a ruin of carnage. Only one of them seemed alive. It squirmed at his feet, gasping from a blood-pulped face.

"We ok?" Alex asked, dazed. His stomach rolled and his hands were shaking. He felt like he had just walked out of a dream.

Luna looked around and then nodded, "I think so. You didn't even give me a warning, you just went charging in like a lunatic. One of them almost got you."

Alex stared at her bloody knife, "Oh...thanks."

"Let's find out what this son of a bitch knows before we draw any more attention to ourselves."

Alex collected the remains of himself and crouched, staring down into the beaten Red Eye. It looked back at him with venom, its swollen lips curled into an ugly snarl. Alex had to fight against the boiling lava in his gut.

He grabbed it by the throat, his voice a hiss, "Looks like you're in rough shape, pal. Doesn't feel very good, does it?"

The Red Eye spat a wad of blood into his face, "Fuck you."

With great patience, Alex wiped the gore from his cheek, his chest a burning furnace, "Ok. Fuck me. Now that we got that out of the way...*where's Empire?*"

"Like I'd tell trash like you," The Red Eye growled, struggling beneath Alex's iron grip.

Alex stood quickly, bringing his victim up with him. He slammed the Red Eye into the car, banging its head against the hard surface.

"Last chance," He warned.

The Red Eye began to gather more saliva into its mouth, but Alex stopped him by ramming a fist into its mouth. In one brutal motion, he ripped out a handful of loose teeth, bringing with it a splash of blood.

"Fucking *talk*," Alex commanded, tossing the freed teeth aside.

The Red Eye's face contorted in extreme pain, its fragmented mouth a cavern of broken ruin. Blood and drool leaked from its swollen lips, its mouth hanging ajar. It stared at the ground, defiant, its fists clenched.

"He's not going to talk," Luna said.

Alex tightened his hold on his captive, "That true? You being stubborn? I don't know how many more teeth you got, but we can find out."

The Red Eye kept its eyes to the ground, its body quivering, but silent.

"To hell with you then," Luna said suddenly. She buried her knife in its skull, rocking its head back and out of Alex's grip. It dropped to the ground with a thump, blood sluicing from the open wound.

"I guess that's that," Alex muttered, stepping back.

A voice rose from the side of the truck, a gruff, weak call, "I…I know you two."

Alex and Luna turned as one and faced the voice. Alex had almost forgotten about the prisoner. When they saw who it was, their shoulders relaxed and Alex stepped forward, offering his hand.

"Jesus…Percy? Is that you?"

The big man emerged from the shadows, his overalls stained with blood. He looked shaken, his face bruised and filthy. His left eye was swollen almost completely shut.

"Fancy meetin' you here," he said wearily, "Can't say I'm disappointed though. It's good to see a friendly face after what I been through."

"We just saw you this morning," Luna stated, "What happened? How did you get captured?"

Percy huffed a sigh, "We went to retake the town like I told you. Thought we had the numbers. Turns out we didn't. We put up a hell of a fight, but it just wasn't enough. Now, most of my people are dead and here I am."

"What were they going to do with you?" Alex asked.

Percy wiped the side of his face with a meaty hand, wincing, "I think they were taking me to Empire. Seeing how I'm kinda in charge of the people opposing him, I'm guessing he was going to make an example out of me or something. Glad we ran into you though. I wasn't looking forward to the next couple hours."

"Hold on," Luna cut in, "They were taking you to Empire? There?" She pointed to Tower 12.

Percy shrugged, "That's what they said. Say, you got any water on ya? I'm terribly thirsty."

Alex opened up the truck and dug out a water bottle from his pack, "Here man. Drink up."

Percy practically tore the top off as he upended the bottle down his throat. It spilled across his beard and dripped down his chest. Gasping, bottle empty, he wiped his mouth and smiled.

"I appreciate your kindness." He eyed Alex's cleaver, "and your blade. You're like a wild animal with that thing. You got rabies or something?"

"Not that I'm aware of," Alex said, wiping his weapon on a dead Red Eye. He strapped it back to his leg and glanced at the

Tower, making sure the forces under the dome hadn't noticed them.

"You ever find that friend of yours?" Percy asked.

Luna shook her head, "No. We think he might be in there though." She jutted her chin toward the Tower.

Percy cocked an eyebrow, "So what…you two planning on just charging in there? Hope you run into him?"

"We're still working on that," Luna said.

Percy pointed to Alex's cleaver, "Seeing how you work with that thing, I'm sure you could take out a couple of them. But after? Hell, son, I ain't a preacher, but I'll just go ahead and say a couple words in your memory now."

"Well, what the fuck are we supposed to do then?" Alex snapped.

Percy held up his hands, "Hey, keep your bullets in your gun, not your tongue. I was just making an observation. You want it straight, son? You're not going to find your friend. If they've taken him, then he's gone. I'm sorry to say it, but it's the truth and you know it. Now, I'm not saying you should abandon him, but you gotta use your head."

"Is there a point to this lecture?" Alex rumbled.

Percy jammed a thumb over his shoulder, "Come back with me to our base. We're mounting up for a massive assault on the Towers. Biggest yet. You come along with me, maybe you'll find your friend. Maybe you won't. Who knows. But at least you'll have a better chance of survival."

"You just lost all your people," Luna said flatly, "and now you're going to go round up some more and try again? Why? I don't mean to sound like a cynic, but we've been throwing ourselves at these Towers for years now and not once have we made any kind of difference."

Percy stepped forward, his voice hardening, "So what? You think we should just stop trying?"

"That's not wh-"

Percy cut her off, "Look, I'm no fool. I know what we're up against. But if we stop trying, then that means we lose. That means the Red Eyes have beaten us. It means those creatures, those Gargoyles, they own us. And missy? I'm not a man to be owned by anyone, man or monster. You throw yourself against a wall enough times and it's going to start to crack. At some point, we're going to break through. And if we can do that, then we are going to ignite a fire that will spread like fireworks and gasoline. We're not the only organized group. There's a big one up in Vermont. There's another in Colorado. We're out there. We're trying. And one of these days, we're going to break these beasts."

Percy looked at Alex and then back at Luna. He held their eyes, waiting for a response.

Luna let out a long breath, "Ok. You win. We'll come with you."

Alex looked at his feet, "This is so fucked."

"We're not giving up on him," Luna said quietly, "we're just making sure we can save him, ok?"

Alex finally nodded, "It doesn't feel right, but ok. We'll take you back to your group, Percy. If Sam is here, we're not going to be able to do anything about it. At least not without help. I hope to God he's ok, but there's nothing we can do for him if he's actually in there. So yeah, Percy, you win. We'll go. And I hope you're right because if not, we're just going to be leading more people to the grave."

Percy grinned and patted Alex on the back, "Have faith. That'll help."

Alex snorted, "Right. Where is this base of yours anyway?"

"Memphis."

Luna raised an eyebrow, "Tennessee?"

"Yes, ma'am. We'll have to stock up on gas on the way. It's about a seven-hour drive from here. I know a couple outposts and Lodges we can fuel up at. They know me."

Luna shrugged, "Alright then. Let's do it."

Without warning, before they could move, a sound exploded across the sky. It was a deafening rumble, like a low horn, so loud that Alex slammed his hands over his ears, wincing. Luna and Percy did the same, the groaning eruption rising into the night, shaking the earth beneath them. The air vibrated and Alex thought his skull would split, his vision shaking. It spread out and seemed to consume the silence, a massive, powerful blast that thundered deep into the darkness.

Finally, mercifully, the echo faded.

Wide-eyed, Luna turned to Alex, "What…the *hell*…was that?"

Alex, head pounding, looked toward the dome, "I…I think it came from Tower 12."

Percy dug a finger into his ear, "Lord almighty, that was quite a ruckus."

"I don't think we should stay here any longer," Alex said, eyeing the Tower. "Whatever that was, it can't be good. I'd rather not stick around to find out."

Percy turned to the truck, "Let's saddle up."

Chapter 9

They were running on fumes by the time they rolled into a Lodge, three hours later. They had entered a town in Mississippi called Pickens, just as the sun peeked over the low horizon. Percy gave Alex instruction as they drove and had promised there was gas ahead.

Shutting the engine off, Alex hoped he was right.

They were parked in front of a run-down apartment complex, dead trees and wild grass lining the brown building. Out front, a man stood with a gun in hand, eyeing them warily. He was the first person they had seen since leaving Tower 12.

The man relaxed when Percy climbed out of the car, throwing him a wave.

"Easy Kent, it's just me."

The man, Kent, lowered his rifle, his shoulders slumping, "Well shit, I haven't seen you in ages Percy!"

Percy stretched, "We're heading to Memphis. We were hoping you'd have some gas."

Kent nodded, "Sure do. Only two cans, but it's something. Should get you the rest of the way."

"Fantastic," Percy said, clapping his hands together. "Tell me where and I'll go and fetch it."

"In the lobby bathroom," Kent said, staring at Alex and Luna, "Who're they?"

Percy walked toward the front of the building, shooting a look over his shoulder, "Who, them two? Just some good people who helped me out of a bind."

Kent nodded approvingly and stepped aside as Percy entered the building. He refocused his attention back to Alex and Luna.

"Where you from?"

Alex leaned against the truck, "California."

"And what you doing all the way out here?"

"We're looking for someone," Luna answered flatly.

Kent chewed on his lip and looked around the empty streets, "Ain't a whole lot of folk round here. Who exactly you looking for?"

Alex was about to speak, but Luna cut him off.

"My kids. I have two boys. Twins. They're probably about twelve now."

Kent spat idly, "Sorry to hear that. You think they're out this way?"

"I have no idea."

"Well, you certainly picked a funny place to look."

Alex pushed himself away from the truck, "Any news from up north?"

"Wha'cha mean?"

Alex found his patience thinning with the man, "I mean, has anything of consequence happened in the northern states?"

Kent rolled his head slowly, "Oh sure. Well. Kinda. That group outta Colorado tried to assault one of the Towers up there. Heard it was a bloody affair and they lost a lot of folk. Damn shame if you ask me."

"What happened?" Luna pressed.

"The hell you think?" Kent said gravely, "Empire turned up. Just like he always fuckin' does. They didn't stand a chance."

"When was this?" Alex asked sharply.

Kent shrugged, "Bout a week past."

Luna and Alex looked at one another.

"How is that possible?" Luna asked. "We've been on his trail this whole time."

Kent stepped toward them, slinging his rifle over his shoulder, "Thought you two were looking for your kids?"

"They're not mine," Alex said.

Luna silenced at that, casting her eyes to the ground.

Alex noticed and clamped his teeth shut. He felt a wave of guilt roll through him. He touched her arm and she spoke again.

"We caught word Empire was close when we passed through Texas. It just doesn't add up."

Kent snorted, "Don't you two know?"

"Know what?"

"That he can travel between the Towers. There's something inside, some room, that allows him to pass on to the others."

Alex felt his breath hiss between his teeth, "What? How do you know that?"

Kent snickered, "We interrogated some Red Eyes back in Memphis. Percy captured em. Put the screws to em, so to speak. I tell you what, no man on this planet hates those monsters more than Percy. He was an absolute terror with those scissors. Took him but five minutes to loosen their tongues," he balked at that, "literally."

Alex blinked, "…Percy? I would have never guessed."

"This changes everything," Luna whispered at his side.

Alex nodded in agreement, "It's certainly going to make

things harder once we get Sam back." Luna kept silent at that remark.

"What else did you extract from them?" Alex continued.

Kent chewed his lip some more, "Not a whole lot. Something about using the Red Eyes as a power source once the time is right."

"A power source? For what? How?"

Kent grunted, "Shit, you two ask a lot of questions. I have no idea what for. Do I look like a damn Gargoyle? What don't you go and ask one of them?"

"Ok, take it easy," Luna said, "we were just asking."

It looked like Kent was about to retort, but Percy interrupted as he came bustling out of the building holding a pair of red gas cans.

"We're in luck, folks!" he announced jovially, "Turns out Kent wasn't lying!"

"Course I wasn't," Kent defended.

Percy passed one of the cans to Alex and the other to Luna, "Get this in the tank, we'll be on our way shortly. Just gotta talk to Kent real quick."

"Sure."

Luna helped Alex fuel up as Percy went and conversed briefly with Kent. The morning sun spilled across the road before them, soft orange rays running down the pavement. The air was already filling with humidity and Alex wiped a handful of sweat off the back of his neck. When the truck was filled, he tossed the empty cans into the bed.

He turned to see Percy approaching, a grim look on his face.

"What's up?" Alex asked.

Percy shook his head, his cheeks flushed, "Sounds like there was some trouble up north. A lot of people died."

"Yeah, Kent told us," Luna said.

Percy sighed heavily, his belly rolling, "Breaks my heart to hear. I swear one of these days we're going to get through these monsters. And we're going to make em atone for all this senselessness."

"We all hate the Red Eyes," Luna assured.

Percy nodded, "They're a cancer. They don't belong here. Once those eyes change, they ain't one of us anymore. Don't care how they look or talk. Nothing makes my blood boil hotter."

"We should go," Alex said, looking toward the sky.

Percy wiped his hands on his overalls, "Of course, of course. I can drive for a while if you'd like. You two can get some shuteye. You look like you could use it."

Alex handed him the keys, "All yours."

The trio climbed back into the truck, and after throwing Kent a wave, Percy pulled back onto the road and encouraged the engine.

Luna sat between the two men and after a moment, she gently laid her head against Alex's shoulder. Alex closed his eyes and hesitantly put his arm around her. He felt her body relax against him and for the first time in ages, he felt at peace. He placed his head against the window and sleep came easy.

The dream approached him like a shadow.

He was standing in the ocean, up to his waist. He could see the shore, a thin black line in front of him. Rising from the shore was a single Tower, its summit scraping the ceiling of the sky.

He looked down and saw the waters surrounding him were blood red, the color matching the clouds overhead. He lowered his hands and the liquid ran thick between his fingers. He inhaled, the smell overtaking him. His stomach buckled beneath the harsh aroma. It smelled like charred earth. It smelled like ash.

It smelled like death.

He looked toward the shore once more. The Tower stood like a watchman, a black pillar against the crimson sky. His eyes roamed its summit and he felt fear tickle the back of his throat.

A Gargoyle stood motionless at the peak. It was pointing at something. It was pointing at something in the sky. Alex turned, the water like a nauseous syrup. His eyes scaled the clouds.

His blood froze and a scream crawled up his throat.

Something was emerging from the heavens, a titanic monstrosity of horrifying proportions.

Gasping, Alex awoke.

The sun glared through the windshield, a relentless wave of heat that coated his skin and burned his eyes. He raised a hand against it and sat up, Luna stirring at his side. Percy shot him a look from the driver's seat, the road rumbling beneath them.

"You ok?"

"Bad dream," Alex muttered, wiping a sheen of sweat from his face.

Luna suddenly opened her eyes and for a moment, they were wild with fear. Alex looked down at her and squeezed her, his arm still wrapped comfortably around her shoulders.

"You're awake," he assured softly.

Luna rubbed her eyes and brushed a strand of sweaty hair out of her face, "God that was a bad one…"

"Nightmare?"

Luna nodded, "Something like that."

Alex flipped the visor down to guard against the glaring sun, "Where are we, Percy?"

Percy pointed down the road, "Round that bend and we'll start hitting the outskirts of Memphis."

"How long were we out?" Luna muttered.

"Long enough to shed most of the journey," Percy said.

"Thank God."

Percy offered them a speculative look, "You know...I snagged a cellphone from the Lodge when I was there. It's almost dead, but it's got a voicemail if you two wanna Listen. Don't know what you were dreaming about, but it looks like it left a sour taste."

Alex shook his head, "Thanks, but we're fine."

Percy shrugged, indifferent, "Suit yourself. We're practically there anyway."

"Anything happen while we were out?" Luna asked.

"Heard another one of them horn blasts. Couldn't believe it didn't wake you two."

"You mean like last night?"

"Yup. Scared the bejesus out of me. Don't know what the hell is going on, but it left my guts crawling."

"Nothing else happened?"

Percy squinted, "Well, not long after I saw a couple Red Eyes along the side of the road. They barely even looked at me, though, which was strange. It seemed like they were walking the other direction, back toward Tower 12."

Alex turned this over in his head, "You think they're getting called back?"

"Could be. Lord knows. I didn't exactly stop to ask."

"Just so long they're not following us."

"Naw, I made sure they weren't. Relax, there's the city, see?"

True to his word, Memphis slowly came into view. Having never been there, Alex wasn't sure what to expect. He soon found that it wasn't much different than the rest of the world he had seen during his travels.

As they drew closer to the sprawling flat rise of buildings, his eyes went to the empty streets. Garbage littered the road, cars sat abandoned, and storefronts were smashed and picked clean. The rising structures looked like colossal gravestones, gray tributes to a life long past.

They passed signs and billboards that offered exclusive deals to a consumer who no longer held interest. Familiar brands and labels stirred something in Alex's mind, the advertisements reading like a dead language.

Percy guided the truck down a street and turned left, avoiding a cluster of rusted out cars. They were entering the heart of the city now, the sun blocked intermittently by a scattering of phantom skyrises.

"Where are your people?" Luna asked.

Percy took another turn, "Inside. We're almost there."

"What's the closest Tower?"

"That'd be Tower 15 about fifteen miles north of us. We've had a couple run-ins with the Red Eyes, but it was mostly small gathering parties during the early days. They don't really mess with us anymore."

Alex's eyes scanned a burned out grocery store, "Do you have power at this base of yours?"

Percy grunted, "Sure do. Got a couple of gennys and plenty of fuel. You see all these cars? We've siphoned all of em. Got to say, I always hated those little electric cars, but never more then when we were hunting for fuel. Neither one of you ever had one of them cars did ya?"

Luna sniffed, "No. I was always a pickup girl."

Percy cocked a grin, "Woman after my own heart. Chevy?"

"Dodge."

Percy's grin faltered, "And now you lost me again."

"I mostly rode my bike," Alex cut in.

Percy's eyes lit up once more, "No kidding? Harley?"

"Honda."

Percy's brow furrowed, "The hell is wrong with you two…?"

"How much further?" Alex asked.

Percy turned into a parking garage, nosing the truck down the ramp, "Actually, we're here."

They took the ramp down to the sublevels and parked. Alex observed quite a few other vehicles parked alongside them, all looking like they had been used recently. This included four Hummers painted in camo. One of them had a fifty-caliber gun mounted to it.

He gestured to it, "That thing work?"

Percy turned the truck off, smiling, "Sure does. We got others hidden nearby throughout the city."

"How many?"

"Enough to make a difference.

Luna pushed Alex ahead of her, out into the parking garage, "Not like they'll matter."

Percy heaved himself out of the truck as well, "Well, not with an attitude like that they won't." A noise drew their attention and together, they turned to face it. A cluster of women were emerging from a side door, guns in hand. When they saw Percy, they broke into smiles.

"Well I'll be damned, our fearless leader returns!" One of them exclaimed, a tired looking woman with long black hair, streaked with gray.

"Miranda, my dear!" Percy bellowed, a smile cracking his face, "Now, don't tell me you didn't miss me!"

The woman shook her head, huffing, "You know…for a second there, I think I did."

Percy turned to Alex and Luna, "This here is Miranda. She keeps an eye on things when I'm out running around."

The other two women shifted where they stood. They were about Miranda's age and looked like they had seen their share of hardship. One of them pointed to Alex.

"Who's this? And where's everyone else?"

Percy slumped, a somber tone slipping from his tongue, "This is it. Everyone else…they didn't make it. Seems we severely underestimated the Red Eyes. I myself was captured by them, but these two here saved me."

Miranda raised her eyebrows, "Shit. Well, I hope you said thank you."

"Do you guys wanna come inside?" One of the other women asked.

Percy clapped his hands together, "Yes! I gotta piss like a racehorse."

Together, the small group entered the building, the large faceless door leading to a series of blank concrete hallways. Their footsteps echoed around them as they passed room after room on either side. Each one was stockpiled with supplies, guns, canned food, and clothes.

"Impressive," Alex noted, "How many of these rooms you got?"

Miranda was the one who answered, "This is most of them, but we have a couple others throughout the city in case this place is compromised."

"Did I miss anything while I was gone?" Percy asked.

"How long were you gone this time? Two weeks? Nah…nothing much. We finally fixed that goddamn Toyota though. We got her running yesterday."

Percy snorted, "Piece of Japanese garbage…don't know why you wasted your time. Glad to hear it, though."

Miranda rolled her eyes, "It's another set of wheels, what does it matter?"

They ascended a stairway to the next floor, pushing out into an open area that looked like it had once been an office. The spacious room was filled with people of all ages. Lining the walls were makeshift beds, pressed tight against the floor-to-ceiling windows. Tables had been intermittently placed around the massive room, some of which were filled with people. They ate and drank and chatted with one another like nothing was wrong in the world. A bustle of noise filled the air above everyone, a jumbled conversation passed between dozens of varying lips. Children ran through the adults, playing with one another, giggling, adding to the gentle chaos. The older folks sat against the walls, watching the whole thing with ghostly smiles.

"Holy shit," Luna muttered, taking it all in.

Miranda chuckled, "This is probably not what you're used to, huh?"

"Not at all."

Alex stepped aside to avoid being run into by a laughing boy, "Why's everyone so damn cheery?" Luna elbowed him in the ribs. Percy saw it and snickered.

Miranda waved to someone in the corner, an elderly couple, "They're just excited."

Alex rolled his shoulders, "Why?"

"Because we're about to have a Raffle."

This seemed to excite Percy who's face lit up, "Looks like I picked just the right time to return! We doing it upstairs?"

"Just like always. In fact, we really should head up. We were about to when the lookouts spotted your truck."

Percy nodded, "Alright then, let's get to it then!"

Bewildered, Alex and Luna stepped back as Miranda and Percy silenced the crowd with a series of sharp whistles. When everyone saw Percy had returned, he was met with an onslaught of good cheer and enthusiastic greetings. After silencing them once more, Percy cleared his throat and addressed them.

"Sorry I was gone for so long!" He called, the crowd stilling, almost clinging to his words, "I'm afraid to say that our endeavor did not end well."

A muted hush swept through the room, eyes cast the to ground.

Percy wasted no time lifting their spirits, "I grieve our losses, as I know you will as well. But! This doesn't change a damn thing. We've built a wonderful community here and ain't nothing going to change that. It's no secret that I hold each and every one of you dear to my heart. I will keep fighting the Red Eyes for as long as you allow me. Sure, the Red Eyes outnumber us, but they can't outmatch our spirit. They cannot kill our will to survive. To fight back. This world is not theirs and we will NOT give it up willingly."

Percy stepped into the crowd, his voice rising, "We are the last towers of humanity. And we will *not* crumble before them."

A cheer rose to that, along with a hundred odd fists.

Percy raised his hands, smiling, his voice carrying over the crowd, "Now I hear we have a Raffle ahead of us, is that true?!"

A flurry of voices hurried to assure him it was, an excited babble filled with chittering anticipation.

"The hell is a Raffle?" Alex whispered to Luna. She just shrugged.

Percy brought his hands together like thunder, "Well, if that's the case, then let's get to it! Up we go, come on everyone!"

Like a gaggle of sugar high children, Percy turned and led the crowd back out the door and up the stairs, leaving Alex and Luna pressed against the wall, trying not to get run over. A few of the older people stayed put, leaving the activity for the younger audience.

"Jesus, they're riled up!" Alex yelled over the din, holding Luna tight against him as they were brushed by.

When the last of the crowd had exited the room, they found themselves standing face to face with Miranda who jammed a thumb toward the open door where a wave of noise echoed down to them.

"You wanna check it out?"

"What is it?" Alex asked.

"Come find out."

Alex and Luna looked at each other. Not sure what else to do, they followed the noise up to the next floor, Miranda on their trail. They came out into a large room, similar in size to the one below. Instead of beds and tables though, a large cage had been built in the middle of the space, about twenty feet by twenty feet, floor to ceiling. It was empty.

The crowd pressed in around it and Percy could be seen amidst the bustle, trying to calm the excited voices.

"Alright, simmer down everyone, simmer down!" He boomed, raising his hands above his head.

The noise receded slightly, but the chatter continued to buzz.

Percy produced a notebook from his back pocket. He waved it around, drawing a round of applause.

"You know how this works!" He called, "Everyone form an orderly line and I'll take down your times. The closest one wins the Raffle!" He paused for dramatic effect and placed a hand to his ear, "What's that? What're the winnings!?"

He nodded to Miranda who handed him a small satchel. Taking his time, he plunged his hand inside and mock awe-filled his face. Smiling, he finally pulled out a pair of cellphones for all to see.

"Well look at this!" He laughed, "We have not one, but TWO phones for your Listening pleasure! I'll be damned!" The crowd cheered and shuffled in place, eager to get things under-way.

"Ok everyone, line up and place your times!" Percy shouted, "Then we'll get this party started!"

Alex and Luna stayed near the back, unsure what was really going on. Something about the whole thing made Alex feel uneasy. Everyone was far too worked up over whatever was about to happen.

He placed his arm around Luna and looked down at her, "This is weird," he muttered.

Luna looked up at him, "Yeah, I'm glad I'm not the only one who thinks so."

Miranda wandered to their side, parting the crowd as they pushed to form a line in front of Percy.

"You wanna enter?" She asked casually.

"Enter what?" Luna asked, "What's going on, exactly?"

Miranda's eyes filtered through the crowd, "Percy is keeping everyone's spirits up. He knows how important that is, now more than ever."

"How so?"

Miranda gave them a dead-eyed look, "Look around. The Red Eyes are growing in number by the day. It won't be long before we're all extinct or turned."

Alex cocked an eyebrow, "I see you don't share the same optimism as your leader."

Miranda snorted, "He's a big talker, but these people need him. They need his hope. I don't know how much he actually believes, but he despises the Red Eyes and what they've done to us. Even if it's meaningless, he *will* lead us against them. For as long as he can."

"How noble," Alex said.

Miranda looked at Alex's arm around Luna and then pushed away from them, back into the crowd. The line was almost through and Percy was jotting down the last of the contestants in his book.

When he was finished, he raised his hands once more and quieted the noise, his voice rumbling over all, "Ok, it looks like we're ready to go! Miranda, where are you!?" He scanned the sea of faces and spotted her leaning against the back wall. He motioned for her to come forward.

"My dear! Would you please be so kind as to gather our contestants?"

Miranda nodded and motioned for two others to follow her. Alex watched her progress through the crowd, his stomach unexplainably sinking deeper and deeper into itself. She opened a door he hadn't noticed before and disappeared inside. As the door swung shut, he saw that a massive red X had been painted across its surface.

After a few seconds, she reappeared.

"What the fuck…?" Luna hissed, tensing against him.

Miranda held a pair of chains in her hand. Attached to the ends were two naked children who had been blindfolded. They looked like they had been beaten, their skin covered in scabs and bruises. One of them was openly weeping.

They were both boys.

"Oh my god…" Luna whispered, her voice dropping out.

"It's ok," Alex assured with confidence he didn't feel, "They're both Red Eyes. I think…" Stomach churning, he watched Miranda lead the children through the crowd and into the cage. Before pushing them inside, she undid their leashes and tossed them aside.

Luna was now hyperventilating, her chest rising and falling rapidly.

"What is it?" Alex dared.

Before she could answer, Percy was at their side, his hand on Alex's shoulder, pushing him toward the cage, "It's something, isn't it? Come on forward and get a good look, don't be shy!" Alex let himself be led to the front row, Luna at his side, her eyes wide and terrified. Percy stopped before the cage, his fingers curling around the iron grates.

"The blindfolds were my idea," he said proudly, "so Empire can't snoop on us. At least, not before it's too late." Still in the cage, Miranda looked at Percy. He nodded to her and she turned back to the two boys. In one swift motion, she removed the rags around their eyes.

Red light poured from their sockets, a radiate, brilliant explosion. The boys stumbled backwards, terrified, clutching one another. They looked at the angry faces leering in at them, snarling, spitting, mocking. One of the boys pissed himself, urine streaming down his leg and onto the bare floor.

At his shoulder, Luna let out a cry.

Alex looked at her, concern filling him, "What's wrong?"

Luna's voice shook, a pained horrified rattle, "Those…those are my boys. Oh God, Alex, those are my *children*."

Alex felt his chest turn to ice, "What? Are you sure?"

Luna nodded, her face pale, her eyes wide.

Suddenly, one of the boys clutched his head, screaming. He covered his eyes and fell to his knees. A split-second later, he recovered, his face a mask of fury.

And his eyes radiated.

"He's here!" Percy cried jovially, "He's here with us!"

A roar shook the room as the crowd pressed tight against the bars, spittle flying, rage creasing every face.

"Let him look!" Percy yelled, "Let him look at who we are!"

The child scanned the faces, neon smoke wafting from his sockets. He met every gaze, every growl, every obscenity spat at him.

When his eyes fell on Alex, he stopped.

Alex felt like his head was on fire, like the universe was boring into his skull. His jaw clicked as he met the boy's look.

The child smiled.

And then he was back, stumbling, crying, rubbing his eyes painfully.

Someone from the crowd yelled over the noise, their voice a haunting prophecy.

"Bring out the dogs!"

Another cheer followed and the onlookers rattled the cage with hungry anticipation. Luna clutched Alex's arm, her face desperate, her voice a rattling moan.

"Help me. Stop this. DO something!"

Alex looked around heart hammering. He knew he had to stop this or at least try. Fear tickled the back of his throat and he fought a sudden impulse to vomit. The people around him jumped with excited need, eyes lost in madness, a driving thirst to kill these boys, to torture the Red Eyes. Men, women, and children, spitting, screaming, faces flush with violence, lost in the wave of it all.

From the back, Alex heard dogs begin to bark.

The crowd stepped aside as two rottweilers were dragged forward, chained in the same fashion the boys had been. The pair Miranda had recruited to get the children held the leashes. The animals were thin and appeared to have been starved. Their eyes rolled wildly in their skulls, their jaws snapping at anyone who got too close.

"NO!" Luna cried. She stepped forward, reaching for her gun, desperation and terror fueling her into action.

Percy was suddenly by her side, his hand snatching the pistol from her grip as she half drew it.

His voice was like thunder, "What the hell do you think you're doing?"

Luna struggled to release herself from his grasp, but he held her tight. Her voice shook, her eyes watering, "Please, I'm begging you, don't do this! Those...those boys! Those are my kids!"

Percy's brow furrowed, "What's this all about?"

Luna finally jerked herself away, pointing to the caged children, "Those are my sons! You can't do this! I'm their mother! Percy, I'm begging you, stop this!"

Percy's teeth clacked together, "You ain't their mother. Red Eyes have no mothers."

Alex finally ripped himself free from his stunned paralysis, "Percy, she's telling the truth. Look at her face. I know they're

Red Eyes, but Jesus, man, have a heart! Aren't there others you could use? Can't you let them go?"

Percy turned on him, practically quivering, all traces of cheery charisma vanishing, "Let…them...*go*?"

Luna grabbed a handful of his shirt, her voice a thin plea, "I'm begging you, if you have an ounce of humanity left in you, don't do this!"

Percy's eyes turned to midnight slits, "You feel sorry for them, don't you?"

"They're my fucking KIDS!" Luna exploded.

Alex, chest heaving, ears ringing from the crowd, lowered his voice, "No one has to know. Just let them go. No one will think any less of you. We saved you, man, you owe us."

Percy's face twisted into a snarl, "I don't owe you shit. Not anymore. I see you for what you are now. A pair of Red Eye sympathizers. And between you and me? That's worse than the Red Eyes themselves."

Alex felt the situation falling apart and it terrified him. He shook his head violently, "What? No! Percy, listen, I *hate* the Red Eyes! This isn't about them though, it's about Luna! Those are her fucking kids. She's their goddamn mother! Please! We'll do whatever you want, just don't let those dogs in there!"

Percy swung his eyes from Alex to Luna, his voice suddenly quiet, "You want to save them, huh?"

Luna nodded viciously, "Please, we'll do anything!"

Percy suddenly stepped forward and grabbed her by the back of the neck, his voice hissing in her ear, "Then get in there and fucking save them."

He dragged her forward, the crowd cheering, and flung her into the cage, ahead of the rabid dogs.

Fuck this, Alex thought, mind splintering into madness. One hand went for his cleaver, the other for his gun.

Before he could draw, a dozen different hands grabbed him from behind. Crying out in surprise, struggling, he whipped his head around and saw Miranda behind him, gun pointed at his face.

"I hoped you wouldn't be trouble," She said, her eyes tired. His weapons were yanked from his hands, like the last gasps of hope.

Four men held Alex as he thrashed about, trying to get free, "Jesus Miranda, how can you let this happen!? What if those were your kids in there!?"

Miranda shrugged, "I never had kids." She nodded to the men holding Alex, "Get him up front so he can watch. He should know what happens to Red Eye sympathizers."

"You've all lost your fucking minds!" Alex screamed as he was dragged forward and slammed face first into the cage. He felt his lip split and blood dribbled between his teeth. His throat ached and his head thundered. His eyes snapped to the center of the cage, finding Luna.

She stood in the center, her eyes huge and terrified. The mob jeered and laughed at her, calling her names and spitting in her direction. She spun in place, finally settling on her two boys. She ran to them, going to her knees and pulling them into her. They tried to push away, confused and scared, but her voice whispered gently into their ears.

From where he was held, Alex couldn't hear what she was saying, but it seemed to calm the children. Luna pulled away, still on her knees, and kissed each one on the cheek. Tears ran down her face and her chest hitched as she tried to suppress a sob.

Percy's voice cut through the noise once more.

"We got a sympathizer among us!"

A chorus of boos swept through the room, followed by all manner of vicious death threats. The mob rattled the cage, eager to see their sick justice dealt, their game met.

Percy pulled out a stopwatch and turned to the dog handlers who were struggling to keep the beasts restrained.

"On my mark!"

This is insane, this can't be happening, Alex thought desperately, his heart in his throat. He tried to buck his captors off of him, but he was slammed roughly back into the bars.

Percy raised the stopwatch over his head, "And... RELEASE!"

The two dogs were set free inside the cage and the door slammed loudly shut behind them. Luna spun and stood, her arms outstretched to protect her sons. They both clung to her shirt, their eyes wild with terror.

The dogs snarled at them and snapped their jaws. They crouched low, their hackles rising, drool leaking from between yellowed teeth. Luna kept her eyes locked with theirs and backed away slowly, pushing her kids into the corner of the cage.

As she did so, the crowd reached between the bars and grabbed the boys by the hair, a cheer rising. Luna turned, panicking, as her kids were jostled against the iron, their faces bashed against the side of the cage. The boys cried out, blood spilling from split lips, teeth rattling loose as their oppressors continued to beat their heads against the hard surface.

Snarling, Luna sprang forward and grabbed at the hands holding her sons. She was quick to pry fingers away, twisting them every way they weren't supposed to. Cries of pain accompanied the breaking bones and finally, the boys were free once more.

Get them, Luna, get them! Alex thought hopelessly, his pulse thundering in his ears, the taste of blood on his tongue.

But then the dogs charged.

Luna didn't have time to turn around before the first one buried its fangs into her arm. She screamed as it pulled her back, its jaws a flurry of sharp jerks, shredding the skin down to the bone. Luna went down on one knee, almost falling over completely as blood splashed to the ground. She raised a fist and beat at the animal, trying to rip her arm away from its vice-like hold on her.

The second dog charged one of the boys. Terrified, the child shrank away from it and backed into the bars, a cry echoing around the room. As his back connected with the cage, a dozen hands reached out and grabbed at him, holding him in place, rendering him helpless against the oncoming attack.

The rabid animal went for his stomach.

It sprang on the boy, its teeth sinking deep into the soft exposed flesh. The crowd roared their approval as they kept the child pinned where he stood, watching in fascination as the dog buried its snout deeper into the boy's abdomen, its jaws shredding through the tissue and muscle like a wood chipper.

Luna, hearing her son's cries, became overwhelmed by a burst of adrenaline. Howling, she kicked the dog holding her. It whimpered as her boot made contact and finally released her. Wasting no time, Luna lunged for her son and tackled the dog eating his stomach. They rolled across the floor and Luna fought to keep the snapping jaws away from her throat.

The gored child slumped to the floor, screaming, as his insides emptied in a puddle before him. The other boy, untouched, weeping, shaking, rushed to his brother's side and frantically tried to shove the tangle of organs back into the gushing hole.

Hands bloodied, face tear-streaked, his voice could be heard among the roar.

"It's ok, it's ok, it's ok, it's ok…" he sobbed, uselessly trying to put his brother back together, the organs slipping from his trembling hands.

Luna, still wrestling with the dog, finally got her hands around its neck and slammed the thing into the bars as hard as she could. The dog let out a yelp of pain and writhed in her grasp, trying to bury its teeth into her face.

Before she could deliver another blow, the second dog attacked. It found Luna's ruined arm and clamped down on the already raw flesh. Luna howled and released her hold on the first dog, spinning and striking at the fresh pain.

The dog chewing on her arm jumped back, still holding fast, and yanked Luna halfway across the cage, leaving a bloody streak in their wake. It snapped its head violently to one side and then the other.

Luna's arm tore free, the bone shattering.

The dog dug into its prize, making short work of the flesh, consuming it in quick, hungry bites. In seconds, it had stripped the bone, blood dripping from its jowls. It turned back to Luna, it's eyes alight.

Luna, screaming, tried to stand, her face snow white and covered in sweat, her eyes rolling in agony. She got to her knees and clutched her gushing stump, gasping, crying.

The dog she had stunned had recovered and directed its attention to the untouched boy who was still trying to help his brother, his back turned. Growling, the dog lunged for him.

Luna saw it and cried out. She tried to leap into its path but stumbled and fell as the other dog bit down on her leg, dragging her back and away from her children.

"No! STOP IT LEAVE HIM ALONE!" Luna shrieked, helpless, spilling blood across the floor.

The dog had reached her son and brought him to the ground. It pinned him on his stomach and bit down into his shoulder, bringing a horrific scream rattling from the boy's throat.

Blinded by tears, Alex watched, his teeth clamped over one of the bars, his whole body shaking uncontrollably.

The dog who held Luna took another massive bite out of her leg, tearing calf muscle away from the bone. Howling, Luna sat up and kicked at the thing, but it jerked its head back, and she watched it swallow a mouthful of herself.

Taking the brief second of freedom, she tried to crawl across the floor, tears pouring down her face. Her son continued to be eaten alive before her, his room-shattering screams fueling her forward.

With her good hand, she reached out and grabbed the dog's hind leg and jerked the beast off her boy. It spun, causing her to lose her grip, and faced her. Luna rolled away from it, strength failing, and looked at her children.

One of them lay motionless by the bars, his stomach emptied.

The other was alive, but the entire left side of his body was a mangled mess of bleeding, exposed muscle. From the floor, he turned his head and met his mother's gaze with dim, red eyes.

Weeping, Luna tried to stand once more, but her shredded leg gave out and she came down hard on her severed arm. She gasped, more tears spilling from her bloodshot eyes. She met her son's fading gaze.

"I *love* you."

The words rattled from her throat with all the pain of motherhood behind it.

The dogs attacked once more. One of them fell over Luna, the other on her remaining son.

Alex closed his eyes, tears streaming down his face, and listened to them die.

Slowly.

Every scream, every crunch of bone exploded inside his skull like fireworks. Every tear of flesh and desperate cry for help punched him in the gut with all the horror in the world.

When he opened his eyes again, the screaming had stopped, lost in a wave of uproarious cheers from the bloodthirsty crowd.

When he saw what was left of Luna and her children, his stomach threatened to empty itself.

Somewhere in the haze of madness, Percy's voice could be heard announcing the time of death and who had won the Raffle. Applause followed, the echoes of mankind lost beneath the storm of hands.

As he was jostled and bumped around, a thought entered Alex's head that terrified him and brought overwhelming grief.

I am completely and utterly alone now.

Suddenly he was spun around and found himself face to face with Miranda. Her face was grim and she held her pistol to his face.

"Once things settle down, I'll let Percy decide what to do with you," she said darkly, "but for now, you're going into isolation."

Before he could react or defend himself, Miranda brought her pistol down over his head and darkness took him along with an eruption of pain.

Chapter 10

Sam stood beneath Tower 12, the sun painting gold across his face. He watched as hundreds of Red Eyes continued to file inside, disappearing without a word into the massive structure. Each one of them looked excited, an air of anticipation crackling through the quiet dusk.

The Towers had sounded.

The time was approaching.

He felt an unexpected swell of pride to be a part of this. To finally do something to make up for the waste of human existence. The room had shown him a lot. Not just about what was coming; it had also uprooted the disease that was mankind. The hurt, the violence, the complete meaningless of existence. Humans had corrupted this planet with selfishness and malicious desires, clawing and stabbing anyone who threatened to take that away.

But not the Gargoyles.

They were pure. They existed without…without all the fucking *noise*. The brief intrusion into their history had assured him that they were incredible beings. The planet-eaters, burning up and consuming all the filth in the cosmos.

Humanity was next.

And we deserve it, Sam's mind whispered.

Straying from his thoughts, he watched as a pair of Red Eyes shuffled toward the entrance. They were slumped over, great buckets creasing their forms as they carried them inside.

Sam walked to one of them, a hand raised, "What are those for?"

The Red Eye paused, shifting the bucket on his back, irritated at having been stopped, "It's ash for the Gargoyle."

The other Red Eye hefted his load higher up on his back, "It's growing weak, it needs to be fed."

Sam stepped away, raising his hands, "Carry on then."

"Who made you in charge?" One of them muttered, pushing past back into the steady line.

Ignoring the remark, Sam watched the two disappear inside. He felt a desire to follow them, to ascend the stairs to the top, and see the Gargoyle up close. To take in its presence, to reflect on it. As he thought about it, he realized he wanted to apologize to it. To ask for forgiveness. To tell it he was honored to serve it, to feed it with the broken remains of this planet.

Despite his inclinations, he stayed where he was. He had a job to do.

Empire emerged from the bowels of the dark doorway, his face calm and pleased with how things were progressing. He scanned the line of Red Eyes, making sure everything was in order. He turned and spoke briefly to one of them, muttering orders and instruction. The Red Eye nodded, practically brimming with pride.

Cutting across the land between them, Empire strode to Sam's side.

"Tower 12 is almost ready," he said, watching, contemplating.

"What about the others?"

"I'll need to check on them, make sure they are being filled without incident," Empire said, running his tongue across his bottom lip. "What are the odds..."

"But the Gargoyles can control them, direct them when they're under the domes," Sam said, "Why do you need to be there?"

Empire pointed past the shimmering, transparent bowl in the distance, "And what about beyond that? There are Red Eyes out there who have heard the call but are still traveling back to their Towers. I need to make sure every one of them is filled, that each one has the numbers required to activate. Most the world is dead or broken, but there's still some out there clinging to hope, thinking they can still make a difference." His eyes casually fell upon Sam.

Sam raised his own to the sky, "And what about me? Any idea where I should start looking for Alex?"

Empire nodded, "I saw him."

"What?"

"A couple of Red Eye boys were taken hostage about a month ago. I've been keeping tabs on them, trying to see where they're being held. They were blindfolded for most of their captivity," Empire sniffed, "clever bastards."

"But you got through?"

"Yeah. And when I could finally see through their eyes again, I saw him."

"Alex? Where?"

Empire shot him a distant look, "I'm not entirely sure. But I can guess."

"Did you see Luna?"

"Who?"

"The woman he was with."

Empire waved his hand dismissively, "I don't know. She's not important."

Sam found himself agreeing. Luna was a part of the problem now. She would never understand what Sam knew now. Not unless she was dragged into that chamber and shown just how pathetic the world was. If she wouldn't do that willingly, she was better off dead. With her out of the picture, it'd be easier to convince Alex to join his brother. The less distractions the better. He didn't need a chittering conscious whispering into Alex's ear as he tried to sway him over to this side of things.

"So where is he?" he finally asked,

Empire snorted, "Well, he was surrounded by a lot of angry looking people. They were inside somewhere, surrounding a cage. Looked like they were revving up to kill the kids. The Red Eyes."

"How many people?"

"I'd say about a hundred. Maybe more," Empire mused, his eyes drifting over to the line entering the Tower. "There's only three places I'm aware of with that many people and that kind of set up. There's a group in Vermont, one in Colorado..." his eyes found Sam's, "and the other is in Memphis."

"Memphis? Shit...that's not exactly close. What makes you think it's Memphis?"

"Nothing, other than the fact that it's the closest of the three. Plus I saw someone else. Someone I recognized. He was leading the assault on that town, the one you were trying to pass through when I found you. His name's Percy."

"So what's the move here?"

Empire looked back at Tower 12, "You're coming with me."

Sam cocked an eyebrow.

"There's a lot of places I need to be," Empire continued, "and the end is drawing very, very close. I don't have time to wait for you to walk or drive all the way to Memphis. I'll take you there myself, between the Towers. Once we've found Alex, I'll leave him to you. Something tells me he's not going to want to see me. At least, not until you've spoken with him. And like I said, I have places to be. I need to make sure the other Towers are going to be ready. When I'm sure they are, I'll meet you back here." Empire leaned in close, his voice lowering, "with Alex. You can't screw this up, Sam. I'm counting on you."

Sam's eyes briefly flared, a rolling wash of red, "We'll be here."

Empire heaved a great sigh and motioned for Sam to follow, "Then let's go."

Curious, Sam followed, questions bubbling from his tongue, "Wait, we're going to use the Towers? How?"

Red Eyes parted for them as they continued toward the open door, faces full of respect and awe. Empire didn't even seem to notice.

"We're taking the Overroad," he said, his voice grave. "It's the fastest way I know. Tower 15 is about a dozen odd miles north of Memphis. That's where we'll go."

They entered Tower 12, the darkness looming around them. Hundreds of Red Eyes filled the interior, all waiting impatiently to take their place inside the slots lining the walls. Sam craned his head back and saw the bottom half had already been filled, the circular chamber impregnating the Red Eyes in the strange, half-coffins. The ones who had already been slotted stood motionless as the strange divots seemed to contort and compress around their bodies, almost coming alive in the process. It reminded Sam of cocoons, coming up to just below the neck.

He refocused back to the task at hand, realizing that Empire was ahead of him now. Brushing past the line, he caught up to him and saw they were headed for the central pillar.

Where the room was.

"What's the Overroad?" Sam asked, matching Empire's stride.

They halted before the rising black column. Empire ran his hands over the surface and after a moment, the door came alive and granted them access to the core of the Tower. The familiar cool fog wafted ahead of them, pulsing lazily with eerie blue light.

Before they stepped inside, Empire turned to Sam, his voice low, "Listen to me and listen closely. Where we're about to go is incredibly dangerous. Once we're inside, I won't have my…abilities…until we've reached the other side. Do you understand?"

Sam nodded, his curiosity peaking.

"The Overroad is the pathway connecting the Towers together," Empire continued, "I've used it many times and each time it grows more dangerous."

"I'm not following," Sam faltered.

Empire stepped toward Sam, his voice a whisper in his ear, "There's…*something*…that walks the world we're about to enter. It knows me. It's seen me. Every time I go to this place, I can sense it."

Sam felt his stomach twist, "What…what is it?"

Empire shook his head, "I have no idea. There's a lot about the Overroad that I don't understand. But it's useful and it's one of the main reasons I've been able to protect all twenty-six Towers over the past decade."

"How did you discover this place?" Sam asked quietly.

"The Gargoyles showed me. But they didn't tell me about the thing that hides behind its hills. Sam, I'm not fucking around here. We get in, we get through, we get out."

Sam nodded, "Yeah, ok. I'm with you."

Empire turned back to the open door, "Then let's get this over with."

He stepped inside and Sam was quick to follow. He heard the door slide shut behind them and silence engulfed the hidden space. He watched Empire closely, feeling uneasy about what he had just been told. Something about Empire's tone, the way his eyes had moved…he was afraid of this place they were about to enter.

And if *he* was afraid…

Sam steeled himself and waited.

Empire stood at the center of the room, the cobalt mists reaching up to him from the floor. He spread his arms and closed his eyes, letting the fog wrap itself around his body. After a moment, his fingertips glowed red and seemed to do battle with the blue.

Then the world disappeared.

Sam felt like he was suffocating, the air releasing from his lungs in a sudden rush of freezing pain. He clawed at his throat but was horrified to realize he didn't have one. His entire body was gone. In the darkness, he opened his mouth to scream, to call out, but he didn't have the ability to do so.

Blink.

Gasping, Sam staggered forward, feeling the sudden return of his body. A hand gripped his shoulder and he leaned over, eyes bulging, trying to retrieve his bearings.

"Quiet…quiet now, Sam," Empire's voice urged over his shoulder.

When he finally got himself under control, Sam righted himself and stood, his eyes rising to meet an expanse so alien he feared he would lose his hold on reality once more. Empire sensed his panic and his hand tightened on Sam's shoulder.

"W-where are we?" Sam whispered.

"The Overroad."

Sam slowly absorbed the eerie land before him, his heart racing. They were standing on some kind of road, a purple stretch of seamless design. It rolled out before them and disappeared over countless dark hills, rising and sinking across the strange landscape like ripples in an ebony ocean. Splintering off from the path were countless other routes, all twisting and contorting through the rising world.

The horizon was a sliver of cool purple, a deep shade that melted into night as Sam's eyes climbed the sky. Above them was a canopy of shivering stars, also purple, the tiny pinpricks seeming to buzz and vibrate silently in the canvas of black.

The earth was the color of tar, the ruffled hills like rising crests of dark ink. There were no trees, no rocks, not even dirt. It was like the blueprints of some unfinished world had been abandoned by a god who lost interest. Painting the perfect dark hills was a grid that laid itself over the earth in perfect symmetry. The lines were thin and colored a soft purple, overlaying the entire plane except for the roads.

As the jarring visuals settled around Sam's fraying mind, he realized something else.

The world was completely, utterly silent. There were no winds, no call of birds, no rustle of trees. Nothing. His own heartbeat sounded enormous in his ears, his breath like a hurricane across his lips.

Empire shifted behind him and his footsteps echoed loudly

up into the night, into that horrible sky filled with trembling purple stars. It was like they were standing in an empty, open warehouse with marble floors, completely devoid of anything but the intrusion of their own presence.

"Are you ok?" Empire asked, his voice echoing and reverberating around them.

Sam took a moment before nodding, "Yes. I think so." He shivered violently despite the complete lack of temperature.

Empire finally let his hand fall from Sam's shoulder, "Then let's go. I don't want to be here any longer than we have to."

Bewildered, Sam slowly followed Empire down the road, their boots clacking loudly against the purple path. His eyes roamed across the grid-painted hills, those strange, awful dark rises. He chanced a glance over his shoulder and almost stopped walking, his heart seizing up for the briefest of moments.

A doorway stood directly behind them, a shimmering frame filled with glowing blue light. Rising from the top corners of the door, hidden mostly behind it, was a towering Gargoyle, its long claws gripping the edges of the light. After the initial jolt of surprise, Sam realized that it was just a statue, its construction immediately apparent after the shock released him.

"Keep up, Sam," Empire edged, throwing a look back at him.

Shaking himself, Sam obeyed, trotting back to Empire's side. He stayed close, making sure his feet remained on the road.

"This is…" Sam started.

"I know," Empire cut in, his voice low but still retaining the echo, "try not to think about it. Let's just get to the doorway we need. It's not far."

The oppressive silence settled down around them, the fall of their boots like drums striking back against the insistent quiet. The road rose slightly to crest a hill and a smattering of snaking side trails slithered away from them, disappearing over the horizon.

"Where do those lead?" Sam asked, making sure to mute his voice.

Empire offered a tilt of the eyes, "I don't know."

"Do they lead to the other Towers?"

"No. I know the way to all twenty-six and these paths don't run to them."

"So then…"

"I don't know, Sam," Empire hissed.

They continued on, all too aware of the noise they were making. The sky overhead remained static except for the quivering stars, their purple light offering little illumination. The world had a strange hue to it, like a dusk that was never meant to be seen.

Sam let his eyes absorb it all. He felt small and intrusive, like this was a place he was never supposed to see. Behind his shocked awe, he realized that his skin was crawling. It was an unpleasant reminder of how little he knew.

His gaze was suddenly captured by something in the far distance, a pink glow that emanated faintly from the long horizon. He studied the color for a moment, the soft neon wash bleeding up into the purple twilight, like mixed paint.

He pointed to it, making sure to keep his voice down, "What is that? That pink?"

Empire shifted his eyes toward it. When he saw where Sam was pointing, he snorted and shook his head.

"That is something I never wanted."

"What do you mean? What's over there?"

Empire turned away from the pink horizon, "A gift from the

Gargoyles. Something they created for me when this is all over, if I wanted."

The pink enraptured Sam and filled his curiosity, "But you don't want it?"

"No, Sam. When this is over, I want it to be over. For all of us. Just like it should be."

After some time, Sam spoke again, barely a whisper, "Can I ask you something?"

Empire didn't slow, didn't divert his eyes from the road, "What is it?"

Sam walked even closer to Empire, "This might be a stupid question, but it's something I've been thinking about ever since I came out of that room.

"Just ask, Sam."

Sam licked his lips, his eyes darting around the still landscape, "I understand the importance of the Towers and what they were sent here to do. I understand the need to create Red Eyes to charge them. But if the Gargoyles found Earth, then why do they need help finding it again?"

Empire's brow furrowed, almost surprised by the question, "Because it's not the Gargoyles that need to find Earth this time."

"What do you mean?"

Empire shook his head, "You saw their homeworld, right? You saw what came out of it, what cracked its surface and emerged from inside? You saw what is crawling towards us at this very moment?"

"I...I did."

Empire nodded, "*That* is the thing we are guiding here. It knows the direction the Towers were sent. But just because you know the geography of the sea, we still have lighthouses, right?

Just because you're looking for someone in a forest doesn't mean you'll find them. You know they are there, inside, somewhere, but wouldn't it be easier if someone shot out a signal flare?"

"I see," Sam said quietly, his mind catching up, "that makes sense. But...that thing...what is it? Where did it come from?"

"I don't know," Empire said in a hushed voice, "All I know is that it has been with the Gargoyles since the beginning. It's like their ship, their engine. Once a planet has been drained of ash, the Towers go out again in search of a new food supply." Empire turned to Sam, his tone turning sharp, "But not just any planet will do. It needs to be lived in. The soil needs to have been...contaminated by life. Once they find a suitable port – planet – then they go. And when they arrive they use the life-forms on that world to charge the Towers and restart the cycle all over again."

"That's...incredible," Sam breathed, feeling awe seep through him. He felt this new knowledge dig into his mind, behind his eyes, and cement his belief that humanity was truly, completely, useless. Who were they to stand against such a perfect, eternal machine? Why should they be allowed to continue their meager, petty, horrible existence when such elevated forms of life needed their extinction to continue their own journey?

The road dipped and they descended down a slope, the purple path taking them to the left across another series of rippling, gridded earth. As they traversed further into the strange world, Sam began to see beacons of blue light in the distance, seemingly at random. He squinted, trying to make out what they were.

"Doorways," Empire informed him quietly, "to the other Towers."

"Just how big is this place?" Sam asked, counting at least eight visible squares of light.

"I hope I never have to find out."

"Have you ever gone beyond the paths? Seen what else is out there?"

"That would be a very bad idea."

"Why?"

"Because-" Empire paused and stopped walking completely.

"What's wrong?" Sam whispered.

Empire pressed a finger to his lips and crouched low, "Shhh. Listen."

Sam squat down next to him, his pulse rising. He waited.

"I don't hear anything," he muttered, almost silently.

"Listen."

And then he *did* hear something. It was so far off that he almost missed it.

It sounded like static overlaying a deep rumbling voice that was speaking nonsense, almost like a garbled transmission in a different language. It echoed gently across this hills and reached for the sky before swooping softly down into their ears.

"What…is that?" Sam asked after a moment.

Empire's face had gone pale, "It's found me again…" He didn't move, he barely seemed to breathe. He remained low to the road, head cocked to the side, listening to the bizarre sound whisper through the silence.

"Go," he finally urged, "we need to go, *now*."

Sam followed him up and together they continued down the road, their pace quickened. He became painfully aware of how loud their footsteps were, especially now. He made an effort to walk softer, but it seemed useless.

They crossed the next series of hills before the sound grew louder, the buzzing static and muffled, deep voice growing closer. As it did so, Empire became increasingly nervous, his eyes darting across the dark hills, his fingers twitching at his sides as they hurried along.

Suddenly, Empire dropped to the ground, pulling Sam with him. Grunting, Sam came down on his stomach, his shoulder bumping into Empire's. The eerie sound of the transmission has stopped.

"What-" Sam started but Empire slammed a hand over his mouth, his palm sweaty and trembling.

"Be quiet," He whispered, his voice shaking. "Be very, very quiet…"

When he saw that Sam understood, he slowly removed his hand, and pointed ahead of them toward the summit of a small hill a hundred yards ahead.

"Do you see it?" He hissed, his chin scraping the surface of the road.

Sam shifted on his stomach and looked ahead of them, feeling the silence press his body closer to the ground.

He didn't see anything.

"It's looking right at us," Empire trembled, "*Do-not-move.*"

Sam felt fear tighten around his throat like a vice. His eyes swept east to west, tearing apart the landscape, desperately willing himself to see whatever Empire had spotted. But no matter how urgently he searched, he didn't see anything.

He shifted his eyes over to Empire and saw he was shaking with terror, his skin pasty white. He had his face pressed to the road, his forehead kissing the purple surface.

The static voice came again, rising from the silence without warning. Sam slammed his eyes shut and grit his teeth against it, the buzzing, mumbled voice cutting through the thick screeches and chirps of the transmission, rumbling in a language he didn't understand. It seemed to be coming from ahead of them, a dozen feet from where they lie.

Empire curled his hands into fists, and stared down at the blank road, refusing to look up at the source. His breath came in short bursts and sweat stood out on the back of his neck. Sam felt himself infected with the same terror, his heart thundering, his pulse a drumming roar in his ears. He chanced a look up but still couldn't make out what the cause of the sound was. Ice tickled his spine and he realized he was hyperventilating, every alarm in his mind blaring with furious fear.

A split second later, Empire disappeared.

It took Sam a moment for his mind to catch up with what his eyes had just seen. He blinked, panicking, and stared at the empty space that lay vacant before him. There had been no warning, no sound, no indication...Empire had simply vanished.

"What...?" Sam cried uselessly. He got to his knees and realized that the sound of the white noise was gone as well. The world shook with utter isolation, coming at him from every angle.

"No, no, no, *no*," he croaked, getting to his feet, continuing to stare down at the place Empire had been mere seconds ago. He spun in place, his brow furrowed into a fearful expression of absolute terror. He turned helplessly, his eyes uprooting every hilltop, every rise, a prayer flowing silently from his trembling lips.

"Please, no, oh my god what the *fuck* is happening?" He

sobbed, feeling lost and incredibly exposed. But no matter where he looked, Empire was nowhere to be seen. He was simply...gone.

Terror rippled through him and rooted him in place. And it only grew as he realized that he was totally and completely alone now.

"Fuck," he choked, coughed, and spat. He took a tentative step forward, continuing to search the road for something, anything, please god *anything.*

The Overroad offered nothing but the deafening silence.

Not knowing what else to do, he took a couple hesitant steps forward, willing himself to move. He looked down the long road, across the altering, splintering paths, his heart and mind screaming to move, go, get the fuck out of here.

He risked another few steps and then another. He chest felt like it was seizing and his breath blew raw across his lips. He had to continue on. He had to keep walking. He had to get anywhere that wasn't in this horrible, terrifying world.

He picked up speed, forming a plan as he did so. Whichever door was closest, he would take. He didn't care where it took him, which Tower he emerged from, he just had to escape this place.

Sam began to run. The stars overhead shimmered indifferently down at him, the black hills and strange grid offered no answer, no direction, no clue. The distant doors he had spotted earlier seemed impossibly far away now and he prayed there was one closer just over the next hill...or the next...or the next...

Suddenly, without any prelude of warning, Empire appeared directly in front of him. It was as if he had just blinked back into existence, popping silently from the nothing before Sam.

He staggered forward, his hair mangled with sweat, his eyes bloodshot and wild. He was bleeding profusely from the nose and fear radiated off him so thick Sam could almost taste it.

He looked up, still in motion, his eyes meeting Sams.

His voice was a bellowing roar that rumbled from his throat with terrifying urgency.

"RUN!"

Ignited, Sam felt both overwhelmingly relieved and monstrously fearful. It only took a second for his legs to follow Empire's desperate command as the two of them tore down the road like hell was on their heels. Questions sparked through his mind, but he kept them locked behind his chattering teeth as he followed Empire in a flat out sprint.

Empire, his eyes wide and brimming with fear, threw a look over his shoulder, past Sam, at something behind them.

"We're almost there, come on!" Empire yelled, the blood from his nose leaking into his mouth and spraying across his lips.

They ran to the crest of another hill and the road jerked sharply to the left and then descended. Ahead of them, Sam could see a blue square of light backed by a towering Gargoyle statue.

They were almost there.

Again, he felt relief sweep through him, a hopeful, trembling surge that fueled his footsteps and pressed him to run faster.

And then the static returned, a maddening, horrible screech overlayed with that insane babble, the voice like thunder that muttered and echoed nonsense across the world.

"No, no, please, NO!" Empire screamed suddenly, looking over his shoulder, his eyes impossibly huge and radiating a fear so real Sam thought it would destroy him.

Mid-stride, Empire disappeared once again.

Sam skid to a halt, fresh terror erupting from his throat in a howling cry, *"FUCK!"*

His voice crashed into the silence, the static gone once more. He stood panting, sweating trickling down his spine.

He cupped his hands to his mouth, shaking, horrified, and alone, "Where are you!? WHERE ARE YOU!?"

Sam looked down the road, toward their destination, toward the door. It was only a couple hundred feet away now, standing, glowing just across a series of hills. Indecision crashed across his mind in waves. It was right there. Escape was right there. But he couldn't leave without Empire. Every sense burned with the desire to, but he simply couldn't. He wouldn't. But what if this time he didn't return? What if he stood here, waiting for him and then that…thing…came back? What if it took him next? And where would it take him? Where had it taken Empire?

"Goddamn it," he sobbed, "oh fuck, what am I supposed to do?"

Again, the horribly still world offered no answer.

The road remained empty, the sky silent, and the hills darker than ever. He looked down at the doorway again, at the statue looming behind it. The Gargoyles. They needed Empire. They needed his help and the power they had given him.

"Help us," Sam begged uselessly, locking eyes with the statue. "Please…someone…"

Suddenly Empire appeared again, staggering and falling across the road in front of Sam.

He clutched his eyes and he was *screaming*. His voice cracked the sky with a pain and terror that dug into Sam's skull like a drill.

"It took my eyes!" He screeched, "IT TOOK MY FUCKING *EYES!*"

Sam raced to his side, head thundering, and pulled Empire to his feet, hands shaking, throat closing. When he looked into Empire's face, he felt his body go cold and repulsion ripped through him with the ferocity of a bullet train.

The sockets that once held Empire's eyes were empty. There were no traces of blood or violence, no whisper of gore or trickle of carnage. Instead, Empire's eye sockets were empty craters, two dark holes that sunk far too deeply into his head.

"Help me!" Empire begged, hands outstretched, grasping for Sam, "God, please HELP ME SAM!"

Horrified, shaking uncontrollably, Sam fought against the repulsion that rocketed through him, the sight of Empire in such a terrible state twisting his stomach with churning unease.

"*SAM!*"

"I'm here," Sam assured, reaching out and grabbing Empire by the arms, "I got you."

Empire's voice shook beneath rising madness, "I can't see, Sam, I can't fucking *see!*"

Sam felt a sob crawl up his throat, pushed across his tongue by insanity, "I know, it's ok, come on, we're almost out! Hold onto me! I'm getting us out of here!"

Stumbling, crying, the two of them staggered forward down the road, pressed forward by a hammer of panic and dread. Behind them, the static returned, the mumbled voice calling to them through the cracking transmission.

"We're almost there!" Sam screamed, dragging Empire down the road, his feet tripping and stumbling blindly along.

"Don't let it get me again, please, don't let it get me!" Empire begged, his breath ragged.

"The door is just ahead!" Sam urged, his hands fumbling to retain their grip on Empire's arms.

Together, fighting against the roar of white noise at their back, they sprinted the final distance to the door. The blue frame glowed brightly before them, its shimmering surface backed by the rising statue.

The static at their back screeched, sensing its prey's escape.

Sam took one last look back into the empty world, and then pulled himself and Empire through the light.

Again, he was overwhelmed with the sensation of absolute nothingness. It wasn't as jarring this time, but he still felt panic as he lost feeling throughout his entire body. He lost his grip on Empire, but could still hear his labored breathing somewhere from the claustrophobic darkness.

The limbo passed in a matter of seconds and Sam found himself crashing to a hard floor, a gasp escaping his lips. Cool air swirled across his face and he scrambled to get his bearings, fighting back against a sudden rush of vertigo.

"Sam?!" Empire croaked, his voice raw and full of fear. "Sam, where are you?!"

Sam blinked and shook the dazed feeling from his mind. He scrambled up from his hands and knees and saw they were in the inner room of Tower 15, the soft blue fog drifting lazily up from the floor.

"I'm right here," Sam called, reaching down for Empire. "Here, take my hand."

Shaking, Empire grasped it and Sam helped him up. The fog drifted up his body and filled his empty sockets before dancing away, leaving them as barren as before.

Empire jerked his head left and right, searching with eyes he no longer had. Sam could see the disbelief, the reality of his situation twist the corners of his mouth down into a pitiful quiver.

Sam took his hands in his, his voice soft, "I got you. We made it through. We're back."

"I can't see," Empire cried, "Jesus Christ, Sam, I can't see anything."

Sam just stared at him, searching for words of comfort, but he came up blank. He squeezed Empire's hands and waited for an order, a plan, something to make sense of what had just happened.

Empire pulled his hands away from Sam's and brought them to his face, his fingers exploring the dark craters that once housed his eyes. On contact, he inhaled sharply and dropped his hands back to his sides, almost repulsed by what he had felt.

"No," He whispered, his voice low and weak, "No, no, no this can't happen...not now when things are so close to the end..."

Sam put a hand on his shoulder, feeling useless, "It's ok. I'm here. I'm not going anywhere. It's going to be ok."

Empire spun toward him, his voice suddenly rising into a snarl, "Ok? Do I look fucking ok!?"

Sam dropped his eyes to the ground and stared at the blue fog, "I'm sorry."

After a moment, Empire deflated, his shoulders drooping, "I can't let them see me like this. Not the Gargoyles, not the Red Eyes...I couldn't bear it."

"I can help with that," Sam offered, "hold on." He pulled at his shirt and ripped a length of fabric from the bottom. He stepped forward and wrapped it around Empire's head, covering his empty eyes.

When he was finished, he stepped back, "Is that ok?"

Empire, blindfolded, nodded slowly, "Yes…yes, this is good. Thank you, Sam."

"Of course."

Empire seemed to settle slightly, his voice finding balance once more, "Where…where are we? Are we in the inner chamber of the Tower?"

Sam observed the blue light and circular walls, "Yeah. This should be Tower 15, just like you said. Unless something changed."

Empire nodded, the frayed knot of cloth falling down the back of his neck, "Good. Then we stick to the plan. Memphis is only a couple miles south. We go there."

"What about the Tower?" Sam asked.

"What about it?"

"Didn't you want to check up on it first? Make sure the Red Eyes are preparing and filling their pods?"

Empire waved a hand at the empty space, "They Towers have sounded, they've heard the call to return. If they can make it back to the domes, the Gargoyles can take control of them if need be. I'm going to have to trust everything is going as planned, for the time being. This…" he motioned to his covered eyes, "incident…is going to fuck things up. Besides, if anyone's going to try to stop the Towers from activating, it'll come from Memphis. Which is where we're headed. If an attack comes from one of the other groups, we're just going to have to cross our fingers. I'm not going back in there, Sam. Never again. I didn't wait ten years for this only to get killed days before it happens. That was the last time I travel the Overroad. I *will* be there when the end comes for us."

Sam nodded confidently, "We'll get there. Both of us, with Alex at our side. Just like when we were kids."

The corners of Empire's mouth twisted slightly, "Yes…just like when we were kids…"

"Let's go get him."

Empire placed a hand on Sam's arm, stopping him, "Hold on. There's one more thing."

"What is it?"

Empire cocked his head, "I'm going to need your eyes, Sam."

Sam stood motionless for a moment, and then understanding swept through him, "Of course…"

Empire's mouth formed a thin line and his hands opened out before him. A red aura briefly flared around his body and then Sam gasped.

"That's better," Empire said slowly, deliberately.

Sam's eyes radiated neon crimson, thick trails of heavily colored smoke rolled from his face. He could feel something dark in the back of his mind, like something was hiding in the shadows of his thoughts. His vision blurred and he fought to regain focus.

After a moment, everything righted.

Sam raised his hands to his temples, "Are you…here?"

Empire's voice came back cold and low, "Let's go see what my dear brother is up to, shall we?"

Using Sam's vision, he positioned himself before the wall and traced his hands across its surface. A door slid open and together he stepped out into the pod chamber with Sam.

Sam felt awe fill him as he craned his neck back to take in the view. The interior walls of the Tower were filled with Red Eyes, hundreds of them. Red light glowed and lit the dark space, extending up to the summit, each of the strange coffins filled with a body.

"I've waited a long time to see this," Empire said, taking it all in from behind Sam's eyes.

"I...want to join them," Sam said quietly, feeling a need rise up in his chest, a desire to offer himself up in this monumental movement.

Empire placed a hand on Sam's arm, "I know and I'm sorry you can't right now. I understand the pull you must feel, but what you're doing for me is more important right now."

Sam nodded, "You don't have to explain yourself to me. I'm with you."

Empire shifted, his fingers absently rising to the cloth around his eyes, "Could you do me a favor? Come stand behind me, over my shoulder. This change in perspective is a little disorienting, especially when we're moving."

Sam obediently went and took his place behind Empire, "Like this?"

"Much better. I won't take further control of you, I just need to see what you see."

"Should we go outside?"

Empire grunted and led them to the outer door. The pod chamber was completely empty except for the Red Eyes that filled the coffins. Their footsteps echoed across the floor and Sam shivered. He could do without that sound. The echoes.

Guiding his hands once more, Empire activated the door and daylight spilled across their faces. Empire raised his hands to shield his eyes and then snorted, realizing what he had done.

Sam shaded his eyes for the both of them.

They stepped out of Tower 15 and found themselves standing atop a hill, the rolling earth rippling out below them in a series of dips and rises. Trees littered the land, crooked dead things that bent and twisted awkwardly like mangled bones.

The sky was growing dark in the west, a wall of heavy gray cloud moving toward them across a labored wind.

The dome bubble fell from the summit of the Tower and spilled out across the world, its reach dipping miles in every direction. Sam and Empire turned their eyes to sweep across the space and Sam found himself mildly surprised at the absence of Red Eyes. He so used to seeing hundreds, if not thousands, of them milling about the base of each Tower. But they were nowhere to be found. Empty earth greeted them silently save for the wind.

"Looks like it's just us," Sam said. The air seemed to pulse with energy around the Tower, a pregnant stirring that begged to be released.

"Which way?" He asked after a moment.

Empire pointed south, past a grove of broken trees, "That way. Just over a dozen or so miles. We should be there by nightfall."

Sam glanced at the approaching storm, "We're going to get caught in that."

Empire began to walk, his voice a growl, "Good."

Sam hurried to catch up, taking his place just behind the blinded man. As they walked, he found himself thinking about what it would be like to see Alex again; what he would say in order to tame his rage. That was something he could count on. However they found him, Alex was going to be a handful. Especially now, after Sam's transformation. How the hell was he going to convince Alex to join them? To stand with them when the world ended and die knowing they were doing the right thing? He mused this over as the dry grass crunched beneath his boots. Luna…maybe he could use Luna. That was, if she was still with him. Sam grunted to himself. Of course she was. She had had eyes for Alex ever since she had joined them.

I was a detour, a mistake, he thought bitterly, *then she abandoned me for the real prize: the emotionally crippled wrecking ball.*

"Stay close, Sam," Empire muttered from ahead. Sam shook himself from his thoughts and quickened his stride, muttering an apology.

"You're thinking about Alex, aren't you?" Empire asked, taking them down a set of small hills and between a cluster of trees.

"I am," Sam admitted, "I'm wondering what I can say to him. It's not going to be easy."

"Of course it's not," Empire sniffed, "that's why I enlisted you."

"What makes you think he'll listen to anything I have to say?" Sam asked, "As soon as he sees my eyes, he's going to go for my throat."

"No he won't."

"What makes you think that?"

Empire's voice grew soft and filled with something that almost resembled sorrow, "Because when he finally left, when he escaped the hell we grew up in…you were the one he went with. Not me. You, Sam."

Sam closed his mouth, taken back. He didn't know what to say. He stared at the back of Empire's head, at the cloth around his eyes, and suddenly found himself feeling extremely guilty.

"It wasn't your fault," Empire said quietly, as if sensing the discomfort. "In a way, I understand why he didn't want to be around me after we got out." His shoulders tensed, "But that doesn't excuse it."

Sam licked his lips nervously, "Can I ask you something?"

"We got time."

Sam took a steadying breath and then asked, "Why do you need him so badly? You're the most powerful man alive. You've single-handedly prepared this world for its end. We're standing at the very extinction of mankind, preparing ourselves for something incredible. You've done something no one else could do. You were given this gift, this power, alone. Why is it so important that Alex be there when we all die?"

Empire slowed, his pace staggering until finally, he stopped altogether. He lowered his head and his body seemed to drain of all its strength. He let out a long, tired breath and it was the most exhausted exclamation Sam had ever heard.

"Just one, Sam…" Empire said quietly. He paused and when he spoke again his voice softened, revealing a humanity that had been hidden for years, "Because I want just *one* person who actually cares about me to be there when I die. Not because their hand was forced, not because they have a gun to their head, but because they want to be." His voice dropped to barely a whisper, "Before all this, before The Impact, before people started calling me Empire…Alex was the only person in this whole fucking world who ever gave a shit about me."

Sam felt his chest sink.

Empire raised his head, "I know you were there too, Sam, but hell, we were kids, you didn't know what my parents were doing to me and Alex. And I know you didn't want to. But it was hard to miss the bruises, the swollen lips, the months where I was so skinny you could count my fuckin' ribs…"

"I'm sorry," Sam said softly, "I…I didn't know what to do…"

"It's not your fault," Empire muttered, "What the hell could you have done anyway…"

"I tried asking Alex about it once…"

Empire shrugged, "He didn't want anyone to know. He was embarrassed. I get it. I was too. Why were we the only ones showing up to school looking like we had just gone twelve fucking rounds?"

"I should have done something…said something," Sam offered weakly.

Empire shook his head, "Wouldn't have done any good. Alex tried that a couple times. Just earned him more pain. Earned us *both* more pain." He grit his teeth suddenly, "God, he couldn't take that. Alex, I mean. Watching me get beat on. He was just a kid, but he'd lose his fucking mind. Scream, yell, taunt my parents, try to get them to stop what they were doing to me. It usually worked. Then we'd get locked away for a couple days and I'd be the one crying. Not because of how badly I hurt, not because my face was all puffed up, but because I couldn't *stand* laying there in the dark listening to Alex try to just fucking *breathe*. Christ, I thought he was dead a couple times…*fuck*…"

Sam shifted miserably where he stood, his mouth pulled down into a frown, his brow furrowed.

Empire shook himself of the memory, "Doesn't matter. He made sure we both got out alive. And when we did, I thought we'd stick together for the rest of our lives, two fucked up kids just trying to make the most of things. But he left. He left me. I'll never forget that day and how much that hurt, watching him go. It was worse than any beating I took. I remember feeling so…so…" his voice slowed to a whisper, "So fucking *alone*…"

The wind took his words and silence grew around them. In the distance, thunder began to rumble, a prelude to the coming storm. Sam let the heavenly growls fill his mind over the next couple miles, the Tower shrinking at their backs.

He didn't know what else he could say to Empire and so he let the conversation die. He sensed that Empire didn't want to continue anyway, his pace increasing, his back now turned, so Sam let him be, a sorrow in his chest.

His mind roamed as his feet trod heavily over the dry earth. The end really *was* coming. For everyone. Every remaining man, woman and child that hadn't been converted inside the Towers. He wondered if they knew, if they could feel the approaching doom.

Did they know what was coming? What was crawling through the cosmos at this very moment? He brushed the thought aside. It didn't matter. He had seen what the Gargoyles did to the planets they feasted on. No one could stop it. No one could end the cycle. But would they try? Would the remaining outposts of hope try to fight back one last time?

They'll all be burned away, Sam thought absently, *let them try to resist. It won't make a difference. They were spared during The Impact out of sheer luck. When the Gargoyles arrive, the rest of them will be turned to ash. The only difference is they've had ten years to think about it.*

The thought encouraged him, if only a little. He looked at Empire in front of him, took in his staggered walk, the cloth around his eyes, the way the tendons stood out on his neck. He could practically smell his will to go on, to push forward all the way until the end.

Isn't that what he's always done? Pushed through the shit until he came out the other side? Sam thought.

Except this time there is no other side.

"Hey..." Sam said quietly, catching Empire's attention, "I'm glad I'm here. You know that, right?"

Empire said nothing, but his body relaxed slightly. Sam suddenly felt himself deeply impressed with the man before him. He respected him, but it was different now, knowing Empire had confided in him, chosen him, seeing and hearing just how much he had gone through to be here...

"Something's happening," Empire said suddenly, stopping, snapping Sam from his thoughts. The wind blustered through the trees around them, taking some of the heat with it. Sam paused and attuned his senses. Empire was right...something was happening, he could feel it tingling through the air, like some unseen energy.

And then, without warning, a blast echoed at their backs so loud that Sam slammed his hands over his ears, his skull rattling. He spun, wincing, and looked back toward Tower 15, now nothing more than a black column against the horizon.

Roaring from its summit, up into the sky, was a pillar of fiery red so bright that Sam had to turn away. It seared the heavens and split through the gathering clouds, rising to heights lost beyond the limits of the eye. The vermillion glow pulsed once, twice, and then a low horn shook the world. Sam grit his teeth against it, pressing his hands even tighter over his ears. The blast seemed to compress his head and he felt dizzy, the light and sound working in unison in a display of power that rattled his bones.

After a couple seconds, the horn subsided, fading into echoes.

But the pillar of light remained, a burning torch reaching hungrily for the unseen stars.

Empire walked to Sam's side, his voice soft, "The Towers have been activated. It sees us now."

It was then that Sam realized that he was grinning.

Chapter 11

Alex awoke in total darkness. The first thing he became aware of was the thundering pain in the back of his head. It burned and pulsed with every heartbeat, an insistent reminder of where Miranda had knocked him unconscious. He groaned and realized he was lying on the floor.

A *hard* floor. He crawled to his knees, the total black threatening to throw him into a panic. Where was he? What had happened?

The recent memories trickled back into his exhausted mind and he wished they hadn't. The Raffle. The boys. The dogs...Luna...oh Christ, *Luna*...

His chest shuddered as he exhaled, the scene of her brutal death crashing through him with all the violence in the world. He clenched his fists and squeezed his eyes shut. She was gone. She was gone and he was alone now. Alone in the darkness.

"Fuck," he cried, the exclamation rattling from his chest, "Oh, fuck I'm so sorry Luna..." a heaviness descended atop his mind and sank into his stomach, a thick dread and sorrow that ate away at him as the memories progressed. He curled his hands into fists and squeezed his eyes shut, fighting against the rising tide. He could feel the agony, just under his tongue, begging to be released.

He swallowed it down, a bitter gulp of air accompanying it. He couldn't cry. Not yet. There would be time for that later.

"You don't know that," Alex realized miserably. He rose from his knees and stood shakily, hands outstretched. He took a moment to center himself and then searched for the walls, fingers grasping blindly in the darkness. Two steps forward and he found one. Cold concrete. He began to walk, dragging his fingers across the surface as he did so. He traced the entirety of his cell and wasn't surprised to find just how small it was.

Two steps to the right, two to the left, and four front to back. He found a door, but it was locked and felt like it was made from pure iron. He pounded on it, tested it, and found it unmoving.

"Shit," he whispered, the word sounding way too close to his lips.

An unexpected claustrophobia suddenly slithered through Alex's mind, a nasty, panicked feeling that curled around his entire body. He wrapped his arms around himself, feeling his heart begin to race. He had to get himself under control, he knew he had to, but it was almost impossible. His pulse quickened and sweat broke out across his forehead. He spun in place, aimlessly tracing the walls of his cell again. He could feel his throat tightening, his mouth going dry. This was too close…everything was too close…everything was pressing in on him, snaring him, compressing him…Christ, it was hard to breathe…why couldn't he breathe?!

"Pull yourself together, Alex," he begged, scraping his teeth across his bottom lip. He hated tight spaces. The darkness, the walls, the locked door…it was all too familiar.

He fought against his shuddering chest, memories snarling out at him from the hidden shadows of his mind. Too tight. Everything was too tight…he would be in here forever…he would die in here…

…it was all so familiar.

The closet. Yes…that was the monster snarling at him from the corners of his thoughts. The closet. How many days had he spent in that closet with Will?

"Stop," Alex cried, head pounding, "don't go there…"

Days? Weeks? How much of his childhood had he spent locked away in that horrible place? How many times did he think he would die in there?

"Shut up, don't do this…" Alex pleaded with himself. But the darkness was relentless.

It had been smaller than this cell. He hadn't even been able to lay down without curling his legs against himself. And that's how he had spent so much of his time in that terrible place…curled up, exhausted, bleeding, just trying to focus on taking his next breath. He remembered how Will had clung to him, his head pressed lovingly to Alex's chest, crying…always crying…begging him to stay alive…

Don't leave me alone in here…

"Goddamn it," Alex cracked, slumping to the floor, "Please…"

He could almost feel his brother's hands wrapped around his neck, his tears dampening his shirt, his labored sobs, the aftermath of the beating they had received. God how they had suffered together in that closet…whimpering…starving…praying someone would come and save them.

But no one had.

Hell holds no sympathy for the young, something that was

revealed to Alex in all its nightmarish might during those longs days of imprisonment. Each time they were allowed back out, Alex remembered swearing he would never let himself or his brother to be locked up again. He would run away, call the police, something…anything…

But he always ended up back in the closet with Will sobbing around his neck.

In the darkness of his own confinement, he had often wondered how anyone could do that to their own children. How anyone could fester such authoritative cruelty. His thoughts drifted miserably from the dregs of his childhood to when he had finally escaped. When he had gotten out, taking Will with him. Christ, how they had fled.

He had never met his unborn child. His wife had been six months pregnant when the Red Eyes took them away. But even if he had been allowed the honor of fatherhood, he knew he would have been a good dad.

If nothing more than to prove they existed.

The unexpected thoughts of his wife and child took him by surprise, filling his mind and pushing away some of the rising despair. With a horrible realization, he found that he couldn't remember the last time he had thought about them.

Guilt flooded through him, a sickening wave that brought bile to the back of his throat. They had been the whole reason he had started this insane march, this search for Empire…for Will…

…the one who had ordered them taken away.

How could he do that to me? Alex's mind cried, *After everything we went through…how could he hurt me like that…?* He lay there in the dark, miserable, and let the memories pour through him.

Time bled away from him. But not without pain. He felt every passing second as if it were nailed into his skull. With nothing to fill the time but his own thoughts, he found himself at the bottom of despair, a helpless, merciless monster that circled the interior of his cell. Before long, the isolation started finding new ways to approach him. It discovered fresh horrors to torment him with. What if Percy's group left him in here forever? What if they let him starve to death? What hell awaited him? What exactly was the point of his imprisonment? Why not just kill him? With no answers to offer, Alex slumped into a corner of his confinement and waited, his knees drawn up to his chest, his arms wrapped tightly around them.

He didn't know how long he sat there before he heard the door open, a sudden intrusion of noise that startled him out of his miserable state of mind. He squinted against the light, raising a hand against it. A massive silhouette filled the doorway and Percy's booming voice called out to him.

"Alex, Alex, Alex…oh boy, what a mess this is, huh?"

Alex stood quickly, his eyes adjusting, Percy's features coming into focus. The big man looked grim, his bearded face pulled down into a scowl. He carried a pistol loosely in his left hand.

Percy flashed it, making sure Alex could see it, "That's right, I'm armed…no need for any stupid acts of rage. Wouldn't end well for you, I'm afraid."

"You son of a bitch," Alex snarled, his back to the wall opposite the big man.

Percy sighed but stayed where he was, "I know you're probably upset. Hell, I'd be too. Brutal thing, wasn't it? What happened to your woman?"

Alex clenched his teeth, his blood pressure rising, "How the fuck could you do that to her after we saved your ass? She was a good person, you *fuck*."

Percy leaned his large frame against the door, his voice calm, "She tried to attack us. That's not something a good person would do. She was a sympathizer – something I loathe more than the Red Eyes themselves."

"You were going to kill her children!" Alex yelled.

Percy shook his head, "No, I was killin' Red Eyes. Those weren't her kids no more. Don't you get it? The world is falling down around us and there's only two sides left. Us and them."

Alex stepped forward, his teeth grating together, "No Percy, now there's just me and you."

Percy tapped the pistol loudly against the door, stopping Alex in his tracks, "Keep your head on, boy. Remember what I said about being stupid? Just simmer down and listen to me for a second."

Alex glared at him, blood boiling, but stayed put.

Percy nodded his approval, "Good. Glad to see you're not a complete idiot. Now listen and listen close cause what I'm about to say is important." He lifted himself away from the door, his voice grave, "The Towers have activated. I seen it myself from the roof of this buildin'. There's a big ol' pillar of light coming outta Tower 15. I reckin' the rest of the Towers look about the same. I don't know what it means, but the Gargoyles are gearing up for something big."

He paused and made sure Alex was listening. Satisfied, he continued, "I made contact with the other group up in Vermont and they are hauling ass our way right as we speak. We're going to give it one last shot, both groups, to try to take down a Tower. It's what we been preparing for and I see no better time than now. I have no idea how much longer we got, but if we're going to go out, I'd rather do it knowing we gave those Red Eye bastards one hell of a punch on the way down. Unfortunately, the group in Colorado can't join us. They don't have the gas, it seems."

Percy crossed his arms, placing his finger against the trigger guard of his pistol, "Which brings us to you."

Alex hadn't moved, Percy's shadow falling across his eyes, "What about me?"

"I'd like you to come along."

Alex barked a laugh, a bitter exclamation, "You want me to *help* you?"

Percy nodded matter-of-factly, "Yes I do. Put aside your emotions for a summer second and think about what we're actually doing here, the difference we can make."

Alex's lips curled back over his teeth, "Oh trust me, Percy, all I've been doing in here is thinking about what you've done. And if you think I'll help you, you're crazier than I thought."

"Is that a no?"

"That's a go fuck yourself."

Percy closed his eyes and exhaled, "Son…there are no more grays."

"What the dumb Christ does that mean?"

Percy's eyes snapped open once more, "Means it's black and white now. It means we don't have time to stand here and compare cocks. The end of the world has arrived and I want everyone who can hold a gun standing with me when we attack Tower 15. What happened to your lady was tragic, but she chose her color and it wasn't ours. You need to see that and get past it."

Alex lowered his voice to a snarl, "She just wanted to save her kids. She wasn't a bad person. She held no love for the Red

Eyes. Neither do I. I fuckin' hate them. But Luna? Luna I cared about and you took her away from me all because she loved her kids." Alex balled his hands into fists, "And Percy? I'm done having shit I care about taken away. So just kill me if you have to because I will never stand with you as an ally."

Percy's face became unreadable, his voice low and calm, "Do you...want to die, Alex?"

Alex blinked, momentarily taken back, "What? Do I want to die? What kind of question is that? Of course I don't want to die. But the thought of helping you, even to kill Red Eyes, makes me sick to my fucking stomach."

Percy nodded slowly, almost sadly, "You sure?"

Alex braced himself and met Percy's gaze.

Percy sighed, "Fine then. If you're not with us, then you're against us." He leaned back and called down the hall, his voice loud and commanding, "Miranda! Bring it here!" He turned back to Percy, his eyes cold, "Last chance."

"Rot in hell, Percy," Alex growled, his nerves tingling.

Miranda appeared behind Percy. She carried a large box in her hands. She looked over Percy's shoulder at Alex, her eyes meeting his, "He won't help us?"

Percy took the box from her, "Nope."

"Idiot," she muttered. She continued to stare at Alex, "She isn't worth it, you know. There are still plenty of women who would spread their legs for you."

Alex felt a rage stir deep within his chest, his vision sparking, "I would rather bury my cleaver between your legs, you *cunt*."

"Leave us," Percy ordered, shifting the box in his arms.

Miranda took one last look at Alex, her face almost sympathetic, and then disappeared back down the hallway.

Percy stooped and placed the box down on the ground,

grunting as he did so. He placed his boot on it and scooted it forward, deeper into the cell.

"What the hell is that?" Alex spat, feeling unease curl around his throat.

Percy tapped the box with the toe of his boot, "What, this? In here?" His eyes twinkled, a smile curling his lips, "This is a big-ass possum. The sonovabitch hasn't eaten in a couple days and I'm fairly certain it's got rabies. We've trapped a couple of these bastards for eatin'. Obviously, if this one is sick then we can't cook it up. So instead of putting it down, I decided to dump it in here with you. Makes sense, don't it? You're both useless to me."

Alex eyed the box and felt his pulse rise, his teeth locking behind his lips. He could hear something scratching against the cardboard, a muffled, frantic noise.

"She's pretty hungry," Percy grinned, witnessing Alex's growing unease, "And let me tell you…she's a *big* un'. Easily twenty pounds. It'd take a lot of meat to fill her up, wouldn't you say?"

Alex said nothing, his heart hammering in his chest. The box scuttled forward an inch before Percy stopped it with his boot.

"Seems like she's eager to meet you," Percy chuckled. "You better watch out. One bite from her and it's going to make dying that much worse." His voice dropped, "And make no mistake, Alex, you're dying in this room. When I close this door, it ain't ever opening again. Sure, you might kill this ol' girl here, but after a day or two…? Oh man, son…you're going to start getting hungry." He tapped the box with the toe of his boot, "Consider this your last meal."

Alex couldn't take his eyes from the box, his stomach twisting, "Die in hell, Percy. I don't know how, but I'm going to find a way out of this room and I'm going to kill you."

Percy snorted, "As your last words, I honestly expected something better than that."

"Fuck yourself."

Percy grinned, "Goodbye, Alex. Have fun." And without another word, he stooped and opened the box. In one swift motion, he stepped back, taking the empty container with him, and slammed the door shut behind him.

Alex had one brief second to lay eyes on the possum before the room was plunged into darkness. It was a massive thing, its black, beady eyes wild, its fur gray and matted, its tail flickering hungrily. It saw Alex, its mouth opening to reveal tiny sharp teeth, and then the light was gone.

"Shit," Alex hissed, quickly backing himself against the far wall, groping blindly. His heart roared in his chest and a cold finger tickled his spine.

The possum scurried for him, its movement broadcast by a hurried skitter. Alex spun away from the noise, the hairs on his arms standing straight up. The rodent hissed to his left, a nasty, eerie sound.

Alex continued to circle away from it as best he could, his pulse drumming in his skull. He felt the door against his back and paused, listening for the animal. It chittered, horribly close. He knew he had to kill it before it bit him. If it really did have rabies, then that was it. Nevermind trying to find a way out of this room.

Without warning, Alex suddenly felt something run across his boots. He cried out and kicked into the darkness, his eyes wide. He missed, the possum scurrying away from the blow. Could it see him? Could possum's see in the dark? The very thought made his skin crawl. He didn't want to imagine this wild animal stalking him, waiting for his guard to drop.

"Come on," Alex breathed heavily, "get it over with…come at me…"

More movement, now to his right. He could hear it hissing at him again, readying for another charge. Alex slid across the wall and pressed himself into a corner, making himself as small as possible.

All at once, he felt something claw up his leg and scurry up toward his waist, tiny paws gripping his pants, a sudden weight wrapping around his thigh. Screaming, Alex jerked himself off the wall, punching down at the animal. His knuckles collided with warm fur and the possum let out a cry of pain, its chittering calls frantic as it scrambled to remain on Alex's leg.

"Get off me!" Alex yelled, panicking, beating down on it once more. His fist connected and managed to dislodge the rabid animal from his thigh. He heard it hit the floor and scurry over to the center of the room.

Panting, shaking, Alex attuned his body to sense if he had been bit.

"You're ok, you're ok," he gasped, hands running down his leg. The weight of the animal against him had been a sickening sensation, its warmth hovering against his skin like a ghost.

Without another moment to recover, the possum attacked him once more. It raced for his leg and he tried to kick out in the darkness before it reached him, but his boot flailed into the empty air. Tiny paws gripped his leg once more and he felt the possum race up his body, shrieking as it climbed.

Alex spasmed, the sensation of the animal mounting his body blasting hot panic throughout his limbs. Howling, he reached down and grabbed at the rodent, his hands finding purchase around the wild creature. Something bit at the air and he felt the animal wriggle violently beneath his grip. Another second, and he knew he'd feel its teeth wrapped around his arm. Screaming, he ripped it from his body and threw it as hard as he could against the ground. He was rewarded with a meaty *thunk* followed by a pained screech. Without wasting a second, he towered over the possum, aimed his boot as best he could, and thundered it down atop the injured animal.

He felt its bones break beneath his sole, a hearty *crunch* accompanying the killing blow. The possum screamed, its death cries sending a shiver running down Alex's spine.

"Fucking DIE!" He shrieked, bringing his boot down again.

And again.

And again.

Until the substance beneath his boots had turned to mush.

Panting, adrenaline soaring through him, Alex collapsed against the wall. He steadied himself, breathing deeply, bending over with his hands on his knees.

"Fucking…*possum*…" he gasped, shaking his head.

After a couple minutes, his heartbeat returned to normal and the darkness settled heavily back around him. He listened for movement, some sudden surge of life from the mangled creature, but it remained a mess of gore beneath his boots. He stepped away from it and went to the opposite corner. He slumped down, his back to the wall, and pulled his knees up to his chest. He rested his forehead against them and closed his eyes.

The walls around him loomed in the black, pressing close against his mind.

"What now…?" he muttered, feeling the approach of misery once more.

Thunder rumbled overhead, the muffled groan reaching down into his cell. Into his head.

Chapter 12

Memphis rose around Sam as he followed Empire down the empty streets. The storm had reached them just as night had fallen. Rain beat angrily against his face and he squinted beneath the gail. The wind tossed his hair across his eyes in wet strands. Lightning ignited the sky, briefly illuminating the rising skyscrapers that lined the road.

Empire had fallen into a brooding silence. He seemed unaffected by the storm, the thrashing sheets of rain whipping and pulling at the fabric around his empty sockets. Sam could sense him, a pulse in the back of his head, a slight pressure behind his eyes.

They were deep into Memphis now, the dark, cloud-filled skies offering no light. Empire walked ahead of Sam, his shoulders hunched, his hands hanging loosely at his sides. Sam had no idea where they were headed or how they were going to find Alex. He could be in any of these buildings, down any number of these branching streets. Empty cars deflected the rain, the water pitter-pattering off the abandoned surfaces.

Empire suddenly stopped and held up a hand. Sam slowed and came to his side, his voice cutting through the wind.

"What is it?"

"Stay still for a moment."

Sam froze, his eyes traveling across the dark city. Thunder boomed overhead and he winced, rainwater running into his eyes. He mopped it from his face and blew it from his lips, shivering.

"Lookouts," Empire muttered.

Sam looked down the empty streets, lightning blinking from the heavens.

"Where?"

Empire didn't move, his voice like gravel, "Building on the left. On the roof. Wait for the lightning."

The seconds ticked by and Sam felt a tightness grow in his chest. Finally, another flicker lit the world and he trained his eyes to where Empire had indicated. Faintly, through the rain, he spotted two figures standing atop the small building.

"What do we do?" Sam asked, the night returning beneath a rumble of thunder.

Empire remained motionless, "We stay put. They don't know who we are. They'll come to investigate. This close to their base, they don't have a choice."

Sam nodded, his clothes soaked and sticking to his body. He pulled at his shirt and shifted in the street, waiting for Empire to speak again. When he didn't, Sam closed his mouth and wrapped his arms around himself.

The storm howled around Empire. His empty sockets were turned toward the building, streaks of rain running down his face. His lips were pressed tightly together and his body language telegraphed a restlessness that stirred through the wet air.

Ten minutes passed without confrontation. Sam blinked moisture from his eyes and rubbed warmth into his arms. He glanced at Empire who remained silent and unmoving, his head trained toward the building.

Finally, faintly, Empire spoke, "They're coming."

Sam dropped his arms from his body, squinting, "Where? You see them?"

"They're on the street, coming this way," Empire muttered, "Sam, close your eyes. I don't want them to see who you are, not until they're close."

"But what about you, wh-"

"I'll be fine. Close your eyes."

Sam obediently did as he was told, his vision joining the blackness of night. Thunder snarled from overhead and he counted the seconds off, his body tense and cold.

After a couple minutes, he heard a female voice call out to them, harsh and commanding.

"Who are you? What are you doing out here?!"

Sam kept his eyes closed as Empire spoke, "We're looking for someone. We heard he was here in Memphis."

A second voice, another woman, "Oh yeah? You still haven't answered the first question. Who are you?"

Empire's voice slithered low into Sam's ears, "Open your eyes."

The world rushed back into view. Two women stood before them, rifles raised, a dozen feet from where they stood.

As Sam opened his eyes, the two women stepped back, alarmed.

"Red Eyes!"

"Shoot him!"

Sam didn't even have time to duck as two reports blasted through the night. Sam gasped, hands going to his chest, a cry rocketing from his throat.

He waited for the blinding pain, but after a moment, he realized it wasn't coming. Confused, he looked to his left.

Empire glowed, a red aura emanating around his body. Amazed, Sam looked down and saw the same light cloaked him as well.

"What the hell!?" One of the women cried.

Empire raised a hand to them, currents of crimson power flowing from his fingertips like electric snakes. They shot toward the two armed women and struck them both in the chest. Heaving a pained cry, the women dropped their guns and staggered back, the red light curling up their bodies, restraining them where they stood.

Thunder growled overhead and Empire took a step toward the two captives, his pace slow and deliberate.

"Jesus Christ," one of the women shuddered, her eyes wide, "oh god, it's *him*."

The second woman went white, realization rippling through her as Empire halted before them, the wind whipping the cloth around his eyes.

"I'm looking for someone," he growled, "a man named Percy. I'm guessing you work with him. Where is he?"

The women, restrained and unable to move, said nothing, fear filling their eyes.

Empire curled his hands into fists, red power dancing across his knuckles, "Don't make me repeat myself. I know you heard me. Answer the fucking question."

The first woman struggled beneath the strange light encasing her, her voice weak and shaky, "We're not telling you anything. We know who you are."

Empire snorted, "Then you know what I'm capable of. Do

you really wanna find out how fucking *thin* my patience is right now?"

The second woman looked at the first, her brow furrowed with unease, "What should we do…?"

"Don't say a word!" the first snapped, "Don't you dare!"

Empire towered over the second, his teeth spitting rainwater, "*Dare*."

The woman shrunk away from him as much as her glowing restraints would allow, her eyes lowered, a whimper crawling up her throat.

"Oh, fuck this," Empire growled.

Without warning, he stepped away from them, raising a hand to the first woman.

He flicked his fingers, drawing a red line across the open air…

….and the woman's limbs tore from her body in one horrific, violent explosion.

Blood splashed to the pavement and a shrieking howl erupted from the gored woman as her arms and legs fell casually to the ground. The red light vanished from around her body and her torso dropped to the street, limbless.

The second woman screamed, a piercing, terrified exclamation as her companion gasped and flopped at her feet.

Empire looked down at the dying woman through Sam's eyes, his teeth clenched in a snarl. The light vanished from his fingertips and he stood panting over the ruined torso, listening to her labored breath.

"No one's going to save you," he whispered, lightning flashing against the towering buildings. "And no one cares about you."

He lifted his boot and brought it crunching down into her

face, dislodging her jaw from her skull. Teeth clacked across the pavement and bone cracked loudly beneath the killing blow. The second woman wept, squirmed, screamed as she witnessed the shocking violence.

Thunder boomed and Empire raised his head to her, his voice like burning coals, "You have four seconds."

"I'll show you!" The woman howled, "I'll show you where Percy is! Please! Don't hurt me! I'll take you!"

Empire nodded and wiped his boot on the ruined torso, "Good girl."

He released her from the red light and she gasped, stumbling to her knees, her lips quivering. She tried hard not to look at the ruined remains of her comrade, but her eyes found the destruction and she whimpered pitifully.

"Get up," Sam said stepping forward and hauling her to her feet. She shuddered away from his touch, but he kept his grip planted on her arm. He felt the toe of his boot touch the bloody mess at his feet and he barely paid it any attention. Empire did the right thing. Set an example, show what happens to anyone who gets in the way.

"Move," Sam ordered, pushing the woman ahead of him through the rain.

Shaking, the woman walked them down the street, her arms wrapped around herself. The rain continued to thunder down around them, a torrential gust that plowed across their bodies in great sheets.

"How far is it?" Sam asked after a little while, blinking against the storm.

The woman shivered violently, her voice small, "Just up ahead."

She chanced a glance at Empire, "What are you going to do when you get there?"

Empire said nothing, the fabric around his eyes dripping darkly.

"Just get us there," Sam said.

They reached the end of the street and she led them down another. As they walked, the woman continued to take small peeks at Empire over her shoulder, like she couldn't believe he was actually there. Fear filled her eyes and contorted her brow into a terrified expression of disbelief.

After some time, she spoke again, "Please...just don't hurt us..."

"Shut up," Sam said flatly.

But she continued, her voice pleading now, "There are children...they haven't done anything to you..."

Empire remained silent.

"Stop talking," Sam growled, growing irritated. He felt a stirring, a desire to extinguish this pathetic waste of life. It was a sensation he had to resist, the need growing the more she talked. The more her toxins poisoned the air.

"We're good people," the woman cried, still leading the three, "we're just trying to survive..."

Without warning, Empire suddenly reached forward and spun the woman around by the shoulder to face him. She jumped, a cry reaching her lips, her eyes expanding.

"Another word," Empire said, his voice dangerously calm, "And I will remove your jaw from the base of your skull."

The woman's mouth slammed shut, her chest heaving.

"Better," Empire nodded, "now walk."

Together, the three continued down the street. The storm seemed to be climaxing, great fangs of lightning reaching across the dark sky with crooked fingers. Rolling thunder followed without pause, a blasting, booming exhale of the inky clouds.

The woman led them down another street, seemingly growing more and more manic as she went. Her head jerked in every direction, willing someone to come and save her. Sam would have pitied her if her very presence didn't disgust him.

Finally, she stopped and extended a finger toward a building on the left, "There. That's where you'll find Percy."

Empire stopped and Sam felt him appraise the high rise through his eyes, "Take us inside."

The woman bit her lip, her eyes practically begging now, "Please...don't make me go in there. I couldn't bear it."

Empire didn't even look at her, "Why? Because you betrayed them?"

Wincing, the woman looked at her feet.

"Keep going," Sam ordered, pushing the woman ahead of them toward the building.

Pained, the woman did as she was told. She guided them through the rain, closer toward the base of the structure. Sam kept expecting someone to call out to them, order them to announce themselves, but the streets remained empty and dark.

They descended into a parking garage, the concrete lot spiraling down to lower levels. They followed it and Sam took note of how many vehicles were parked below. They looked recently used, unlike the rusted out pieces of metal lining the streets outside.

Their feet echoed loudly as they reached the end of the lot and the three halted in front of a plain-faced door.

"Through here," the woman whispered, "go up a couple

floors and you'll reach us." She turned to them, her hands clasped together, "Please...I've done what you asked...now please...please let me go."

Empire faced the door, away from her, his voice low, "You want me to let you go?"

She just stared at her feet, frowning, shaking.

"You've led us right to your people," Empire continued, "and I didn't even touch you."

"Taylor..." the woman sputtered, "you...what you did to her..."

"Did you care about her?" Empire asked.

"She was my friend."

"Do you hate me? For killing her?"

The woman didn't move, dared not to.

"I would hate me," Empire continued. "Hell, most people hate me..." he trailed off for a moment before continuing, "But then again, I've done a lot to deserve it." Sam felt his eyes move to the woman, appraising her.

"You want to go?" Empire asked, almost gently.

The woman nodded, paralyzed.

Empire waved his hand in the air, "Then go..."

She blinked, as if in complete disbelief. She looked at Empire, as if trying to gauge what his angle was.

"Go on," he muttered, "get out of here."

Without waiting another second, the woman ran, her foot-steps bouncing loudly across the concrete.

"What are you doing?" Sam hissed, alarmed.

Empire turned to him, "Giving her hope." His hands ignited with red fire, "But only for a moment." He spun toward the fleeing woman, his whole body glowing now. She had almost reached the first bend, an urgency pushing her forward.

Sam watched as her legs suddenly burst into flames. Before she could scream, the length of her body was wrapped tightly with the crimson fire, muting a shriek. She spasmed and then was lifted into the air, spinning and twirling in silent agony.

Empire remained motionless. The woman's flesh began to cook and smoke, curling from her bones like blackened paper.

Sam watched, his eyes alight.

Still conscious, the woman writhed as she was lifted further up into the air, her head scraping the ceiling. Then, in one brutal motion, Empire slammed her back into the concrete so hard her body exploded like detonated meat. Gore splattered the walls and floor, bone shattered and splintered, and the woman's skull popped like it was a rotten pumpkin.

The flames ate away at the remains, the storm surging outside.

Empire turned away from the carnage, "Let's go find my brother..."

Senses heightened, Sam followed Empire through the door. He was glad he had killed her. She hadn't deserved freedom. She hadn't deserved anything.

None of them did.

They found themselves in a dim hallway, empty save for themselves. Empire took the lead, Sam's eyes at his shoulder. They passed a handful of rooms and Sam peeked inside as they passed. Each one was stocked to the ceiling with supplies, food, ammo, blankets, everything needed to keep living.

They reached the end of the hall and stepped into a stairwell. Without pause, Empire began to ascend, his pace growing more hurried. Above them, Sam detected voices. A conversation. Someone was coming down the stairs.

"You hear them?" Sam whispered, trying to gauge how far up the voices were.

Empire nodded, his body alighting, the red aura returning. It clung to him like a second skin and when Sam looked down, he saw that he was cloaked with light as well.

They rose another two floors and the voices became louder. Sam braced himself at Empire's back.

They twisted around the rise of stairs and found themselves face to face with three men, all mid-stride. When they saw the strangers, they stopped, mouths agape, hands frozen as if unsure whether they should draw the pistols at their hips.

Empire didn't even slow.

He passed through them as he ripped their heads off, massive crimson tendrils rising from his back and making short work of the interruption. Their heads rolled down the stairs, past Sam, blood waterfalling over his boots.

The headless bodies fell, already forgotten.

They reached the next floor and Empire paused before the closed door. His hair ran red and trickled down his face into the cloth around his eyes.

"Here," he said, "this is where they are. Stay close, Sam, and keep your eyes ahead. This is going to get ugly."

Empire opened the door and went through. A short hallway stretched before them and then expanded out into a massive open space. Lightning flashed outside, filling the floor-to-ceiling windows that lined the room. Sam's heart skipped a beat.

There were over a hundred people inside. Beds and tables lay scattered throughout, filled with men and women of all ages. Sam saw children turn and look their way, their eyes curious. The older ones stood, looking not quite as welcoming.

When they saw Sam's eyes, the room erupted.

A chaotic scramble for weapons ensued, a madness that took the minds of the occupants. Frantic orders were shouted, children were shielded, and someone screamed. Guns were drawn and a wall formed before Empire and Sam, a dozen barrels pointed their way.

Before they could shoot, Empire cupped a hand over his mouth and red neon bled between his fingers. A second after, the room reverberated beneath a blaring whistle that bore into the skulls of the attackers. They screamed at the sudden pain, the intrusive, high-pitched shriek rattling their teeth and sending rockets of agony between their ears. They lowered their weapons and covered their ears, wincing, screaming, trying their best to escape the maddening noise.

Empire lowered his hand and wasted no time addressing the stunned crowd.

"Where's Percy!?" He roared over the moaning masses.

No one responded. The dazed attackers scrambled to regain their senses, focus, and raise their weapons once more.

"WHERE'S PERCY!?" Empire bellowed, faint traces of red smoke snaking off his tongue. The crowd winced once again, Empire's voice cracking the air like a whip.

Finally, a man stepped toward them from the back, one hand clutching his head. He was a big man, his massive beard extending down to his overalls. He ground his teeth together as he strode toward Sam and Empire, as if trying to stop the world from spinning.

He pushed to the front, raising his hands in surrender, "I'm Percy!" he called, his voice strained.

"Tell your people to lower their weapons," Empire instructed, "not like they'd do any good."

After a moment, Percy waved to the crowd. They obeyed,

but with great reluctance. Fear sparked between them like currents of electricity, their eyes alight with terror as they stared at the intruders.

"My patience is razor thin right now," Empire continued, hands at his sides, "so don't push it. None of you."

Percy brought his hands together, a trickle of unease creasing the wrinkles around his eyes.

"Who are you?" He asked as if fearing the answer.

"You know who the fuck I am," Empire spat.

A hushed moan swept through the room and Sam saw mothers clutch their children tightly and push them toward the back of the room.

Percy shifted, his hands wringing together, "Empire…"

"I'm looking for someone."

Percy licked his lips, "Now look, there's a lot of good people in here-"

Empire took an aggressive step forward, "I don't give a burning *fuck* about these people," he growled, now standing toe to toe with Percy, "I'm here for one man and one man only. His name is Alex."

Percy's face seemed to melt, a mix of panicked emotions rolling across his pale skin, "Ah…him…o-of course…"

"Here's here?" Sam called from behind Empire.

Percy's head snapped up like he was noticing Sam for the first time, "Um…Alex…yes. He's here."

Empire stared up at the massive man, "Where is he?"

Percy swallowed hard, "Uh…he's locked up right now. In a cell."

Empire's voice hissed between his teeth, "You locked him up?"

Percy nodded, growing more and more uncomfortable, "He got violent…"

"Why?" Sam asked, "What happened?"

Percy struggled to speak, his confidence fleeing, "Uh…look, if you want him, I'll go get him. No problem."

Empire cocked his head back toward Sam, "Why don't you answer my friend's goddamn question?"

Percy looked around the room, as if gauging his chances, "There was an accident," he said slowly, "there was a woman he was with. She died and he…he kind of lost his mind. We had to contain him."

"Luna…" Sam whispered.

Light flared around Empire's body, "You locked up my brother like a wild *dog*?"

Percy blinked, sweating now, "B-brother…?"

"Is he still in his cell?" Empire snarled, neon smoke wafting dangerously from his fingertips.

Percy nodded, eyes wide, "Y-yes…I'll show you…" he paused, summoning his voice again, "He's really your…your brother?"

Empire looked up into Percy's face, fury leaking from every pore, the cloth around his eyes still wet with blood, "Did you hurt him?"

"W-well no, not really," Percy sputtered, "but he was out of control…we had to get him away from everyone before he hurt someone. You understand, don't ya?"

"No, Percy," Empire growled, "I don't." Suddenly Percy's body was enveloped in red light, encasing him completely. Percy let out a cry, back peddling and swatting at his clothes. When he realized he wasn't in pain, he looked up, "What is this? What are you doing?"

"Saving you for Alex," Empire said darkly.

In an instant, Empire stepped back and raised his hands to the crowd. Crimson pillars grew from his palms, sparking, pulsing columns of blazing power. The onlookers shrieked in panic as Empire sent them into the middle of the room, the bars of light floating between them.

"Shoot him!" Someone screamed.

Before anyone found a trigger, Empire raised his right hand high above his head…

…and snapped his fingers.

The pillars of light exploded like glass. Shards of razor red detonated across the room like a bomb had gone off. Screams erupted beneath the wave of violence and the crowd was shredded, a million pieces of burning shrapnel blasting through a hundred different bodies. Blood painted the walls as flesh parted beneath the onslaught, a thousand deadly lacerations cutting the life out of the room. Chunks of gore splattered across the dark windows, screams were cut short, and the bodies fell in waves beneath the mutilation.

In a matter of seconds, the room was silent. A hundred dead in the blink of an eye.

Percy's mouth was open in a silent scream, his eyes wide and rolling wildly in his head. The shield around his body winked out, the protection no longer needed.

Sam surveyed the sea of corpses, blood pooling around the still bodies. He felt a twinge of pleasure ripple through him. So many dead. So many useless, pathetic lives snuffed out. His eyes found the remains of a father holding a pair of little girls. He could barely make out their features beneath the bloody scars that crisscrossed the lengths of their bodies.

Percy finally found his voice, a strained, disbelieving croak, "Oh god…oh my *god*…"

Empire grabbed a fistful of his shirt, his voice like iron, "You going to take me to see my brother or do you wanna look a little longer?"

Chapter 13

Alex stood in the darkness, his heart racing. Something was happening. He had heard screaming. Pained, horrific screaming. He went to the door and pressed his ear to it. Now there was nothing but pregnant silence. Had they been attacked? But by who? Red Eyes?

It didn't matter. Not unless the attackers were going to break him out of this damn room. He raised a fist and began to pound against the door.

"Hello!? Is someone out there!? I'm locked in this room, help me!"

He continued to beat his fists against the stubborn surface until his hands went numb. He paused, flexing his fingers, and listened once again. Still nothing.

"Goddamn it," he muttered, resting his forehead against the door. The darkness crept up his shoulders and slithered back into his mind. He tried to shut it out, tried to edge out the consistent despair, but it was a relentless insistence.

"Someone…" he whispered.

He brought his fists against the door again and began to yell his throat raw. He couldn't die in here. Not like this, not in this room…this closet.

Wincing, he finally gave in to the pain and dropped his hands to his sides. He exhaled miserably and went to the opposite wall. He sat down against it and covered his face with his hands. He had never been a praying man, but the temptation presented itself.

"Fuck that," he whispered.

The silence filled the black. The walls squeezed in around his shoulders and he tried to ignore his rising heart rate. He would not panic…he wouldn't lose his mind in here. Please…

Suddenly, something rapped against the door. It jolted him from his smothering thoughts, a blast of hope bringing him to his feet. The noise came again, a knocking and then a clank of metal.

In a rush, the door pulled open and Alex was momentarily blinded by light. He shielded his eyes and squinted, readying himself for a confrontation.

A shadow filled the doorway and then a voice echoed around him.

A familiar voice.

"Hey, Alex."

In disbelief, eyes wide, Alex lowered his hands.

"Sam?" He whispered, shock rolling through him.

Sam didn't move from the doorway, his voice carefully neutral, "Seems you got yourself into some trouble, huh?"

Alex was about to respond, a thousand questions lining his tongue, but the air seemed to freeze as he looked into his friend's eyes.

They glowed a brilliant red, a flaring certainty that left no room for doubt.

He shook his head, mouth agape, "No…no, no, no…"

Sam raised his hands, as if expecting this, "Calm down, Alex. I'm here to get you out. It's ok."

Alex extended a finger, unwilling to grasp what he was seeing, "Your eyes...Sam, your fucking *eyes*..."

Sam nodded, "I know. Don't freak out on me. I haven't gone crazy or anything, I'm still the same person. I'm still your friend."

But something about the way he said it filled Alex with doubt. There was an emptiness to his words, like they had been carefully scripted and rehearsed.

"What happened to you?" Alex whispered, "Where the hell did you go? We looked for you...Jesus, Sam, you just disappeared. Luna and I..." Alex's heart dropped, "Oh god...Luna...she's...she's dead, Sam."

Sam's face didn't change beneath the news. He simply nodded, "I heard. Awful. I'm sorry, man."

Alex shook his head slowly, a sense of unease growing rapidly in his confused state, "You're sorry? You're fucking sorry? You disappear without a word in the middle of the night, leave Luna and I without a clue, and now you show back up with your eyes looking like that?" He grit his teeth, voice dropping, "And now you're telling me you're fucking *sorry*?"

Sam crossed his arms, "A lot has happened, Alex."

"No SHIT!" Alex roared suddenly, hands balling into fists, "Luna dies and you turn into one of THEM! So what the FUCK SAM?!"

"Calm down."

Alex took a threatening step forward, "*Don't* do that."

"I need to you to listen. The Towers have been activated."

Alex blinked, his anger momentarily leaving him, "...what? What do you mean?"

"It means you don't have a lot of time. You need to come with me."

Alex didn't move, "What are you talking about? Sam, what the fuck is going on!? Where have you BEEN!?"

Sam stared at Alex for a long time before answering, his voice calm, but careful, "I've been with your brother."

The blood drained from Alex's face, his voice a stutter, "W-what...?"

"He was the one who took me that night. He didn't give me a chance to say goodbye. I'm sorry."

Alex's head was spinning, "He took you? Why? Why you?"

"He needed me for something."

"For what?"

"For this," Sam said, stepping into the cell, "for you."

"What the hell are you talking about?"

Sam's face softened, his eyes glowing in the darkness, "He needs you, Alex. He wants you there with him when the end comes. He doesn't want to fight. He just wants to be your brother again. One last time."

Alex stepped away from Sam, his face going blank. After a moment, he began to laugh. It was a soft chuckle that bubbled from his chest and past his lips, a disbelieving exhale of madness.

"Are you fucking kidding me?" He finally asked.

Sam didn't seem amused, "No, I'm not. Alex, think about it. What the hell have we been doing the past couple years? What have we really been after?"

"We've been hunting down my bastard brother," Alex snarled, "the same son of a bitch who took Maddison and my unborn child away from me. Sam, what the hell IS this?"

Sam crossed his arms, his voice soft, "Is that really what we were doing? We had years to catch Empire and each time we got close, something would happen to slow us down. But it was never enough to stop us. We had multiple opportunities to catch him, but we never did. And do you know why?" Sam's voice dropped, "Because you never wanted to. Oh, you talked a big game, but there were so many times your actions proved otherwise. Remember when we found Luna? Alex, we were so close, but you wanted to gather supplies before moving forward. You insisted, even though you knew it'd cost us time."

"You're full of shit," Alex growled.

Sam shook his head, "No, I'm not. You've used your brother as an excuse to run from your heartbreak. From the pain that shuddered through you every time you thought about your wife. And you knew that if we actually caught Empire, then you would be forced to confront that shit. So you always were careful to keep us a couple steps behind because god forbid you ended the manhunt and had to deal with your pain." Sam sighed, "That's always been your problem, man. You never had the heart to heal. That's why instead of mourning your loss, you channeled it into a rage, a burning desire to make someone pay. Anyone. You'd lose yourself in it because it was easier to get angry than to allow yourself to feel fucking *anything*."

Sam stepped toward Alex, "And this isn't the first time you've run away from something."

Alex was trembling, a white-hot rage building behind his eyes, "Shut up. Shut the fuck up. You have no idea what you're talking about."

Sam sniffed, "Really? Who's been with you since the beginning? Who's lived through every torment you've suffered?" Sam jabbed a finger into his chest, "I have. Me. Your best goddamn friend. When we were kids, I knew you were going through hell. I didn't know the extent of it because you never wanted to talk about it and I respected that. But I wasn't blind. I saw the aftermath of your parent's abuse. I stayed quiet when you cried. I never said a word to anyone because I knew you didn't want that. Not from me. But goddamn it, Alex, I was there for you. I always have been. Even when you got out and went to California – who came with you? I did. Me. Because I knew you needed someone who understood *who you were*."

Sam was now toe-to-toe with Alex, his voice quieting, "But you abandoned your brother when he needed you most. Unlike you, he had *no one*. You left him. You cut all ties to the one person you fought so hard to protect all your life. And why? How could you do something like that?"

Sam's voice hissed between his teeth, "It's because you are incapable of dealing with pain. He was the only one who had seen you at your absolute lowest, broken, bleeding, crying, and every time you were around him, you were reminded of everything you went through. Together. But instead of helping one another past that, you left. You didn't even give him a chance."

Alex glared into Sam's glowing eyes, shaking, losing himself, "If you don't stop talking I swear to-"

Sam suddenly grabbed Alex by the shirt, his voice a snarl, "For once in your life, shut the fuck up and *listen to me*. I'm done helping you. I wasted years wandering the country on a hunt that never ended. I didn't do it because I wanted to, I did it because you needed me. Well, guess what, Alex? That part of our friendship is over. Now there's someone who needs *you*."

"What poison has he infected you with?" Alex growled, temper peaking.

Sam gripped Alex tighter, "Poison? No. I've been shown the truth. I've seen what a waste we all are. I've seen the horrors of the human race, the violence, the pointlessness of it all. But you know what? Your brother never needed to turn me. It was there this whole time."

He pressed Alex against the wall, his voice like gravel, "I've seen the pointlessness of your rage. And it's time you did too."

Alex shoved away from Sam, disbelief crashing over him, "This isn't you. I don't know what kind of shit your head's been filled with, but the Sam I knew wouldn't talk like this."

"Just because my eyes are a different color doesn't mean I'm not talking sense," Sam rebutted, "You know I'm right. You know you've been using this vendetta to run from your problems. I mean Jesus Christ, Alex, we've been at it for ten years! How much longer can this go on?!"

"Fuck you."

"Right, of course," Sam said, stepping back, "just deflect. Continue to ignore the problem."

"I think it's time I left," Alex said."

"And where would you go?" Sam asked, "What battle are you going to run after this time?"

"The same one I've been chasing," Alex growled, "nothing's changed. And I'm not going with you."

"Why do you keep using her?"

"Shut up."

"Why are you so intent on disrespecting her memory like this?" Sam continued, "She's just a name you use to justify your actions. I'm talking about your wife, Maddison, in case you forgot."

"Shut the FUCK up, Sam!" Alex yelled, advancing.

"Do you even remember what it was like to love her? Or did Luna wash those memories away?"

Snarling, Alex snapped. He stepped toward Sam and cocked his fist back, roaring, "Fuck OFF!"

He swung, putting the full force of his wrath behind it.

Sam was ready though and caught his fist mid-swing. He twisted Alex's arm away and stepped into the blow. Alex felt pain rocket through his skull as Sam brought his forehead crunching into Alex's face. Blood erupted from his nose and stars danced before his eyes. He stumbled back, surprised and dazed, tripping over himself and against the far wall.

He steadied himself for a moment, his eyes ascending to meet Sam's, "You son of a bitch…"

Sam rubbed his forehead with the heel of his palm, "You swung first, idiot. I'm not here to fight you so please don't do that again."

"Then why the hell are you here!?" Alex yelled, wiping the blood from his face.

"Because your brother needs you," Sam said patiently. His guard dropped a little and his voice softened, "I mean hell, Alex, the world is falling apart around you and you still can't move on. He *needs* you. Can't you just stand with him one last time? Do you really want to die hating your only brother? Is revenge really worth it?" Sam's shoulders slumped, "And I get it, man. I know you think I'm completely insane now that I have these," he motioned to his eyes, "but really listen to me. The end is inevitable. The Towers have been activated. The Gargoyles are coming. Very soon there's going to be nothing left. Do you really want to be alone when you die? Haven't you spent enough time in misery? Because that's all he wants, you know: to feel something other than misery before he goes. To feel like he's not completely alone in this world before it perishes."

Alex said nothing, his nose trickling crimson.

"Just because my eyes are red doesn't mean we can't stand together," Sam said softly, "all of us. Just like we use to when we were kids. I mean hell, aren't you tired? Hasn't this journey drained you? How many more people are you going to kill? How much longer can you really go on? Because for me? I'm *exhausted*...and I just want this whole thing to be *over*."

Alex dropped his eyes, his voice thin, a sudden fatigue overwhelming him, "Goddamn it...what the hell do you want me to say, Sam? I can't forgive him for what he did. You know I can't."

"I'm not asking you to," Sam pressed, "I'm asking you to just...just be with him, just for a little while. No one wants to die alone. Not even you. And if you leave, then that's exactly what's going to happen. Please, Alex. Remember how much he needed you – how much he looked up to you. You were the only person in the entire world to him. You still are."

Alex ran a hand down the length of his face, pulling blood with it, his voice weary, *"Fuck..."*

"I know, man."

Alex shook his head, "Fuck..."

"Do you want to see him?" Sam asked.

Alex looked up, "What...he's here?"

Sam nodded.

Alex pulled himself up, a bubble of nerves coursing through his chest, "Where?"

Sam threw a finger over his shoulder, "Follow me."

"Alright..."

"You're not going to try and hit me again, are you?"

"Go, Sam."

Sam turned and exited the room. Alex followed closely

behind, his heart racing. As he followed Sam down the hall, he tried to prepare himself as best he could. A mountain of conflicted emotions blew through him like a hurricane. Rage, anger, sorrow...and deep down below that...he was terrified. He had spent so long dreaming of this moment, preparing, thinking about what he would say. But now that the moment was upon him, he felt unsure of himself. And that was something he feared more than anything.

They exited the hall and entered a massive office space filled with an array of makeshift beds and tables. He recognized the room. But it was different now and Alex slowed, his eyes growing huge.

Dead bodies lined the floor. Dozens of them, all lying in various states of death, their flesh shredded and gored almost beyond recognition.

Sam stepped over them and directed their path toward the back of the room. He seemed completely unaffected by the carnage, his eyes boring straight ahead. Alex swept his gaze across the corpses, shock coursing through him. Men, women, children, it didn't seem to matter. All had been destroyed and now lay massacred, turning the room into a graveyard.

Sam stopped suddenly.

Alex walked to his side, pulling his eyes from the ruin.

"Go ahead," Sam said quietly, pointing, "go talk to him."

Heart beating like a drum, Alex looked ahead of them.

Empire sat against one of the windows, his legs splayed out before him. His head rested against the glass, a strip of cloth wrapped tightly around his eyes.

As soon as Alex saw him, he felt his heart skip a beat.

He looked so grown up.

Empire rolled his head off the window and stared blindly at Alex, his features hidden, his voice tired, "Hey Alex..."

Something crawled up Alex's throat, an unexpected surge of pain that he fought to keep down. He didn't move, didn't breathe, and felt as if the room was spinning.

"Sorry about the mess," Empire said, still seated, "they didn't seem like they were going to let you go peacefully."

Alex took a hesitant step toward his brother, his voice cracking, "Will...?"

Empire smiled, a sad twitch at the corners of his mouth.

Alex took another step toward him, a gale raging through his chest. Words clawed at his tongue but he couldn't seem to release them. He was assaulted by a surge of rapid-fire emotions and impulses, unexpected and terrible thoughts clashing violently with a sorrow so deep he felt he would throw up.

Empire sighed and pulled his legs up, resting his forearms on his knees, "There's a lot of things I need to say to you."

Alex stared down at him, a current racing up his throat, turning his legs to jelly, his hands into fists. He clenched his teeth, the sight of his brother rattling him to the bone, a vicious, terrible surge of memory and pain.

"Goddamn it, Will..." Alex whispered.

Empire smiled again, the sadness remaining, "I know...I'm sorry. You probably don't believe me, and I know I can never make things right, but I am sorry. You're the last person I wanted to hurt, but I fucked that up because I'm a selfish son of a bitch. Fuck, man, I... shit..."

"What happened to your face?" Alex finally managed to ask.

Empire touched the cloth around his head, "Heh...that. I lost my eyes. They were taken from me."

"How?"

Empire waved the question away, "It doesn't matter. I'm using Sam's eyes for now. He's been a real trooper. You look like shit, by the way."

Alex snorted, almost in disbelief that he was having this conversation, "I've been having a rough time, lately."

"When have we ever had it easy?" Empire asked quietly, that sad smile still lining his lips.

Alex exhaled through his nose, a quiet acknowledgment.

"Look," Empire said, standing, "What I did…"

"Stop," Alex said sharply, "don't."

Empire shook his head, "No, I need to say it. I'm sorry for…" he paused, struggling, "…for taking her away from you. There's a lot of things I've done that I regret and that…that one leads the pack. I'm not going to make excuses, I wouldn't do that to you." He sighed heavily as if he hadn't slept in years, his voice quieting, "I just…missed you…"

Alex closed his eyes, his teeth grinding together, "You have no idea what you did to me…"

"I know…and I know I can never make it right. I won't ask for your forgiveness because I wouldn't want you to give it to me," Empire said gently, "I was lost. Alone. When you left me, I didn't know what to do. In a way, it was worse, because even though I was away from Mom and Dad, I didn't have you anymore. You…you *left* me, Alex…"

Alex turned away.

"You left me all alone," Empire whispered.

"I couldn't," Alex hissed, struggling with himself. "I just…couldn't."

"You didn't even try."

"What the fuck did you want me to do?" Alex snapped suddenly.

Empire paused, taken back, "I…I just wanted you to be my brother."

Alex wheeled on him, "And I wanted to forget about mine and live a happy life. Funny how that turned out."

"Why am I so repulsive to you?" Empire asked, standing, "Just what the hell is so sickening about me? Because that's all I appear to be to you. A tumor in your otherwise perfect life."

"Perfect?" Alex spat, "Nothing about my life has been perfect, but leaving you and the memories of our youth behind certainly helped." He stepped forward, voice rising, "And meeting Maddison pushed all the shit in my head even further away. I know you think I'm some fucking pillar of strength, but that's some bullshit fantasy you concocted, not me. When I left you I was a goddamn disaster. Ask Sam. Ask him what those first couple months were like. Since you two are such good buddies now, I'm sure he would be happy to share."

Empire said nothing, his hands hanging limply at his sides.

"But you just couldn't let me be, could you?" Alex growled, "It wasn't enough that I got us out of that fucking house alive, was it? You couldn't stand the fact that I wanted to forget. That I moved on. That I found someone that I loved and wanted to be with. Someone that wasn't you."

Empire stared blindly at the ground, his voice soft, "You still don't get it. It wasn't that you left me. It was that you stopped loving me. As fucked as it was in that house growing up, at least I knew someone cared about me. That someone loved me. Once we left, so did that feeling."

"Of course I loved you!" Alex yelled, voice cracking, "But the world doesn't revolve around you, you stupid son of a bitch! If you weren't so GODDAMN selfish then maybe you'd realize that! Maybe you would have seen how much pain I was in! I mean Jesus FUCK, Will! Did you ever stop to think about what I needed!? That maybe – just FUCKING maybe – that in order for me to move past all that SHIT that I had to get the hell away from you? Couldn't you just let me do that!? Couldn't you just let me go!? Wasn't it enough that I got us away from Mom and Dad ALIVE!?" Alex was fuming, sorrow and rage clashing in his chest like an avalanche.

Empire's voice came out low and pained, "The world didn't get any better once we got out…"

Alex stormed Empire, a fist roughly gripping his shirt, his lips twisted into a snarl, "That's not my fucking problem. I can't live your life for you. I can't be there every mother*fucking* second to make sure my damaged brother is ok!" Alex slammed Empire up against the window, spittle flying from between his teeth, "I needed to be ok. I needed to get away and start a life for myself. Because if I didn't then I would have fucking *killed myself* in a matter of weeks."

Empire didn't struggle as Alex roughly slammed him back once again, his voice lost in a rage.

"And instead of moving forward, instead of building something for yourself without me, what did you do?!"

Empire stayed silent, his head bouncing off the glass.

"WHAT DID YOU DO!?" Alex bellowed.

Finally, quietly, Empire spoke, "I saw an opportunity to not feel powerless for *once* in my fucking life."

"You helped the Gargoyles destroy EVERYTHING!" Alex roared.

"SO WHAT!?" Empire suddenly yelled, hands at his sides, "Who CARES!? What the FUCK did the world ever do for us!? Where the hell were all these goddamn people when we were kids!? These people you are suddenly SO concerned for!?

Well!? Where the FUCK were they when Dad was beating the fucking CHRIST out of us!? Where were these people when Mom wouldn't let us eat for days!? WHERE THE FUCK WERE THEY ALEX!? Because if there's one thing I learned growing up in that house…if there's one fucking thing…it's that people are cruel and selfish beings. No one gives a SHIT about anyone else. Not if they become an inconvenience or a burden. I mean WAKE UP ALEX! We spend our lives in this cycle of fucking MISERY! The good times are there only to build up for the inevitable fall! They exist only to remind us of how great things COULD be! Christmas morning comes around and everything is wonderful, but one day later and it's back to the fucking closet for us! Why do you – YOU of all people – care that I decided enough was enough!? That I was presented with an opportunity to stop this horrible pattern and TOOK IT!?"

Alex bunched his fists tightly into Empire's shirt, his breath hissing between clenched teeth, "Because not everything is like that, you fucking little *cunt*. If you had tried to get over your shit, tried to move past our childhood – past ME – then maybe you could have seen that. But no…instead you decided to wipe it all out. To erase the goodness you couldn't see because you *couldn't fucking have it.*"

"You have no idea what you're talking about," Empire fumed, "You have no clue how isolated I felt after you left. I spent my entire life looking up to you. Would it have killed you to see how I was doing? Just once? Or would that have been too hard? Would that have been too painful? I mean Jesus…have you always been such a fucking coward?"

"Coward?" Alex spat, feeling white hot magma building in

his lungs, "Is that really what you think of me? After everything I did?"

Empire leaned into Alex, his voice a grating snarl, "Only a coward would hunt down his own brother. Only a coward would want to kill me instead of trying to fix things. So yeah, Alex, I'm calling you a coward."

Alex's vision went white.

He felt himself cock his fist back and plow it into Empire's face. A pained grunt followed and a flash of red. His knuckles came away wet, his mind receding into the darkness. His fingers wrapped around his brother's throat. He craned his head back and then brought it smashing into Empire's face so hard it made his teeth hurt. He could feel himself fading, losing himself in his anger, his rage.

At his back, he became aware of Sam calling his name. Rough hands grabbed at him, but Alex spun and delivered a vicious punch that drew blood from his friend's nose. In the brief flashes of sight he was allowed, he saw Sam fall to the floor, clutching his face.

He turned back to his brother who was still pinned against the window.

"You ruined EVERYTHING!" Alex roared, gripping Empire's face and slamming the back of his head against the glass. His brother grunted and his body slumped in Alex's hands.

Alex hauled him up and threw him against the wall, driving a knee into his stomach. Without pause, he grabbed Empire as he doubled over and delivered an uppercut.

"Come on!" Alex screamed between the white-hot anger, "Fucking FIGHT BACK!" He threw another blow across his brother's jaw. And then another. And another.

He grabbed a fistful of Empire's hair and slammed his face against the wall, once, twice, and then his knuckles did the rest. Blood splattered the floor as Alex brought his fists back into his brother's bleeding lips, ejecting a tooth. He threw an elbow, followed by a knee, and then he shoved Empire back against the wall, his head bouncing off the hard surface.

Empire was gasping, his hands at his sides, the cloth around his eyes slipping.

"HIT ME GODDAMN IT!" Alex screamed, planting a fist into Empire's stomach.

Panting, he let his brother fall to the floor, his face bleeding profusely.

Alex towered over him, quivering, on fire with anger, "Get up. GET THE FUCK UP!"

Slowly, Empire rolled up into a sitting position, bloody drool hanging from his lips. Grimacing, he adjusted the rag around his eyes.

"Come on," Alex taunted, "Show me how fucking powerful you are."

Still sitting, Empire leaned against the wall and rolled his head back to stare blindly at Alex. His voice shook as he spoke.

"Dad would be so proud of you."

Alex froze, his blood turning to ice, his voice a panting rasp, "What did you say?"

Wincing, Empire touched his beaten face, "You hit harder than he did."

Alex felt his vision clear, the rage ebbing away like black waves.

Empire ran his tongue across his split lips, "You're just like him, Alex, and you don't even realize it."

Alex took a step back, an unexpected surge of panic racing

through him, "What the hell are you talking about? I'm *nothing* like him."

Empire grunted, "You sure about that? That rage…that loss of control…it's so fucking familiar it makes me sick."

Alex shook his head, heart racing, "No…"

Empire stood, legs shaking, "Oh really? Because just now I felt like I was five years old again. I felt like Dad just got home and I knew it was going to be a bad night. You remember those times, don't you? When we knew, from the second he walked in he door, that we were dead meat. And we knew that once he threw that first punch, he was gone. Poof. Lost in his anger. You reminded me of those memories just now."

Alex heard Sam rise from behind him, but Empire held his hand up, "I think we're done, Sam."

"Are you ok?"

Empire stared vacantly at Alex, "I've taken worse."

Alex suddenly felt sick to his stomach. A sharp pain rolled through his gut and he wrapped his arms around himself. His head spun, the world tilting unexpectedly. His pulse pounded in his ears and his throat went dry. His licked his lips and ran his hands through his hair, his eyes wide.

"What the fuck am I doing here…?" He whispered, feeling terribly lost.

Empire placed an arm against the wall for support, rolling his shoulders, "I don't want to fight you, Alex."

Dazed, Alex looked up into his brother's covered face.

"But I deserved that beating," Empire continued. "I told you I wasn't going to ask for your forgiveness and I'm not going to. But you're all I've got left. And things are in motion that can't be stopped. The Gargoyles are coming and the end approaches. All I want is for you to be with me when they arrive. I just want to see the end. After that…" he sighed, an exclamation that bore a world of exhaustion behind it, "After that, I just want to die…I just want this…all this…to be over. I'm tired, Alex. I'm so *fucking* tired."

Alex just stared, disbelief and chaos roaring through him, "Why…? Why the fuck would you want something like that?"

Empire shook his head, "Because if there's good in this world, it was never meant for me."

"That's not true…"

Empire smiled weakly, "You don't have to try anymore, Alex. You don't have to love or hate me. My mind is made up. And despite the ass kicking you just gave me, I don't want you to die."

Alex blinked, "Die…? What are you talking about?"

"When the Gargoyles arrive, the Towers are going to erupt once more," Empire said gravely, "Just like they did ten years ago. Except this time, they're going to destroy everything. They don't need us anymore. Humanity has served its purpose. Everything will be turned to ash and no one will be spared."

Alex exhaled, a shaking, pained realization, "So it really is over then, isn't it?"

Empire nodded, "But if you come with me, if you stand with me atop one of the Towers, we will be spared from the blast and I can get you to safety. Consider it my final act of penance."

"It doesn't have to be like that," Alex whispered.

Empire snorted painfully, "Aren't you quick to change your tune. Alex…I want this. It would be a blessing at this point. But before that happens, I want to see the end. I want to see my journey to its completion. Despite how you feel about me, about what I've done, I still believe in in what I'm doing. And if you're with me then I think I can spare you the end. You and

Sam both. I owe you two so much and if I can help it, I'm going to get you away from the hell that's coming. You do want to live, don't you?"

Hating himself, Alex nodded.

Sam came to Empire's side and faced Alex. His eyes burned a brilliant crimson.

Empire patted his shoulder, "If you want it, then I'll do what I can for both of you. I can't promise anything, but I'll try."

"How...? What could you possibly do?" Alex asked.

Empire's voice went low, almost a whisper, "I'm going to take you to the Last Tower."

Chapter 14

Alex felt lost. More lost than he had ever felt before in his life. He watched as Empire wiped blood from his mouth, Sam at his side. He had spent so long hunting down this man, his brother, and now that same person wanted to save him. He ran his hands through his hair, turning away from the pair. What the hell was he supposed to do…? What was he supposed to think? When he looked at his brother, he was overwhelmed with conflicted emotions. He saw the terror and power of Empire, the whirlwind of destruction that had helped tear the world apart after The Impact. He saw the blood on his hands, the need to end humanity, the spite and hatred he had for everyone around him. But he also saw a scared little boy. He saw Will, the frightened child who had clung to his chest and cried when all seemed lost.

Alex closed his eyes and let out a frustrated, anxious breath. Deep down, he realized that he couldn't kill him. As much as he wanted to, as badly as he wanted to murder the one responsible for Maddison's abduction, he found that he didn't have the heart. And that sickened him. It made him feel pathetic. It made him feel like less of a man. If it were anyone else, anyone at all, he would have had no problem putting a bullet between their eyes.

But it wasn't just anyone…it was Will.

And despite years of hardening himself in preparation for this confrontation, he found that he couldn't do it. Not because the desire had vanished, but because he knew what his brother had already suffered. And seeing him now…confronted with the cruelty of his own bloodlust…he felt it ebbing away. It was an unexpected sympathy, a gentle voice that whispered from the back of his mind. And he knew now, that if he killed Will, then he would be no better than the others he had grown up to hate.

Dad would be so proud of you…

Alex opened his eyes, disgusted with himself.

Maybe Sam was right, Alex thought, *maybe I have been using this journey as a way to fill my mind with something other than pain.* He sniffed.

Am I really that pathetic?

"Alex?"

He turned, emerging from his thoughts.

"Are you coming with us?" Sam asked, adjusting the cloth around Empire's eyes.

Alex looked around him, at the dead bodies littering the room. His mind pulled him in different directions, a vicious tug-of-war that left him exhausted. He let his eyes fall to the floor, across the puddles of drying blood, the gore, the death. If he stayed, it would only be a matter of time before he joined them. If what Will said was true about the Towers erupting again…

What the hell do you have to live for?

The thought shocked him. He blinked and shook his head,

trying to rid himself of the clinging realization. What *did* he have to live for? Why go on? Why keep this violent, miserable existence up? Now that Sam had turned and Luna was gone…

Thinking about her sent a tremor of sadness through him. Flashes of her death rolled through him like a toxin. He felt a heaviness settle over his shoulders and sink into his chest. He discovered that he missed her terribly.

But despite the overwhelming sadness, despite the loneliness, he realized that he didn't want to die. The thought almost ashamed him. Why should he get to go on when everyone else didn't? What did he do to earn that?

"Alex?" Sam asked again.

Alex turned, his head thumping painfully beneath his tormented thoughts, "What?"

"What do you want to do?"

Alex sloped a sad smile, "What do I want? I want to disappear. I want to know what the fuck I'm supposed to do here."

Empire wiped the last of the blood from his lips and remained silent, letting Sam speak for him.

"Where else would you go?" Sam asked. "We've all made mistakes here. We've all fucked up. But it's not worth thinking about when we're all about to die."

Alex ran a battered hand across his mouth, "What is this place you mentioned? This…Last Tower?"

Empire looked up, "It's a place the Gargoyles built for me. My own personal paradise."

Alex furrowed his brow, "Then why do you want to die? Why carry out this death wish?"

Empire smiled sadly beneath his blindfold, "I already told you why. And I don't want to talk about it anymore. I've made up my mind. If you're with me when the Gargoyles come, that'll be enough for me."

Alex let his eyes fall, his voice a frustrated mess, "Goddamn it…"

"Let it go, man," Sam said evenly, "just let it go. Everything. Just bury it and come with us."

Alex let his eyes wander between Sam and Empire.

"I just have one more thing I need to ask," he said slowly.

Empire waited as if expecting the question that came next.

"What happened to her?" Alex asked softly, "What happened to Maddison after the Red Eyes took her?"

Empire sighed heavily, pausing a moment before answering, "She was never turned. I couldn't do it. We took her into Sacramento and she…" his voice dropped sorrowfully, "and she died in childbirth. I'm sorry, Alex. Neither of them made it."

Alex just stared at them, his heart thundering.

"I wouldn't lie to you about this," Empire said gently. "I knew how much she meant to you. I didn't hate her, I just wanted her away from you. And when her pregnancy came to an end…so did she."

Alex felt his eyes watering and turned away. He bit his lip and simply nodded.

"I'm sorry," Empire said again.

Alex turned back to them, dragging a hand across his eyes, "Yeah. Me too. Let's go."

Empire raised his head, "Yeah?"

"Don't make me say it again…"

Empire almost smiled, but caught it before it escaped, "There's something I want to give you before we leave." He nodded to Sam who reached behind his back and pulled something out of his shirt.

It was Alex's cleaver.

"Found this," Sam said, handing it to Alex, "figured you'd want it back."

Alex took it and turned it over in his hands, "There's a couple people I'd like to introduce this too."

"We know," Sam said, "come with me. One last thing and we'll be on our way."

Alex looked at Empire who simply nodded, "Go ahead. I'll be downstairs. Take your time."

Sam looked over at him, "You need my eyes?"

"I'll manage. Let him enjoy himself."

Confused, Alex followed Sam down a hallway, leaving Empire in their wake. The cleaver felt heavy in his hand, his fingers tightening around the grip. Sam walked ahead of him and for a split second, he envisioned himself burying it in the back of his head. He shuddered the thought away. What the hell was wrong with him...?

Sam stopped before a closed door and fumbled with the lock. Alex waited patiently at his side, confused and slightly on edge. Sam pulled the bolt aside and pushed the door open to reveal a thick darkness inside. He stepped away from the entry and allowed Alex to peer inside.

When his eyes adjusted to the dim light, he felt rage erupt in his chest so violently he lost his breath.

Percy. He was naked and strung up by his arms, his wrists bound with thick chain that had been thrown over a cross-beam. His beard was stained with drying blood and the left side of his face was puffy and purple. When he saw Alex, his eyes went wide.

"Aw, hell no, not you!" He groaned, twisting in his bindings.

Alex felt his teeth slam together in a snarl, anger coursing through him so intensely he felt like he would throw up.

He stepped into the room, "Well hey there, fucker," he hissed.

Percy tried to writhe away from Alex, but the chains held him fast, "Now hold up, son! Take it easy! Don't look at me like that, we just had ourselves a misunderstanding!"

"You got that right," Alex said, stopping before him.

"I was gonna let you outta that room! Swear to Abraham I was! I just wanted to give you some time to clear your head out!" He begged.

"You waited too long," Alex said darkly, circling the strung up man.

Percy whipped his head around, fearfully eyeing the cleaver, "I'm not your enemy! Come on now, let's let bygones be bygones!"

Alex stopped pacing, staring hell into Percy's eyes, "Shut the fuck up. You sound *pathetic*."

"We can make this right," Percy bumbled, "I'm sorry about your woman, truly I am!"

"Her name was Luna," Alex said, the words heaving from his boiling chest, "and yes, I intend to make this right."

Without waiting for a response, Alex raised his cleaver and ripped the length of the blade across Percy's armpit. The skin parted easily and blood immediately began to spill down across the big man's chest. Percy screamed and twisted in his chains, fighting to escape the pain. Alex didn't give him a chance to recover. He slashed his cleaver beneath Percy's other armpit, drawing a similar gash across his fatty skin. Percy arched his back, his screams echoing around the room. The splits beneath his arms vomited torrents of blood across the floor. Alex watched grimly, gaining a sick satisfaction from the sight.

When Percy had settled slightly, tears clinging to his eyes, his breath coming in shuddering gasps, Alex circled around behind him.

"This is going to hurt even worse," Alex whispered. He stooped and brought his cleaver back once more.

In one violent motion, he severed Percy's Achilles tendons, the wide blade making quick work of the exposed flesh.

Percy's shrieks rattled the walls, his eyes bulging and his throat tearing beneath a mountain of pain. Blood gushed around his feet and he struggled to remain standing, caught between his torn tendons and the cuts under his armpits. Every time he slumped down, unable to take the pain, the gashes beneath his arms widened, the skin parting as it took the full brunt of his weight.

Alex stepped back, his eyes murderous. Sam stood at the doorway, arms crossed, his face unreadable.

Alex wiped the blood from his cleaver and his eyes rose to meet Percy's, "Fuck, that looks like it hurts."

Percy whimpered and screamed, his ankles giving out, his arms tearing.

Alex turned to Sam, "I'm done here. Leave him up and lock the door."

Sam cocked an eyebrow.

"I want to give him plenty of time to understand what dying feels like," Alex growled.

"Suit yourself."

Percy, sliding in his own blood, howled at them, "Don't leave me in here! Please!"

Alex placed a hand on the door and took one last look at the squirming mess, "Goodbye Percy." He shut the door on the man, Percy's screams now muted behind the barrier. Alex slid the deadbolt in place and turned away.

"Let's get out of here."

Sam led them down the hall and back into the room with all the bodies. Alex paid them no attention this time, his mind numb beneath the fading rage. He felt no sympathy for Percy, no regret. The man deserved every hell he got.

They walked to the stairwell and began to descend toward the street. Their footsteps echoed loudly above their heads and Alex wondered again if he was making the right choice. As they reached the next floor, he decided it wouldn't do any good to dwell on it anymore. He realized that at the end of the day, he was tired of thinking about it. He was tired of always wondering what the next move should be. He had grown weary. It was the bags beneath his eyes, the darkness around his heart, the ache every step brought. It was the death that surrounded him wherever he went, the sadness that seemed never-ending.

He was ready to just...stop...fighting...

Sam halted ahead of him.

Alex slowed and was about to ask why, but before he could, he saw Will sitting on the stairs, obstructing their progress. He had an arm wrapped around his side and his breath came in short, halting pulls. A small puddle of bloody drool oozed at his feet.

"You ok?" Sam asked, helping Empire to his feet.

He grunted, "I'm fine. Figured I'd just wait for you guys. I'd feel pretty stupid if I broke my neck walking down some steps. I need your eyes again, Sam."

Sam nodded and waited. After a moment, his sockets flared red and Empire nodded, "That's better. Don't care much for the darkness." He turned to Alex, "You take care of your business?" Alex just nodded. Empire winced and stood, hissing quietly between his teeth.

"Good. Let's get outside then."

Together they traveled the last of the stairs and stepped out into the parking garage. As they exited the office building, Alex noted the sky had taken on a soft glow. Sunrise was nearly upon them.

But as they walked toward the empty street, something appeared to be different. It was the colors.

They reached the end of the garage and stepped out into the open air. As they did so, all three of them slowed and Alex felt his pulse quicken. He looked up past the rising skyscrapers and slowly spun in place, taking in the eerie glow.

The sky was thick with red clouds, a rolling ocean of smog that drifted silently overhead. It filled the heavens and sent a worm of unease crawling through Alex's stomach.

"We don't have much time," Empire muttered, gazing through Sam's eyes at the strange display of eerie light.

"Where exactly are we going?" Alex asked, unable to take his eyes away from the crimson expanse above them.

"Tower 15," Sam answered, "It'll take a couple hours to reach it on foot and that's if we hurry."

"Hold on," Alex said slowly, finally pulling his eyes from the clouds, "We just passed a ton of vehicles in that garage. Why don't we take one of them?"

Sam blinked.

Empire placed a hand on his arm, "Go get one and hurry up. These clouds, the sky...the clock is ticking." Sam nodded and sprinted away, back into the garage.

"You ok?" Empire asked at his side.

Alex turned, "What? Yeah...I'm fine."

"I gotta say, I'm a little surprised you decided to come with us," Empire said.

"At this point, what fucking difference does it make?"

Empire nodded, "Yeah…can I ask you something?"

"Sure."

"Do you still want to kill me?"

Alex turned and looked into his brother's beaten face. He studied it for a moment and then let his eyes fall away, "I don't know…"

"I wouldn't fight it, if that's what you wanted."

"I know you wouldn't."

Empire let his arms hang at his sides and exhaled wearily. He tested his swollen lips with his tongue and ran a hand across his ribs. He seemed to be in great pain and Alex saw his hands were shaking. An awkward silence drifted between them, filled only by a gentle breeze.

Alex closed his eyes and kept his voice low, "Look…when we get to wherever we're going…I need you to do something."

"And what's that?"

Alex looked toward the parking garage, "I need you to let Sam go."

Empire said nothing, waiting for Alex to continue.

"I don't even know if you can, but if I'm going to keep on living…I don't want to do it alone. I don't think I could bear it."

"I was wondering when you would ask…" Empire said quietly.

"So you can do it? You can make him normal again?"

Empire snorted, "Normal…sure Alex, I can make him normal. I won't need his eyes anymore anyway."

"Promise me, Will."

Empire let his head fall back across his shoulders and sighed, "You know, part of me wishes you could see like he does, if only for a moment. I've thought about that a lot over the years. I've considered turning you into one of them. A Red Eye. Not so that I would have you under my control, but so that you could really understand why I'm doing what I'm doing."

"You've been brainwashed. Everyone knows that's what the Gargoyles do," Alex said.

Empire shook his head, "You're wrong. All they do is show us what a pathetic people we are. We don't deserve existence. I mean Jesus…what have we done with it?"

Alex remained silent, his gaze returning to the rolling red clouds.

"You know why I never turned you?" Empire asked, "Why I couldn't?"

Alex shot him a look out of the corner of his eye, "Why?"

"Same reason you can't kill me."

Alex let his eyes fall back to earth, a wave of exhaustion pouring through him.

Before either of them could speak again, a loud noise erupted from the garage.

"Seems like he got one running," Alex muttered.

Sure enough, a couple seconds later, Sam pulled out onto the street behind the wheel of a beat-up Toyota. He kicked the door open and motioned toward them.

"Come on, she's got plenty of gas," he called.

"Let's finish this," Empire said, his voice worn.

Chapter 15

Alex sat in the back seat with Sam at the wheel and Empire riding shotgun. Memphis slowly disappeared behind them as the small car accelerated toward Tower 15. The sky continued to heave thick red clouds across the heavens and once or twice, Alex thought he heard thunder.

Empire rested his head against the window. Alex listened to him take labored breaths, small tugs of air that he seemed to struggle to get down. He continuously shifted in his seat, adjusting himself and grunting every time he moved.

Sam noticed and shot him a look from behind the wheel, "Are you ok?"

"I'm fine. Just drive."

The road opened up once they reached the city limits and took them across an array of sprawling hills and flatlands. Clusters of trees and empty gas stations littered the roadside, both equally dead. The land had taken on a strange red hue, a reflection of the sky overhead. Sam kept his eyes on the road and applied generous encouragement to the car. The engine whined in protest but dutifully obeyed. Alex let his eyes drift across the landscape, his mind a crowded chamber of dark thought. No matter how he looked at it, he kept coming back to the same conclusion.

This isn't going to end well.

"How much further to the Tower?" He asked.

"Just up ahead," Empire coughed, his voice heavy with effort, "Look, you can see it."

Alex glanced out the windshield and saw his brother was right. Tower 15 loomed in the distance, its dark summit poking sharply toward the stratosphere. His stomach dropped when he realized that it was alive with energy, a massive beam of light soaring from its twin spires, cutting through the clouds and into space.

"Jesus," he whispered, soaking in the spectacle. The pillar of red pulsed, its center white with power, a beacon of dread reaching out toward the end times.

The next few minutes passed in muted awe. Alex leaned forward in his seat, unable to tear his eyes away from the Tower. The sight of it brought reality into razor-sharp focus and he found himself deeply unnerved.

How did we get here? He thought hopelessly. *How the hell did we get here?*

Sam edged the car up a rise, the Tower coming fully into view. As he did so, his knuckles tightened around the wheel and his voice rose with a concerned cry.

"Empire!" He cried, pointing toward the structure.

Empire sat up, suddenly alert. Through Sam's eyes, he saw the cause of concern.

"What the hell is this?" He asked weakly.

Alex leaned forward and looked ahead of them. When he did so, his throat tightened and his stomach dropped out.

An army of vehicles roared toward the Tower from the

opposite side, their numbers in the dozens. Trucks, cars, buses, and a scattering of military automotives kicked up a thick cloud of dust in their wake. As Alex's eyes fell upon them, they opened fired upon the Tower.

Men and women hung out of the windows, armed to the teeth, their automatic weapons popping loudly across the hills. RPG's were hoisted and aimed from the flatbeds of pickups. Fifty-caliber guns spat shells from the roofs of the military Hummers, a trail of white fire that peppered into the walls of Tower 15. A moment later and the rockets were loosed, a screaming line of explosions that connected with the dark walls, blowing chunks of it away.

"No," Empire whispered, "no, no, no!" He spun around to Alex, his lips lined with dried blood, "What the hell is this!?"

"Percy," Alex whispered, watching as the convoy fanned out and reloaded their firepower. "He did this."

"What are you talking about!?" Sam yelled, stomping down on the gas.

"He told me this would happen," Alex said, his ears picking up the chatter of gunfire as the barrage continued.

"Who are they!?" Sam practically screamed, his eyes flaring.

Alex watched as four trucks split off from the pack and unleashed another wave of rockets at the Tower. They detonated on impact, blowing a large piece of black substance away.

"ALEX!"

He fumbled, trying to recall what Percy had said, his voice strained, "They're one of the northern groups. He told me about them when I was in captivity. They were supposed to make one last push, one more effort to take out the Towers."

"Why the FUCK didn't you say something!?" Sam roared.

"I've been a little busy trying to stay alive!" Alex yelled back.

"We have to do something," Empire said, rolling his window down, "If we don't get on top of that Tower, we'll be caught up in the blast." He pointed toward the cluster of trucks with the RPGs, "Get closer to them, Sam. NOW!"

Sam gunned the engine and jerked the wheel, the small car bouncing off road and down a small slope toward the attackers. They were about a hundred yards away, circling the Tower and preparing for another assault. The main force began to curl around from the other side, a steady stream of gunfire cracking the air. Alex looked up toward the summit of the Tower and saw a Gargoyle peering down at them, hands at its sides, its eyes unmoving upon its stalks.

"Hurry Sam," Empire urged, sitting up on the window and sticking half his body outside. He coughed violently as dust entered his lungs and Alex saw his fingers come away bloody as he wiped his mouth.

Sam directed the Toyota toward the trucks, trying to cut them off before they unleashed another volley. Now only fifty yards away, it appeared as if they hadn't been spotted yet, all eyes trained on the Tower. Alex could see the passengers in the back, scrambling with their weapons. The drivers focused on navigating the rough terrain, unaware that Empire was preparing to unleash fury upon them.

At twenty yards, the car bouncing violently, Empire began to glow. His body became engulfed in red light as he raised a hand toward the trucks.

A moment later, he unleashed a wave of raw power at them, a wall of crimson that exploded from his fingertips and raced viciously across the open ground. The drivers finally took notice of their attackers and only had a split second to gasp before they were obliterated beneath the roaring destruction.

The trucks exploded violently backwards, flipping high into the air, ablaze with searing flame. The passengers in the beds were incinerated instantly, shadows of darkness that vanished beneath the onslaught. Crunching metal collided with dry earth and fragments of debris thundered heavily to the ground.

Empire slid back into the car, the light around him vanishing. He leaned over in his seat, clutching his chest, gasping. His body shuddered violently and he winced beneath a series of throat-tearing coughs. He covered his mouth and when he finally stopped the brutal hacking, his hands were splattered with blood. He leaned back, breathing heavily, and swallowed the rest of it down.

"What is going on?" Sam asked, concerned, continuing to skirt the car around the Tower. The roar of engines could be heard in the distance, followed by more gunfire and explosions.

"I'm fine," Empire wheezed, a trickle of blood escaping the corner of his mouth, "we just have to get inside the Tower."

"This is your fault!" Sam growled, spinning back to look at Alex, "look at what you fucking did to him!"

"Stop Sam," Empire grunted, "it doesn't matter."

Suddenly, without warning, Alex became aware of something growing quickly in his backseat window. Distracted by Sam's outburst, he hadn't noticed it until right at that moment. He turned, eyes going wide, heart leaping into his throat with frantic urgency.

"Look out!" He screamed, seconds before a truck plowed into the side of the Toyota.

The impact was immediate and terrible. Alex's side of the car took the full brunt of the collision, his body whipping painfully across the backseat and slamming into the opposite side. Stars exploded across his vision and he heard Empire yelling from somewhere in the chaos. His vision rattled as the Toyota flipped over on its side, a deafening screech of metal and shattered glass ringing in his ears. The world went sideways and then upside down, a trembling shift of perspective that brought blood gushing from his nose as it struck the door he had fallen against.

Blinking back a blackout, he felt the car mercifully stop rolling and come to a halt. He smelled gasoline and tasted copper on his tongue. Dazed, vision shaking, he tried to orient himself. Glass crunched beneath his body as he shifted in the debris, hand outstretched to grab at the broken frame. Grunting, head pounding, he pulled himself upright out of the shattered window and onto the red-tinted earth.

He wiped blood from his face and put a hand to his temple, squeezing his eyes shut. Noise swam in and out of the background. Someone was calling his name. He got to one knee and opened his eyes, the Tower looming before him. More explosions detonated against it, a blossom of fire that filled his head with their thunder.

"Alex! Sam!"

Alex turned back to the overturned Toyota and saw Empire crawling from the wreckage. His hands shook as they grasped at clods of dirt, painfully wriggling his body free from the smoking ruin.

"I'm here!" Alex called weakly, limping over to his brother. He grabbed him from beneath the arms and hauled him to his feet. Empire fell back weakly against the car and clutched his head in both hands, the cloth around his face whipping in the growing wind.

"Sam!?" Empire called, his voice thick.

Alex ducked down and peered into the flipped car and saw

Sam crumpled against the wheel, upside down. His eyes were closed and he seemed completely unresponsive to Empire's cries.

"Oh shit," Alex croaked, dropping to his stomach. He wriggled in through the passenger window and reached out to grab his friend.

"Sam? SAM!" Alex yelled, terrifyingly aware that the clock was ticking. He shook Sam aggressively, trying to remain conscious himself. Sam flopped limply onto his side and remained unresponsive.

Outside the roar of his own pulse, Alex became attuned to a growing thunder, a symphony of engines headed in their direction.

"Shit, Sam come on buddy!" Alex pleaded, grabbing him by the arms and tugging him back out of the car with him. He tried to ignore the glass beneath his stomach, a thousand tiny teeth that bit into his shirt, arms, and legs.

"Alex what's going on!?" Empire yelled.

Alex heaved Sam completely out of the car and laid him gently down on the ground. He checked for a pulse and was relieved to find one.

"ALEX!"

Spinning, Alex stood, his senses filled with the growl of approaching vehicles.

"Fuck," he hissed, dread filling him.

Ten trucks were racing their way, armed to the teeth with a furious mob. He guessed they would reach them in less than a minute.

"What's happening!?" Empire yelled, "I can't fucking SEE!"

Alex felt his throat tighten as he realized what had happened. He hopelessly looked down at Sam, heart racing, the convoy approaching. Already he could hear gunfire wildly being shot in their direction.

Alex grabbed Empire by the shoulders and pulled him forward, "We're fucking dead if you don't do something!"

Empire stumbled, hands outstretched, "Where are they!? How many!?" He suddenly coughed painfully and doubled over, an onslaught of agony ripping through his body. Alex caught him before he could fall over, his eyes shooting to the approaching trucks.

"Ten, directly ahead of us!" Alex yelled into his brother's ear.

Empire raised his hands to them, trying to gauge their approach by the snarl of speeding motors and scattered gunfire. Blood oozed from the corners of his mouth and his chest rose and fell with hellish effort. His shoulders slumped weakly and his knees buckled as he directed his outstretched hands.

Alex stood behind him and gently gripped Empire's forearms, "Over to the left," he whispered in his ear, "there."

Gasping, body trembling, Empire began to glow. As he ignited, bullets whistled past them, the trucks almost upon them, a wall of guns, gasoline, and explosives.

Alex squeezed his brother's arm, his voice low in Empire's ear, "Give it all you got."

Red power sparked from the tips of Empire's fingers, his mouth twisted in pained effort. Lightning grew and expanded, taking shape before them.

"Hurry!" Alex pleaded, a bullet streaking dangerously past his head.

Empire screamed, body convulsing, as the dancing power took shape. Beneath his hands, Alex felt Empire's muscles cramp and tighten, the bones shifting as he poured himself into the attack.

The crimson lightning spun and twirled, forming a towering tornado of devastating destruction. The heat burned Alex's skin and he squinted against it as it continued to grow and expand, a massive funnel of swirling chaos and death.

Empire screamed as the bones in his arms suddenly snapped and popped through the skin, bringing with it an explosion of blood and flesh. Alex, temples throbbing, panic erupting across his scattered mind, desperately compressed the exposed bone, his fingers slipping as they tried to hold his brother together.

Howling, spasming, Empire unleashed the tornado.

It traveled the short distance to the trucks in less than a second, a whirlwind of metal tearing power that barreled into the convoy with the force of a locomotive. It connected in a blinding eruption, a booming collision that annihilated and scattered the trucks like they had been punched by the fist of some titanic force. Alex watched as the vehicles went airborne and came apart, the frames blown to bits as if a bomb had gone off. Flaming pieces rained down before them like a storm, an iron rain that collided with the dry earth.

Empire immediately fell back into Alex's arms, his face sickly pale, a sheen of sweat coating his skin.

"Did I get them?" He asked faintly, his voice horribly distant.

"You got them," Alex assured, taking his brother's weight.

"Sam? Is he alright?"

Alex glanced at his friend's motionless body, "He's alive."

"I need him," Empire winced, forcing himself up.

Alex made sure Empire wouldn't fall over with exhaustion before kneeling next to Sam. He stole a quick look toward the Tower, toward the attackers. Someone was shouting through a bullhorn, instructing the remaining thirty-odd vehicles to focus all firepower at the Tower. Pieces of the black construct continued to pepper away as it was struck.

"We need to get inside," Empire wheezed, "get him up."

Alex shook Sam by the shoulders and checked his pulse again, "Hey, Sam, wake up man. Come on, buddy, I know you're still with us."

Sam's eyes stirred behind his eyelids and then with a troubled groan, he opened them. He looked disoriented and in pain, his face contorted with discomfort.

His voice was thick, "What happened?"

"We got blindsided. Nothing we could have done about it," Alex said quickly, "get up, we don't have much time. Are you ok?"

"I'm goddamn wonderful," Sam coughed, pulling himself to his feet with the aid of Alex. He looked at Empire and his entire face drained, "Jesus Christ, what happened to your arms?"

Alex glanced at the exposed bone lifting out of the skin, the trickles of blood running down Empire's hands and dripping off his fingers. Both of his arms looked like they had been smashed with a hammer.

Empire swallowed hard, his voice heavy with effort, "My body's failing."

Sam seemed to push his own pain aside and ripped his shirt into rags. He went to Empire and grimaced.

"This is going to hurt," He warned. Slowly, he began to wrap Empire's arms, using the cloth to compress the bone back beneath the torn skin. Empire grit his teeth, spittle escaping from his lips as Sam worked, his breath terribly stunted.

Alex watched the convoy, the assault still in full bloom. It sounded like a war, a barrage of explosives and gunfire splintering the red heavens. The trucks and buses continued to trace a slow circle around Tower 15.

And the damage was starting to show.

"Your eyes," Empire hissed when Sam was finished, "I need them for just a little longer."

"Of course."

Empire nodded and suddenly Sam's eyes flared once more. Empire's shoulders seemed to relax, just a little.

"Into the Tower," He breathed, hobbling forward without waiting. Alex and Sam followed closely, watching intently as the cluster of vehicles disappeared around the opposite side of the Tower.

"Why have they stopped attacking us?" Sam asked, limping slightly, boots churning up dust.

"Because their best chance is to hit the Tower, not me," Empire panted. "They had to learn the hard way, just like they always do."

They ran as fast as their battered bodies would allow, an insistent willpower fueling them past their pain. Empire was clearly struggling, each breath coming in wet gasps. Blood began to soak through the rags around his arms and it dripped lazily from his chin. His legs threatened to give out as he hurried along, each step bringing a strained grunt. Sam offered help, a silent gesture, but Empire shrugged him off.

They were almost to the base of the Tower when the roar of engines filled the air once again as the small army completed their circuit.

Stumbling, tripping, panting heavily, the three reached the looming black walls and practically slammed into it. Alex looked over his shoulder as Empire weakly activated the door, his ruined arms streaking scarlet rivers through the bandages.

The head of the pack rolled into view, a trio of trucks and a single bus, each packed with militants. When they saw Alex, Empire, and Sam, they let out a roar of hatred and took aim, clouds of dust obscuring their vision.

"Get inside!" Empire ordered roughly as the door slid open. Alex and Sam pushed through as gunfire erupted at their backs. As they fell into the interior behind Empire, the Tower took the brunt of the assault.

Mercifully, the door slid shut at their backs.

"Christ," Alex gasped, panting, hands on his knees. Empire slumped against the wall and then threw up, his chest heaving, his mouth ejecting a torrent of bloody vomit. Sam went to his side and wrapped his arm around Empire's shoulders, pulling him up.

"We're almost there, don't give up," he urged.

Empire wiped his mouth and spat, "I can make it. Come on...we have to climb."

Alex stood up and let his eyes sweep the inside of the Tower, allowing himself another moment to catch his breath. The walls were lined with Red Eyes, each one encased in their pod. From his position, it looked like a thousand rubies sparkling from the recess of some dark mine. The strange half-coffins rose all the way to the high ceiling, each one filled with an unmoving body.

"Alex, are you ok?" Sam asked, shaking Alex from his daze.

Alex blinked and exhaled, "What? Yeah...let's get this over with."

Empire finally allowed Sam to help him as they began to climb the spiraling stairs that wrapped around the inner column. Alex trailed them, listening to the walls groan and shake beneath the attack.

Halfway up and his legs turned to anchors. His muscles burned fiercely as he fought to just put one foot in front of the other. Empire threw up again, a violent ejection that left him dazed.

"Almost there," Sam assured, his own chest rising and falling, sweat standing out on his brow. Empire's face was white beneath the rag, great beads of perspiration rolling thickly down his cheeks and neck.

"I can make it," he gasped hoarsely.

They continued, the twisting stairs seemingly never-ending. Alex gripped the rail fiercely and stared at his feet, his thighs screaming, his feet heavy, his lungs dying. Sam had taken almost the full weight of Empire, his body slumped awkwardly across Sam's shoulders. Once or twice, Alex almost slipped in the trail of blood left in their wake.

Finally, when he thought his body would simply not go on any further, they reached the summit.

The ceiling pressed down on top of them and the stairs seemed to just disappear through it. Empire, half-conscious, raised a trembling hand and activated the hatch. It hissed open and blinding red light filtered through the square opening.

Sam hauled himself and Empire through first and Alex followed. As he stepped out onto the summit, he collapsed, his legs giving out. He rolled onto his back, dazed. He closed his eyes and fought to just pull down the next breath, his whole body burning. A hot wind whipped across his face, filled with dust and grit.

Finally, after a couple of seconds, he forced himself to open his eyes once again. The vermillion sky filled his vision...and took his breath away once more.

Extending from the thick ocean of cloud was something that

grew from a nightmare. It turned his blood to ice and a scream rose in his throat as his vision was consumed by the sky-filled horror.

It was a giant humanoid face, unlike anything Alex had ever seen before. It protruded out of the sky and loomed over the earth like some demented moon. Its size was daunting, its grotesque features consuming the heavens. Jutting from its pale snout was a fleshy tube the size of a continent. It slithered around the abhorrent head and back into the planet the beast grew from. Bulging from its eye sockets were similar abominations, twin hoses of squirming pink that had been jammed into its skull. A colossal hand soared past the horizon, beyond the limits of Earth, disappearing into the eternity of space.

Eyes bulging, Alex looked behind the elongated limb and titan sized head. Through the parted clouds, he saw the god-sized monster was attached to something that could only be another planet, a black orb that cracked apart at the surface to make room for the birthed behemoth. The titan, the nightmare horror, leaned over the Earth like some kind of predator, its presence expanding across the length of the cosmos.

"Oh *god...*" Alex whispered, heart thundering, disbelief and terror sparking across his exhausted body.

The giant in the sky moved, a great, creaking explosion of sound, like boulders grinding together. It positioned its head directly over the world and stared down at Alex with eyes that weren't there, the ruined planet like an eclipse behind its head.

Slowly, terribly, the tubes protruding from its face began to shift and detach, pulling away from the planet. The sound was indescribable, the most nauseating thing Alex had ever heard and it turned his stomach to rot.

The ends of the colossal tubes finally tore free from the

planet and hung limply from the titan's face. After a moment, they wriggled in the stratosphere and dipped down, like hollowed out worms burrowing through the air. They cut through the glowing heavens and reached for Earth, the ends of tubes a trio of emptiness that looked like black holes of absolute darkness.

"Incredible..." Alex heard Empire whisper at his side.

Unable to look away, Alex shuddered a question through his quivering lips, "What the fuck *is* that?!"

"The Gargoyle's vessel," Empire replied, his voice lined with awe, "their eternal engine."

The trinity of tubes continued to extend toward the Earth and Alex realized the planet-sized monster was about to attach itself to the world.

The impact happened with earth-shaking force, the mammoth dark tunnels disappearing beneath the horizons like wriggling fingers. The ground shook as they latched onto the world, the Tower trembling violently beneath them, a thunderous groan rising from the broken continents. The face in the sky twisted, its neck creaking as the protrusions from its face made landfall, the planet-sized leviathan docking horribly above the earth.

Alex became dimly aware that he was being pulled to his feet. He couldn't seem to look away from the monster above him, the planet at its back absorbing his attention.

"Alex," Sam was saying from somewhere to his right, "Alex, get up." He let himself stand, a hand guiding him up. He found his feet, his neck craned, his mouth open. Sam shook him.

"Get behind us," Empire muttered, wobbling weakly at Alex's side, "get behind us right now."

Finally, Alex snapped out of his trance and looked at his

brother. Empire's face was pale and rugged, his mouth hanging open as he fought to breathe. He looked like a corpse.

Sam pulled Alex toward him, "You're not supposed to be up here," he hissed.

Alex stumbled forward and Empire pushed him behind Sam and himself. Confused, Alex looked past them, at what had been standing at his back.

Tower 15's Gargoyle rose before them, a menacing statue of alien fury. He had never seen one up close and its appearance turned his legs to jelly. It was at least ten feet tall, its thin black body exposing open ribs of a similar shade. Its long arms hung low, ending in sharp claws that looked like broken rock formations. Its head sat upon a squirming neck, a wide slab of bone that extended outward past its narrow shoulders. Two stalks wriggled out of the face, ending in grotesque red orbs that pulsed and slithered beneath a translucent casing. The Gargoyle stepped toward them, its mouth opening to reveal soft tendrils that hung from jagged pink gums. They looked like a nest of slugs, each one alive with their own desires.

Empire raised a trembling hand to it, his other shielding Alex at his back, "He's with me," he rasped, "leave him alone."

The Gargoyle took another step forward, its stony fingers clacking together, its eyes alive with burning intensity.

"You got what you wanted!" Empire roared suddenly, "you don't need him! Ignite the FUCKING Towers!"

The Gargoyle stopped, a foot away, its neck craning down to stare at the three. Alex met its gaze, fear and exhaustion clashing in his frazzled mind.

The Tower shook suddenly as the onslaught from below continued, a wave of explosions rocketing into the crumbling structure. The Gargoyle snapped its head up and emitted a gurgling groan, a sickening sound that squished from its throat.

"Do you want to die!?" Empire yelled, staring up at the creature, "What are you waiting for!?" He pointed to the sky, at the titan above, "Your planet is here! Ignite the goddamn Towers and end this!"

The Gargoyle glared at Empire, but slowly stepped back. Alex felt himself exhale. The creature walked to the center of the platform, the heavenly fiend immobile above. Alex watched in muted terror as the Gargoyle got down on its knees and pressed its elongated hands against the surface of the Tower. Then, slowly, it began to groan once more, its sickly voice rising in pitch.

As it did so, crimson fog began to seep through the floor and contort around the Gargoyles body, a swirling dance of color that grew with intensity the longer the creature howled. Alex felt the air around him begin to heat, a pulsating sensation that thickened and pressed in around his body.

Empire grabbed him by the arm and pulled him down with Sam at their side.

"What the hell is it doing?" Alex gasped.

Empire said nothing as the groaning moans continued to rattle from the mouth of the Gargoyle, its body almost completed hidden beneath a wall of red mist. Alex felt his throat tighten and all the moisture in the air seemed to vanish.

Then, in a screech of terrible fury, the Tower erupted.

Alex slammed his eyes shut against the magnitude of power, a rippling wall of flame that shot out from all sides and swept over the earth in a tsunami of blazing wrath. In the brief glimpse that he had been allowed, it looked to Alex like a nuclear warhead had been shot directly into the earth, a massive inverted mushroom cloud blooming from the base of the Tower. The heat was incredible and Alex thought his skin would sizzle off his bones as the blast detonated across the world, joining the twenty-five other Towers in a display of devastation that coated the land in absolute annihilation.

Below them, the army vanished into vapor, the trees were swept away, the earth shriveled, and cities were evaporated. The extension of the discharge rumbled monstrously outward, the wall of fire reaching for the very corners of every doomed horizon.

Alex curled into himself beneath the destruction, hands covering his head in a gesture of hopeless fear. His body blasted with incredible heat and a furious gale threatened to scoop him up in its treacherous claws. If he had been able to breathe, he would have screamed, his ears deafened beneath the eruption.

Stars exploded behind his eyelids and nausea punched him in the stomach. He thought somewhere beyond the hellish ruin, he was whimpering.

And then…painfully…miserably…the eternal blast began to fade. The storm around him began to settle. The world stopped shaking and the stars vanished behind the darkness of his eyes. His head thundered, but it was now contained and alone, the outside influence ebbing away to the ash-stained hills.

Still curled into himself, he felt a hand on his shoulder.

"Are you alive?"

He didn't want to answer. He didn't want to move. His ears rang from the aftermath of the blast, his lips were lined with dust, and his tongue stuck to the roof of his mouth.

"Alex?"

Hesitantly, he opened his eyes. Empire leaned down above him, his hands cupping Alex's face.

"You ok?" He asked.

Alex just stared up at him, unable to speak. His head buzzed, a disbelieving charge of shock leaving him paralyzed.

Empire wiped grime from Alex's face and then pointed above them, toward the rolling heavens, "Look…"

Alex forced his eyes past his brother and when he did, he found himself shaken by new horrors.

The planet at the titan's back was alive with activity, a streaking endless wave of red comets that soared across the space between worlds. They were in the millions, an unfathomable number of smoke trails that arched from the surface of the cracked planet and descended down to Earth. It looked like the remains of some explosion, each smoldering trail a red piece of debris.

"Here they come," Empire muttered, his voice filled with awe.

He struggled to stand and Sam came to his side, his face black and covered with soot, but alive. He helped Empire to his feet and threw an arm around his shoulders for support. Alex, feeling like he was trapped in some otherworldly dream, stood and joined them. Together, they raised what eyes they had to the heavens and watched the comets – the Gargoyles – descend to Earth.

"I can't believe it," Empire whispered, watching the scene through Sam's eyes, "I've waited so *long*…"

Alex clawed for his voice and when he found it, it came out ragged and thin, "Is this really what you wanted…? After all we've been through, this is the end you fucking *wanted*?"

Empire faced his brother and smiled, an unexpected display of sadness, "Not this…" He waved his arm across the world, "*This*…"

Alex lowered his eyes and swept them slowly across the charred land. As he did so, he felt his nausea return, an empty twist in his gut.

Everything was gone. Every tree, every rock, every piece of evidence that this planet had ever been anything more than an empty, lonely world.

"It's all...ash..." Empire whispered. "No more noise...no more people...no more misery." He placed a hand on the back of Alex's neck, "Do you hear how quiet it is now? Listen...just...listen...they're gone. They're all...fucking...*gone.*"

His voice softened even more, a gentle trickle, "I know you don't understand this...I know this whole thing is terrifying to you...but even so, I'm glad you're here with me, Alex. It wouldn't feel right without you next to me. Just like it used to be. Two kids standing shoulder to shoulder as everything around them went to hell."

Alex realized he was shaking, his mind trying to catch up with the level of destruction that had eradicated everything before his very eyes, his brother's words ringing hollow in his ears.

He pulled himself away from Empire's touch, his voice a strained whisper, "How the fuck do you think this is right? Do you actually believe this is...better?"

Empire turned his sad smile to Alex once more, "It doesn't matter because we won't ever have to find out..." He raised his bloodied hands to the sky, "It's over..."

Alex shook his head, mind unraveling, "You just...destroyed...*everything...*"

Empire slowly nodded, "You know how you believed there was still good in this world?"

Alex just stared at him.

"Well…" he continued, his voice lowering, "I never got to see it. And now…neither does anyone else. I can already feel the noise in my head receding. Do you know how relieved I feel, knowing I'm not leaving behind a world filled with people who've acquired what I could never seem to find? At the end of the day…that's all I wanted…"

Alex stepped away, his eyes heavy with darkness and sorrow, "God…"

"I don't think so…" Empire said distantly. "Just us."

Sam suddenly stepped forward, breaking into the conversation, his eyes alight with an alien eagerness that chilled Alex to the bone, "Please," he whispered desperately, "let me go down there now…turn me to ash. Let me be a part of this. Let's go down together."

Empire sighed and faced Sam, "You've been an incredible companion through all of this. I couldn't have asked for a better man by my side. But I'm not ready to let you go just yet. There's still one more thing I promised." His voice filled with lost memory, "The Last Tower."

Alex shook his head, confusion and chaos rumbling through him, "What's the point?! This world is EMPTY! There's nothing left!"

Empire sighed wearily, "You still want to live though, don't you?"

Alex found himself unable to understand, a terrible realization that he struggled to find an answer for, "Live? Live for what!? Will, everything is GONE!"

Empire placed a bloodied hand on Alex's arm, "There's a place I can take you. A place you'll be safe." He lowered his voice, "A place you won't have to be alone…"

Alex spread his arms, voice cracking, "Where!? What is this fucking place you keep talking about!?"

Empire turned away, his voice grim and terribly tired, "It's across the Overroad."

"I don't *understand*!" Alex cried helplessly, his mind threatening madness.

"You will," Empire said softly.

Chapter 16

They descended the staircase, leaving behind a world that no longer existed. Alex trailed Sam and Empire, his head just as empty as the land below. With each step, he felt like he plunged further into some terrible dream. A dream that he would wake from at any second. Christ…everything…*gone*…

Not just the roads and buildings, not only the cities and trees but everyone with it. All the hope, desperation, and will to survive wiped out in a matter of seconds.

We are the last three human beings alive.

The thought threatened to tumble Alex the rest of the way down. It was a terrible, overpowering thought that clung to him like a disease.

He had never felt so alone in all of his life.

How could this have happened? How could his own brother help bring about such finality to the world? He looked ahead of him, at Sam and Empire…at Will. His journey was over now. There was no one left to call him Empire. Alex shuddered, his body wrought with pain and despair, writhing beneath an isolation that seemed endless. How had Will's hatred for humanity reached such lengths? How had he grown such infectious spite for everyone around him, an anger that burned so fiercely he had eliminated the entire remaining population? Could it have been stopped? Could someone have intervened?

Could he have?

Instead of spending the past years in a vengeful hunt, should he instead have tried to reconcile the wrath Will had been nurturing? This lonely goal to bring about the end of everything?

As he watched Sam limp Will down the stairs, he saw his brother for what he was. He wasn't some all-powerful monster. He wasn't some creation birthed from the Gargoyles.

He was just a broken, deeply hurt kid who needed someone to watch out for him.

Alex grit his teeth, fighting off a wave of empathy. A battle turned in his mind, a war that's existence enraged him. Will had killed so many on his journey. He had slaughtered thousands without mercy. He had brought about the destruction of mankind in a selfish plight to satisfy his own troubled needs.

And how many did you kill trying to reach him?

Alex almost stopped. The thought traveled down from his head and sank deep into his chest. It spread out like a sickly warmth, extending across his limbs and out his fingertips.

At the end of the day…weren't you doing the same thing?

Of course not…

How many Red Eyes did you murder? How many brainwashed humans fell beneath your cleaver?

That was different…

Was it? What purpose did their deaths serve other than your own? They were simply in the way, weren't they? Obstructions that heeded the path toward your own selfish desires?

Shut up.

You were blind with need. With anger. Anything that got in your way, you eliminated. How is that any different from Will?

Alex pushed his troubled thoughts away, a darkness settling deep beneath his eyes. What the fuck did any of it matter anymore…

Sam and Will continued to descend before him, his brother's clawing breaths coming in shorter and shorter pulls. His legs threatened to give out at any moment, his clothes a bloodstain mess of dirty fabric.

Why are you still following them?

He searched the furthest extent of his mind for an answer and only found one.

He simply was not ready to let go.

The death Will so relentlessly desired was the same thing that kept Alex moving. The promise of nothing more, a longing dream for his brother, was a concept that absolutely terrified Alex. Wherever they were headed…it would be better than that.

Despite every awful heartbreak and tragedy I've suffered, I'm still not ready to give up.

It was a need he wished he didn't possess. A part of him longed to be like Will and just accept that this world held nothing else for him. But no matter how hard he tried, he simply could not accept that. Whatever awaited him he would accept as something better than death.

"We've made it," Sam said in front of him, stumbling down the last of the stairs. Will slumped miserably at his side, his face covered with sweat and dried blood. He gasped pitifully and leaned against the inner pillar, mouth agape, drawing down hungry lungfuls of air.

Alex stepped to their side and for the first time since re-entering the Tower, he looked around him. The walls were no longer shining. The glow had gone out. The thousands of

Red Eyes that lined the pods were silent, still, and dark. Their bodies slumped over in their eternal coffins, their final resting place, their purpose fulfilled.

"It's so...quiet in here," Will said between gasps, wrapping his ruined arms around himself as if he was trying to hold himself together.

"I envy them," Sam whispered.

Will's shoulders slumped and he seemed to be fighting with himself. After a moment, he raised his head and spoke, his voice dragging with remorse.

"Sam...what I did to you...you didn't deserve it. I want you to know that."

Sam shook his head aggressively, "What are you talking about? You showed me-"

"Stop," Will commanded with some effort. He paused as a chest heaving cough rattled his bones. When he finally got himself under control, his voice was thin and weak, "I used you, Sam. You were my only chance to see Alex again before the end and I took advantage of that. You might not have known the extent of my suffering growing up, but you were there just the same. You were with us through that. You were always kind to me. You never asked questions you knew you shouldn't. And after we got out, you stayed by Alex's side and helped him start a life for himself. I can honestly say you're a better man than me."

Sam looked at his feet, "You don't need to tell me that."

Will nodded painfully, "Yes I do because I need you to understand that my brother still needs you. Where I'm taking him, taking both of you...you're going to need each other. And I would feel better if I died knowing you were at his side. You're a good man, Sam. And I thank you for being such a loyal friend to the both of us. But now, it's time to let go. It's time to send you back."

"What are you-" Sam started but was cut short as Will raised his hands and covered Sam's face.

Alex stepped back as Will's body flared red, bringing with it a sharp gasp from Sam's lips. Brilliant light spun and danced around Will's fingers and slowly, carefully, he began to draw them back, away from Sam's face. As he did so, two trails of smoke followed, as if they were being drained from Sam's eyes.

It was over in a matter of seconds. Will dropped his hands to his sides and the light around his body vanished.

As did the crimson glow from Sam's eyes.

Silence filled the space between them. Sam seemed rooted in place, his mouth open, his face contorted in confused shock. He looked first to Will and then over to Alex, his eyes blinking rapidly.

Alex stepped forward, heart thundering in a sudden gasp of life, "Sam…?"

"Oh no…" Sam whispered finally, his voice sounding very far away, "oh no, what have I done…?"

Alex felt a lump form in his throat, a surge of hope that felt impossibly alien. Instead of answering, he embraced his friend in a furious hug.

Sam slowly wrapped his arms around Alex, his face still riddled with cautious fear and confusion. Finally, he pulled away and looked into Alex's face, his voice slow and uncertain.

"It wasn't a dream, was it…?"

Will was the one who answered, his voice somber and low, "I'm afraid not."

Sam stared at him and Alex saw a rising anger begin to emerge from his friend's scattered expression.

"*You...*"

Alex placed a hand on Sam's shoulder, halting any impending aggression, "It's over, Sam. Nothing matters anymore. It's just us now."

"It doesn't...matter?" Sam said, as if sampling the words.

Alex stepped between Sam and his brother, his voice careful, "What he did to you is unforgivable, but it's over now and we're both alive. There isn't time for anything else."

Snarling, Sam jabbed a finger over Alex's shoulder, "That piece of shit-"

"Please," Alex exhaled, his eyes pleading, "I know. I know how fucking pissed you probably are. I am, too. I mean, Jesus, you're my best friend and I've been searching like hell to find you. To get you back." He gripped Sam's shoulder, "And now you are. Let's get out of here and put all this shit behind us. As much as you probably want to kill Will, we need him right now. Let's just...let's just go."

Sam glared at Will, his eyes his own once more. His fists clenched at his sides and his teeth ground together. For a second, Alex thought Sam was going to launch himself past him and attack his brother, but the moment passed and Sam relaxed slightly.

"Do you know what he's done?" Sam whispered, venom dripping from his tongue.

"Of course I do," Alex said, "better than most."

Sam met Alex's eyes, "The only reason I'm not beating his fucking skull in is because you're asking me not to."

Alex nodded grimly, "I understand. Now let's get out of here." Sam nodded slowly. Alex squeezed his arm again, drawing close, "Hey...I'm glad you're back, man. I missed you."

Sam just stared straight ahead, "Yeah..."

Together, they turned their attention back to Will who was leaning heavily against the inner column, a hand to his chest. Blood trickled lazily from between his teeth and his clothes stuck to his bruised body in sweaty clumps.

"We ready?" He asked, his voice like steam.

"Do it," Alex said.

Will heaved himself away from the wall and turned to face it. He raised his hands and placed his palms flat against the cold surface. Before he opened the door, he cocked his head blindly toward Sam.

"If you want to kill me once we get inside…I'll understand. At this point, it doesn't matter how I go, I'll welcome it however it comes. But…if you choose to do it, at least let me show you where you need to go."

"Just get us through," Sam growled.

Wordlessly, Will turned back to the wall and activated the inner door. It slid open with ease revealing a cool blue fog that wafted out from the interior. It fell weakly around Will's feet and without waiting, he entered the chamber. Sam looked at Alex, and together they followed him inside. Alex heard the door close at his back as he strode into the fog, a chill engulfing his legs. It spun and swirled like a vortex up the length of his body and he watched Will through the haze. Sam stood at his side, his face like stone, his eyes like chips of cold rock.

Will held his hands out at his sides and his body began to glow. It was a weak pulse of red that peaked briefly from the tips of his fingers. Alex slowly became aware that the fog was thickening and before he knew it, he was lost in it.

And then everything vanished. In a moment of panicked vertigo, he reached out for something to hold onto as his vision went dark. Empty black surrounded him and he realized he couldn't see his hands. He couldn't even feel them. He opened his mouth to speak but was horrified to find he couldn't. Terrible claustrophobia flooded his frantic mind and he felt as if he would die beneath its insistent rise. He could sense his heart racing, but he couldn't identify where exactly. Right as he thought he would go mad, the world righted itself once again.

Alex blinked and gasped, stumbling forward, relieved to feel solid ground beneath his boots. Sam and Will appeared around him, catching themselves before they fell.

"What the hell was that?" Alex croaked. But before he could get an answer, he raised his eyes and swept them across the landscape stretching out before him.

A sea of rolling, impossibly dark hills rose and fell across a purple horizon. The ebony earth was layered with a strange purple grid that plastered itself across the rippling expanse. Mind reeling, he looked to the sky and saw a smattering of eerie stars that seemed to vibrate in place, a million pinpricks that dotted the heavens.

Pathways snaked and slithered away from him, a twisting maze of roads that spooled out like yarn and disappeared into the strange landscape. His senses absorbed it all with cautious wonderment, his mind trying to make sense of what his eyes fed it.

"Where are we?" He finally managed to get out.

"The Overroad," Will whispered back, his voice echoing gently into the perfect silence. "The world between the Towers."

Alex continued to take it all in, his eyes wide, "Is this...their world?"

Will shook his head, "No. Just the space between. You need to keep your voice down, we're not alone out here."

Alex looked at Sam, a trickle of unease worming its way into his stomach, "You've been here?"

"Once. Briefly. It's where Will lost his eyes." His voice cascaded across the sky, a series of muted echoes.

"I'm powerless in this place," Will explained, "so I won't be able to protect you if it comes for us."

"If what comes?"

Will lowered his voice until it was almost inaudible, "Hopefully you won't have to find out. Come on, we're wasting time. Can either of you see a pink glow on the horizon?"

Alex spun in place, letting his eyes crawl over the gridded black hills. As he turned, his boots clacked loudly on the road and Will shot his hand out and grabbed his arm. He put a finger to his lips.

"Be. Quiet."

Alex nodded numbly and took greater care as he continued his search. The sky looked like it was moments before some alien dawn, the purple hue lifting from the skyline and up into the darkness that held the shivering stars.

Sam pointed to their left, "There. I see it."

Alex saw it as well. It was faint, nothing more than a slight pink glimmer, a soft bloom that rested against the horizon.

"What is that?" He asked, making sure to keep his voice down.

Will leaned in close, "The Last Tower. There are no roads that lead to it. We'll have to cross the hills. It shouldn't be more than a couple miles."

"We're going to abandon the road?" Sam hissed.

"It's the only way to get there," Will said. "I'll need one of you to guide me. And remember, stay as silent as possible. If we're discovered, there's not much I can do for us."

Alex took Will's arm, assessing his brother's battered condition, "Are you going to make it?"

Will grunted, "I don't think so. Come on."

As quietly as they could, the three left the road and began to trek across the hills. Alex felt a shiver run through him as he stepped cautiously across the hard ground. The black was so dense that it gave off the illusion he'd fall through it into some terrible void below. In the distance, he could faintly make out blue squares of light, a littering of contrasting color against the canvas of midnight earth.

"What are those?" he whispered as quietly as he could.

"What are you looking at?" Will whispered blindly.

"Light. Blue rectangles of light."

"Those lead to the other Towers," Sam answered softly from his opposite side.

Alex fell silent, his eyes straining to take in the bizarre doorways. Will held his arm tightly, his breath ragged and labored. He moved slowly, but there was an urgency to his step. Even in the dim light, Alex saw his brother's face was terribly pale.

They walked. The hills rose and fell around them, the ever silent sky a star-filled abyss above their heads. Alex became aware of how loud the sound of his own pulse was. How each breath he exhaled was like a gale across the impossibly empty world. Despite their pained efforts, their boots sounded like hammer falls, each step echoing loudly and bouncing across the grids. He trained his eyes on the pink glow in the sky and focused intently. It was growing, expanding, its presence drawing closer.

And with each mile they walked, something else began to emerge out of the horizon. It was a peak, a sharp rise that poked up toward the discolored sky. It was like an optical illusion slowly unfolding, an unveiling of something that seemed to warp the dull light around its massive presence.

"I see something," Sam whispered.

"I see it too," Alex echoed, "It looks like…it looks like another Tower. I can see its summit."

"Good," Will heaved with some effort, "it's still there…"

Sam shot Will a look, "Did you think it wouldn't be?"

Will coughed wearily, "I don't know…"

Another mile and the Tower grew even closer, a massive, colossal thing. It's size became more apparent the nearer they drew, a mammoth structure that was double the height of the other twenty-six. It rippled from the background, the pink sky at its back acting as some sort of camouflage. Twin spires extended from its summit, a pair of sharp fingers that cut up into the stars overhead. It loomed against the glowing heavens, a silhouette of titanic proportions, a long-hidden relic from some alternate plane of existence.

Will suddenly stopped and grasped at his chest, a lung-ripping cough bellowing from his throat. He slammed a hand across his mouth and managed the mute the last of the assault, but even so, the sky echoed loudly with the pained release. Blood leaked from between his trembling fingers as he pulled away and slumped heavily against Alex, his voice a wet mumble.

"I don't have much left in me…"

Alex looked toward the Tower, "Do you need me to carry you?"

Will suppressed a muted chuckled, "No. Don't think I could bear that. You still hate me, remember?"

Alex pulled his brother's arm across his shoulders, "Then this will have to do."

They took only a handful of steps when Will fell to his knees, pulling Alex with him. Another wave of fitful coughs rattled through Will and he fought to keep the noise to a minimum as he wrestled with his failing body.

"Jesus Christ," Alex whispered, one hand on his brother's back.

Will fought to stand, but fell back to his knees, "Not my finest hour…"

Alex looked up at Sam, "Help me carry him."

Sam looked down at them both, his face filled with disgust, "Are you kidding me?"

"Please, Sam."

Sam didn't move, "Why the hell are you doing this, Alex?"

"What are you talking about?"

Sam squat down and faced them, keeping his voice low, "He's dying. Let him die. We don't need him anymore. Let's just get to the Tower and be done with it."

Alex's face turned to stone, "I'm not leaving my brother."

"It wasn't that long ago you wanted to kill him."

Alex met Sam's eyes, "What's the fucking *point* anymore…?"

Will placed a trembling hand on Alex's arm, "He's right, Alex. You don't need me. You two should just go."

Alex snapped his eyes back to his brother's beaten face, "Shut up and get up. I know you're not done yet."

A weak smile spread Will's lips, "This is what I want, remember? I was never going to go with you through the Tower. That was never a part of the plan. It's over for me so just…just get out of here and let me go."

Alex was about to protest once more, but a distant sound cut him off. It was low and muffled, an echoing wash of static that chirped faintly beyond the hills.

Sam's eyes went wide, "Oh no…"

Alex looked around, trying to pinpoint the source, "What? What is that?"

Will grabbed Alex's shoulder, his voice suddenly urgent, "It knows we're here."

"What does!?"

"The thing that took his eyes," Sam answered, his face pale.

Will struggled to his feet, teeth clenched, his legs shaking beneath the effort. He took Alex by the shoulders and brought him in close, "Get out of here. It wants me, not you. I'll distract it long enough for you two to get to the Tower."

Alex shook his head violently, "I'm not going to just leave you here!"

The static grew louder, closer, a rolling chatter that bounced off the sky and echoed ominously toward them. Underlaid beneath the white noise, Alex could make out a voice. It spoke in a language foreign to him, a rumbling, deep mumble that seeped into the darkness of his mind and unearthed a primal fear.

"Alex, we need to move," Sam whispered, his eyes darting across the hills, his face taunt.

"Goddamn you," Alex growled under his breath. He reached across his brother and hauled him close. Will groaned and slumped miserably across Alex, a strand of pink drool hanging from his lips.

"I'll get us there myself if I have to," Alex panted, adjusting his grip around Will. The static had grown alarmingly close, an insistent buzz echoing toward them from the near distance. Sam tapped his fingers against his leg, his body tense, his voice panicked.

"Hurry, Jesus Christ, *hurry!*"

Grunting, Alex limped himself and Will across the strange grid, all concern for silence abandoned as the haunting voice gurgled from the white noise at their backs. It was gaining and Alex pulled Will along as quickly as he could, his legs bowing beneath the weight.

"Don't do this," Will begged, gasping, the cloth around his eyes slipping, "Please...I'm not worth it."

"Shut up," Alex hissed, feeling his strength fading, "save your breath and *move*."

Sam was ahead of them, chancing quick glances over his shoulder. His eyes were wide and Alex saw fear ripple through them. The static rose to almost a roar at their backs, the muttered phrases coming quicker, the lost language booming in Alex's skull.

"Let me go!" Will exhaled, "It's almost on us! Alex!"

Alex felt his chest hitch, sweat standing out on his forehead, "No! We're almost there!"

The Last Tower sat squarely ahead of them, a black titan of immense size, its walls wide and almost eternally tall. They neared the doorway, traces of a purple outline glowing ominously from the midnight surface.

"Sam get th-" Alex started, but was cut short as something buzzed through him. It was like an electric shock, a massive surge of power that rendered him momentarily paralyzed. He opened his mouth to scream as pain wracked his body, but found his vocal cords were frozen in agony. He felt Will shudder at his side, a jolting seizure that trembled through him like a storm.

The world disappeared.

Color and shadow consumed his eyes, a spinning tornado of chaos. He felt like he was falling, a terrible, helpless sensation that gripped him viciously. He held onto Will with heightened desperation and realized he was screaming.

His shoulder collided with something and he grunted, bouncing away from the contact and spinning face first into something else. It squished beneath his weight, but pain rocked his bones nonetheless.

"Not him!" He heard Will scream, his voice a frayed rattled, "You don't want *him*!"

Alex, still falling, was able to find his sight once again. As the stale air whipped across his face, he tried to gain his bearings. With the world speeding past them, he realized they were falling down some kind of tunnel or hole. The walls were pink and seemed to be composed of slimy, organic matter. It looked like the inside of a throat, a massive, dark abyss that pulled them deeper into itself. Growing from the slick pink walls were tiny arms. They wriggled and twisted, reaching for Alex as he fell with long, pale fingers. Purple light glowed beneath them, a blinding orifice that signaled the end of the drop. As they fell toward it, something began to extend from the bulb of color.

"Grab onto the walls!" Will screamed in his ear, his voice cracking with fear.

Eyes watering, stomach in his throat, Alex only had a moment to react before his brother reached out and buried his hands into the soft organic matter. Immediately, Alex felt Will slip from his grip and barely managed to hold on as they both slammed into the wall. The impact pushed the air from his lungs as his body bounced into the strange, fleshy substance. Hands reached for him, a dozen tiny appendages, a hundred odd fingers, all grasping and stroking his face, arms, and legs.

Alex felt himself about to slip free from his brother and quickly grabbed onto one of the hands reaching for him from the wall. Will panted at his side, his skin soaked with sweat, blood, and grime.

"Get to the top!" Will yelled, his voice hoarse, "Don't stop and don't look down! MOVE!"

Alex looked up, his hair hanging in strands across his eyes, and saw a small circle of white light above them. It looked impossibly far away, a hundred feet at least.

"Climb!" Will roared. He screamed as he pulled them up, his broken arms cracking and splitting all over again, spraying blood across Alex's face.

Alex reached above his head and gripped another mindless hand that grew from the wall. Keeping Will tight against him, he rose. The alien hand he clutched assisted his ascension, pulling him up and toward the next. And the next. And the next. Up and up, the living throat pulsing and squishing around them.

That's when Alex became aware of something below, a presence that rose from the purple, bringing with it a brutal cold wind that hissed and slapped at his skin. As he was pulled up closer toward the circle of white, he felt his eyes drawn down below into the void.

"Don't look at it!" Will screamed into his ear, "Don't fucking look at it!"

Fighting every instinct in his body, Alex slammed his eyes shut, his teeth clacking together. The cold swirled and licked at his face, a maddening sensation that begged him to open his eyes and peer down at whatever was coming.

"Don't stop!" Will cried, "Whatever you do, don't stop! CLIMB GODDAMN IT!"

Alex could feel his brother slipping, his broken, shattered

arms giving way beneath the agony. Blood ran down them in great currents, streaming thickly across his chest.

Suddenly, a voice boomed up at them, a deafening exclamation that threatened to crush Alex beneath its ferocity. It was the same voice from the static, a garbled string of harsh dialect that compressed and rushed over them in a wave of icy exclamation.

Heart racing, lungs burning, Alex frantically pulled them up the long throat, head pounding, muscles aching. He could feel whatever it was below them begin to pick up speed, a gale of freezing air swirling past them. His eyes watered beneath the onslaught and he squinted, trying to focus only on the white light above.

That's when Will slipped from his grasp.

It happened in a second, a sudden release that threatened to topple him as well. A spike of panic speared his senses and he desperately reached out with one hand and snatched Will before he tumbled down the living throat. Screaming, arm trembling beneath the exertion, he pulled his brother up to his side once more, the voice below bellowing and rising at an alarming rate.

Will gasped and reached out weakly with his ruined arms, the walls hugging him limply.

"It's going to get us," he cried, consumed by exhaustion, "you have to let me go. It wants me, not you."

The roar of alien language blasted up at them, a defiant, repeated muttering that's intensity almost split Alex's mind in two. He stared helplessly into his brother's covered face, feeling another wave of arctic wind rush up from the purple light below.

"You can reach the top on your own," Will gasped, the

strange hands on the wall groping and poking his body. "You have to let me go, Alex."

"No!" Alex cried, "Don't give up!" He reached out for another handhold, but Will's dead weight pulled him back down toward the fast approaching horror below.

"It's almost reached us," Will said weakly, "but you can make it if you let me go. Please. Don't throw your life away for me."

"I can't!" Alex cried, feeling Will begin to slip, "Goddamn it, Will, I can't do this!"

Another blast of wind chilled Alex to the bone and he felt something begin to stir thickly below, a massive, terrible energy that seemed to tug at his boots.

Will began to pull away, his voice low, "You've always been my favorite brother…"

Alex reached out toward Will, panicking, "No! Stop it! WILL!"

Will pushed himself away, a terrible sadness filling his throat, "Thanks for always looking out for me…" and then he was falling.

"NO!" Alex screamed, "GODDAMN IT DON'T GO!"

But Will was gone, falling rapidly toward the rising entity, his silhouette disappearing into the blinding purple light. Screaming, crying, Alex reached down for him, tears blinding his vision. As his blurred gaze fell toward the abyss, he felt his blood go cold as his eyes descended upon what crawled up toward him.

He only saw it for a second before he slammed his eyes shut again, but that brief moment seared itself into his mind like a blazing ember.

A sprawl of countless, endlessly long arms pulled the monstrosity up through the wide throat with terrifying speed. Its form pulsed a sickening purple, a dark wash of blinking lights that poured out like spotlights from an array of gaping orifices that littered the length of its body. Long metallic looking structures rose from its back, a twisting glow of sharp spires that cut and tore through the fleshy walls of the throat as it climbed. Its head was a long extension of bone and gore, an eyeless skull that protruded from its mass like a diseased growth. Its snout ended in a massive grate, a circular pattern of iron that bled the darkest black. Reaching out from the colossal prison were a hundred bloody hands, each one alien and unique in its biology. In unison, they gripped the air, clawing for another victim to fill their eternal hell.

Screaming, mind threatening to break, Alex pressed his eyes shut against the chaos. His head felt as if it would splinter apart, his chest heaved with pained loss, and his muscles burned with endless exhaustion.

Tears streaming down his face, sorrow clutching him with red-hot fingers, Alex reached above himself and clawed for another handhold. Arms trembling, he felt himself hauled up. A burst of ear-splitting static screamed from down below, and Alex felt himself almost slip and fall down into the abomination.

His boots kicked into the fleshy walls, his fingers dug into whatever they could find, and through it all, the world shook and rocked as the hell below consumed his senses.

Up…up…up…grab, pull, breathe, *live.*

At one point Alex felt himself throw up from exertion, a violent release that splashed wetly across his chin. But he kept going, each inch he gained feeling like the last he could manage.

Teeth chattering from the insistent cold, Alex suddenly

became aware that something was glowing directly above him. He looked up, vision fading, and saw the circle of white light only a couple of yards above his head.

Gritting his teeth, Alex screamed and heaved his trembling body the last of the distance. Below him, as he disappeared into the glow, he heard the monstrosity bellow with fury.

A moment after, he reached the top and pulled himself out of the nightmare.

Chapter 17

Alex fell to his knees as the Overroad rose around him once again. He stared down at the gridded ground, his eyes wide, trying hopelessly to piece his mind back into place. Drool hung in strands from his lips and his chest felt as if it had been struck by a boulder. He became aware that he was crying, his sobs echoing loudly out across the silent world.

"Jesus Christ! Alex!"

Sam dropped to his side, his hands running over Alex's back, "What happened? Are you ok?! Calm down man, catch your breath, you're safe again."

Alex squeezed his eyes shut, his body expelling a violent shudder. What the hell had just happened? Where had he gone? What *was* that thing? And Will…oh god…

"Are you hurt?" Sam continued urgently, "Can you move?"

Alex opened his mouth to speak, his voice coming out in a croak, "He's gone, Sam…"

Sam leaned close, "What are you talking about?"

Alex waved a hand feebly, "He fell…he fell into it…"

Sam said nothing, his hands pausing across Alex's back.

"That thing…" Alex hissed, "that thing took him…he's fucking gone, Sam."

"Christ," Sam finally whispered.

Alex slowly got to his feet, a wave of dizziness threatening to send him back to his knees. Sam helped steady him, his eyes trained intently on his friend as if trying to gauge the mental fortitude of his mind. Alex let his head fall back and released a trembling breath, a sorrowful exhale as reality squeezed the fragile edges of his psyche.

Will was gone...

Lost in that place forever...to that thing...

"Goddamn it," he sobbed weakly.

"There was nothing you could do," Sam said grimly, "God knows you tried. Are you ok?"

Alex searched himself and stared down at his open hands. Tears budded in his eyes and his voice came out in a thin cry, "I feel... I feel *relieved.*"

Sam placed a tender hand on Alex's shoulder, "That's ok. I get it, man. There was nothing you could have done differently."

Alex turned his eyes to Sam's, his voice a plea, "What kind of person does that make me?"

"You put the weight of the world on your shoulders," Sam said quietly, "I don't think you should regret anything. Will made his mind up years ago about what kind of person he was going to be. There wasn't anything you could have said or done to change that. You did your absolute fucking best with the situation. And at the end of the day, you were there for him. After everything he did to you, you chose to bury your own shit for the sake of your brother." Sam hugged Alex, "And that makes you a good person. Probably the only one left."

Alex clung to Sam and buried his face in his shoulder, "I'm

so fucking tired of this," he cried softly, "I can't *fucking* do this anymore…"

"I know," Sam whispered, "I know, man. And you don't have to. We're done. We made it. The Last Tower is right there. I have no idea what's inside, but it isn't this." Sam pulled away and stared kindly into Alex's eyes, "And I'll be there with you. I'm not going anywhere. We're going to be ok. We always have been because we look out for each other. Now let's get the hell out of this place before that monster comes back."

Alex wiped his eyes and nodded. He took a second to collect his breath and push the impending sorrow away from his thoughts. There would be time for that later. He knew it would come back. And yet through it, he couldn't shake himself from the one sensation that clung to him like smoke from a cigarette.

Relief. It was over. He would never have to worry about his brother again. He would never have to hate or hunt or protect Will ever again. It was *over*. And as much as it sickened him to realize…it filled him with overwhelming *relief*.

Alex dragged a hand across his face and turned his attention to the Tower before them. It soared up into the shivering stars, its twin spires scraping the roof of the sky. This close, its size almost terrified him. Its walls stretched and wrapped around the edges of his vision and he couldn't help but fear whatever lie inside. As he set out toward it with Sam, Will's voice echoed back to him from the pit of his mind.

My own personal paradise…

It didn't take long for them to cross the distance to it. Their footsteps bounced off the horizon and their breath blew like gusts of wind across the black landscape. Alex's mind clouded with a darkness that matched the heavens. Sam kept silent at his side, allowing his friend to deal with his misery and loss in the confines of his own head. He would be there when he needed to be. But right now was not that time.

They stopped before the towering construction and looked at one another. Heavy bags clung to their eyes and the years of travel, violence, and loss traced and bled from their weary faces.

Without speaking, Sam cautiously placed his hands against the surface of the Tower, unsure what else to do. As he did so, a faint outline began to glow and trace across the blank exterior. Thin purple lines cut the shape of an entrance before their eyes and when the pattern was complete, Sam lowered his hands.

The door slid open and Alex stared inside, too tired feel anything but a need to end this journey. Familiar blue fog bubbled from the dark interior and spilled across the Overroad like a quiet exhale.

"You ready?" Sam asked.

Alex looked behind them at the alien expanse, "What choice do we have?"

Sam reached out and took Alex by the hand, "I don't want to lose you in there, man."

Alex nodded, "Let's go…"

As one, they stepped into the fog. Alex didn't even hear the opening close behind them as things began to change. The fog rushed for them and collided into their bodies. It rushed down his throat, up his nose, and into his ears. A cold weightlessness consumed him and everything went dark. He clutched Sam's hand desperately and shut his eyes, his teeth gritted. The floor dropped out from under him and gravity seemed to evaporate. Vertigo came next, a terrible, stomach-churning sensation. It felt as if he was spinning hopelessly his limbs flailing wildly as time and space rippled and tore around them. Wind whipped across his face and he became aware that they were flying at an incredible speed toward something.

Blink.

Time slowed to a crawl and everything went still, his body jerking to a halt in the total darkness. His stomach slammed into the outer walls of his torso and he fought against a sudden need to vomit.

Blink.

Sound wormed toward him from a great distance. He focused on it, forced himself to hold onto the gentle wind that filled his ears, his mind. Something came at him from the noise, from behind the wind. It sounded like water…waves…

Blink.

Heat. A warm, wonderful heat. It tickled his skin and flooded across his face.

Blink.

Light. It was muddled at first, a blinding blast of yellow that erupted behind his eyelids. Then it sharpened into focus. Golden yellow light. Blue. The clearest blue he had ever seen.

Blink.

His feet sank slightly, comfortably. The world shook and trembled and tried to right itself before him. He clung to Sam's sweaty hand like it was the only thing separating himself from madness.

The edges smoothed out. The color softened. The heat cooled. The wind and water settled. Everything rolled together and then split apart into their assigned corners, revealing a new world before them with the clarity of a master painting.

"Holy shit…" Sam whispered, his fingers digging into Alex's.

Alex finally was able to make out where they were and what lay before them. He felt his anxiety ebb away and the knots in his shoulders loosen. His mouth dropped open and he allowed himself to breathe once more.

They were standing at the edge of an endless beach, thick dunes of sparkling white sand sprawling out along a coast that lapped with crystal green water. Frothy waves crested and fell, spilling softly across the perfect sand. The sun hung overhead like a blazing globe, splashing wonderful heat across their worn faces. Seagulls cawed overhead and swooped toward the water, landing gracefully on the glassy surface.

As Alex tore his eyes away from the eternal ocean, he realized that something wasn't quite right.

Sam saw it too and opened his mouth, his voice a hesitant whisper, "Are those what I think they are?"

Alex nodded without speaking.

The beach was littered with thousands of gravestones. They sat silently across the dunes, beneath the radiant sun. Alex let his eyes travel down the beach, his pulse slowing. They were simple in construction, the small gray monuments poking from the white carpet of sand without order or variety.

Every single one was the same.

"What the hell is this?" Sam asked, shaking his head.

Alex cautiously walked to the nearest one, Sam following at his back. He leaned down and wiped a hand across the surface.

"Are those names?" Sam asked, squinting.

Alex felt his blood turn to ice, his throat tightening.

Sam crouched down in front of the headstone and read the names out loud, "Here lie William and Carol." Sam faltered for a moment, realization crashing through him. He turned to Alex, "Is this…?"

Alex covered his face, "They're my parents."

Sam shook his head slowly and stood back up, allowing himself to look down the beach once more, across the millions of head-stones, "Jesus Christ…"

Alex looked at the grave once more, feeling sick, his voice a trembling release of sorrow, "His own personal paradise…" he closed his eyes, "My god, Will…"

Slowly, he stood. The sun bore down on them, the soft waves licking the shore. More gulls cawed overhead and Alex raised his eyes to them and followed their trajectory across the sky.

The beach ended in a row of thick forest, a tropical belly that echoed and filled with the scattered call of wildlife. Beyond that, the land began to rise and in the far distance, he spotted a colossal mountain that soared up into the cloudless sky.

Sam stood at his side, his arms crossed, "You think anything is out there?"

Alex continued to stare out at the foreign world, "I don't know…"

"Do you think we're alone here?"

"Would it be better if we weren't?"

Sam looked sideways at Alex, his voice soft, "I honestly don't know."

Alex gazed out across the lush greenery, at the mountain that pressed itself against the horizon like a picture stuck to paper.

Sam turned around and looked at the ocean, then back at the forest, "What do you want to do?"

Alex said nothing.

Sam shifted in the sand, "Should we go into the woods? That mountain looks like a good landmark to head toward. If there's anything out there, something tells me that's where it'd be." Sam looked at Alex, "Hey, you ok?"

Alex turned his back on the mountain and returned his eyes to the ocean. He let the gulls calm him, the gentle waves ease him. They pushed the endless questions out, dulled the roar of his own mind.

"What do you want to do, Alex?" Sam asked softly.

Alex closed his eyes and let the warmth of the sun fill his head. His voice rose to barely more than a whisper, "I just want to stand here for a while I think…"

Sam walked to Alex's side. He looked out across the sparkling water, the salt water wind blowing lazily between them.

"I could stand here forever," Alex said after a while.

Sam smiled, "We can if you want."

An emerald wave crashed loudly before them, the cool water creeping up and around their boots.

Alex exhaled, releasing a world of exhaustion, "Maybe we will, Sam. Maybe we will…."

About The Author

Elias Witherow lives in New England and continues to explore new ideas and ways to disturb people. But if you ever run into him, he'd be more than happy to buy you a drink and talk writing. With each new book, he strives to grow and provide increasingly entertaining fiction. Find him on Twitter @EliasWitherow and on Facebook at facebook.com/Elias-With-erow-831476890331162.

YOU MIGHT ALSO LIKE:

The Black Farm
by Elias Witherow

The Third Parent
by Elias Witherow

The Worst In Us
by Elias Witherow

THOUGHT
CATALOG
Books

Printed in the USA
CPSIA information can be obtained
at www.ICGtesting.com
LVHW042153130424
777365LV00021B/190